Dog Island

Joseph McConnell

ProcArch LLC, Ann Arbor

ISBN 978-0-9963385-7-8

First Kindle edition, 2020.

Although there is a "Peters Island" in the northern part of Lake Huron, the Peters Island here is entirely fictional. For one thing, the real one is bigger and has trees. For another, there don't appear to be people living close enough to the real island for the action here to be feasible. The author doesn't know if there are any dogs.

Cover photography and design by the author.

This is a work of fiction. All characters in this work are inventions, and they do not represent real people, living or otherwise.

This book is for Linda and for Kerry, Sammy, and Sunny. Good dogs, all of them.

Dog Island

Not exactly foggy. Just the mist off the lake. Temperature's going up, might even be a nice day by ten o'clock or so.

She talked to herself when she was driving. The paved road was in reasonable shape, even for early spring, and it would be easy to lose focus, otherwise. She liked music in a car, but they weren't supposed to have anything but the command radio on. Not that there was any traffic, either on the radio or on the road. But tunnel vision wasn't a recommended thing up here, these days. Few humans to run into, but deer? Oh, boy, were there deer.

Just like Isle Royale, she thought. *When the wolves died out, the moose population went up. When the humans move away, the deer come back.*

With that thought, of course the radio did wake up. "E, you out there?"

She toggled the microphone on. "I'm on the way. Ten minutes, about."

"Okay, E. Let me know."

"Ten-four."

She called herself E, pronounced "Ee". Her parents named her Eden, and she'd hated it since grade school. *Eden Gorsky, for God's sake.* A boyfriend, if you want to call it that – she didn't – called her Edy once, and she stopped answering his texts.

The road ran south ahead of her. On either side, second-growth pines came up to three or four meters from the pavement. No one was clearing the space in between anymore, so each year driving these old routes became more of a daytime activity. Three months ago, as she was coming off her shift and heading home, a wolf walked casually out of the brush, stopped in the middle of the road, and just stood there, looking at her. *That made my day.*

Today, she was driving out to a tiny spot on the shore – it used to be four houses and a fish shed, now just two weathering old homes. The family in one of them said they hadn't seen the guy in the other one for two days. Wasn't answering the door. Light in the back room had been on all the time. He was kind of a cranky old fellow, so they weren't prepared to break in. Typical welfare call. Is old Fred or old Mary still alive? This one's name was Mike, and for once, he wasn't someone she'd met. Whoever he was, though, she hoped he was all right. *I do sort of care.*

She'd been in Security Branch, what? Almost two years now. Six years in the Field Branch before that, and of course on the line during the Separation. That word always made her growl, mentally. *Call a war a war, dammit. Not much fighting, but enough.* She hadn't had to do any shooting, herself, just drive trucks back and forth. But it got her into the Field Branch afterward, citizen card, right to vote. And bored stiff. And since the soldiers were doing more and more support for the police anyway, she transferred. And then she got to come up here to the island. No one else wanted the job. *Why would they? Clear the hell up here, cold as hell seven months out of the year.* But not much pretense, either.

The paved road turned right, going along the shore up to the ferry landing. E's way was off to the left, down a gravel lane, dropping a few meters toward the lake and the little place called Peters. At some point, some guy named Peter had a cabin and a fish dock, and so it was Peters, without the apostrophe. There was a tiny, uninhabitable island off shore, and it was called, naturally, Peters Island. E occasionally wondered about the process the old map makers used. Did they start by wandering around, asking people "where am I?" and writing down the answer? Did they leave off apostrophes intentionally, to save space, or was it just random? And since most of them here would have been English or French, did they tend to favor English and French sources? So Native American names only ended up on the maps, transliterated into whatever the, say, eighteenth-century cartographer heard, when there weren't any English or French around to talk to?

The small collection of ruined houses with two of them less ruined than the others looked like it had, *what? six months ago?* the last time she'd been out here. *Here we go. Better let Ed know.* She picked up the microphone. "Ed, you there?"

Pause. Again, "Ed, you on?"

"Yeah, E. Just, uh, on the phone. You out there yet?"

"Just now. Nothing obvious going on. I'll check with the neighbors first."

"Uh, okay. Let me know."

"Ten-four."

Ed was nominally her superior officer, even though he wasn't an officer any more than she was – they were both sergeants – but he'd been in charge here when she transferred in, and they left it at that. It was just the two of them, plus two private soldier slots as the individual kids rotated in and out, coming and going with their two-year National Service terms. Theoretically, you could request a specific posting, but she'd never met anyone else who really wanted to serve here. Except Ed.

She parked the Army-spec pickup truck across from the houses. The one in question was on the right; gray pine boards and a small porch roof sticking out over grass and dandelions. That was where the subject was supposed to be. Mike something. She checked the note

3

she'd written. Silverman. Mike Silverman.

On the left, next to Mike's house, there was just a space. The house that had been there fell over in a winter storm, and somebody salvaged most of the material. A small stack of very weathered-looking boards remained. To the left of that, the only other inhabited space was better looking, slightly. Part of it had been painted gray, maybe to match the unpainted part. The windows were all there, and a bulb over the door was on. E walked toward it, and before she got there, the door opened.

"Good morning, ma'am," E said. "Did you call us?" The woman at the door was younger than the general demographic on the island, maybe in her forties. But she looked, sadly, very much like her house. Gray.

"Yeah, I did. I went up to the store, there, and called." Of course. There weren't any phone lines out here. And cell coverage? No. "We ain't seen him", she gestured toward Mike's house, "for two or three days, now. And he don't answer the door."

"Okay. Does he have a car?"

"Yeah. Truck." She pointed off toward E's right. There was nothing there.

"Where? Is it gone?"

"Over there. He parks it down the road behind the trees. So it stays out of the wind, mostly. Wind comes in off the lake hard in the winter."

"I see." E looked at the front and side of Mike's place. She noted some kind of shed or garage behind it, leaning hard to the north. "Have you looked around? In that shed, maybe?"

"Nope. He's kind of grouchy. He didn't like people bein' on his place. So I just knocked on his door, last night. To see if he's all right, you know." The mix of present and past tenses in the woman's speech was a characteristic of the people here. For the most part, the difference between *is* and *was* didn't matter all that much.

"All right. And ... oh, are you here by yourself, right now?"

"Yeah. My husband's out with his boat ..." she pointed at the lake in general. "And the girl's off at school. I just got back, drivin' her there." There was a reasonably sound-looking Ford pickup parked at the other side of the woman's house.

"All right," E said again. "So can I ask you to stay inside for a bit while I go and check?" The woman nodded and went back in the house.

E approached Mike's house cautiously. There was just the door and a single window, and she came up from the blank side. She stood at the side of the door and knocked. "Mister Silverman. Security Branch. We just want to see if you're all right." Silence. "Mister Silverman?" A louder set of knocks. "Mister Silverman? Are you okay?"

Most of this was theatre, with the neighbor being the audience. *We knocked. We called. He didn't answer us, either.* Cautiously, E moved closer to the window and looked in. Some kind of cloth – a curtain or a sheet or something – was covering it inside. Outside, the window frame had square metal brackets, common enough in the north: holders for wooden storm shutters. The shutters themselves would be somewhere in the house or in that shed. Nothing to be seen through the window, though, shutters or not. She knocked and called once more. *Okay. Phase two. Around back.*

E hadn't had a look at the right side of the house, the side away from the neighbors. She backed away toward the road first, moving far enough to have some warning if Mr. Silverman or anyone else was hiding over there. As

5

her view down the side wall expanded, she saw nobody, just the shaky-looking side of the backyard shed. In the house wall, there was a small window, head height, halfway back. *Bathroom.* She closed in to the wall and peeked quickly. Nothing. Just another window with a drape of some kind. She looked back and then around the brush and a nearby ruin: nobody. *Okay, then.*

She walked wide of the back corner, looking hard at the old shed. She stopped part way, before she could see the back wall of the house, because the shed wasn't a shed, per se. It had been a small garage, and there was a very sad-looking car in it, just the front end showing. The shed had collapsed on it, probably over winter. Or the winter before. Or ten years before that. If the car hadn't been there, the shed would be flat on the ground. *Returning the favor. The garage used to shelter the car, now the car's holding up the garage.*

Very briefly, she considered the idea that Mister Silverman might be in there. In the ruins. In the car, even. But it seemed very unlikely. Worth checking later, maybe. But it was so much more likely that he'd be somewhere in the house, unconscious, hiding, or dead. Or not here at all, somewhere else on the island. Or even off it. No; next step, check the back of the house. She side-walked three steps further. And there was Mister Silverman, or his legs, anyway. Or someone's. Sticking out the back door, toes down.

E's hand dropped down to her side. She had a pistol – required to have one, of course – and training said you needed to have it in hand for questionable situations. In this case, the situation was questionable enough, but it didn't call for firepower. She convinced herself in less than three minutes that the only person in the house was the one lying half in and half out the back door. The one with an obvious gunshot wound in the back of his head. She holstered her sidearm, took a quick photo with her otherwise useless phone, then walked back around the other side of the house. *Ed'll love this.*

Ed didn't sound as though he loved it. "Aw, hell. You sure?"

"I'm sure. GSW, right in the back of the head. And no gun lying around, either. No brass."

"Aw, hell. Battalion won't like that. Not at all."

"Well ... I don't like it all that much, myself."

The conclusion was that E needed to hang on there while Ed got Company on the phone and gave them the news. She turned the radio up so she could hear it from the back of the house, and started a careful look around, standing away from the immediate scene and just looking hard at the ground. It wasn't rewarding. Grass didn't seem to grow out there in the space between the house and the garage. Mostly just gravel, and there was nothing that looked like tracks. She gave up on that and tried shining her light into the collapsed building, trying to see around the car and some junk piled on it. *It hasn't moved in a while, even before the shed fell down.*

She straightened up, stretched, and looked out at the lake. The water was barely moving, with just a hint of on-shore breeze. There wasn't really a bay here, but the island indented enough that the view had a distinct left and right side, open to the lake on the south and cut off by Peters Island on the north. As she looked, a boat came into the scene from the left, the south side, moving across toward the other side. The silhouette was familiar. *That looks like ...* a Naval Branch patrol boat. Eight meters. High, lake-boat bows. A chief petty officer and six or eight sailors. It went on slowly north and out of sight. E looked back at the garage, walked once completely around it, and then saw the boat come back, still slowly, this time heading south.

The car. *Silverman wasn't using that heap in the*

garage to get around. It would be a long walk to the little store, up at the ferry. The mail boxes were even a couple of hundred meters away, up by the Ferry Road. Bicycle? She realized that she knew nothing about poor old Mike at all – including how old he was. The neighbor's "kind of grouchy" description had given her an assumption about him, but he might have been in his twenties for all she knew. *I'm out of practice. Better go talk to the lady next door again.*

The woman, of course, had been watching from a side window, and she came out as E walked up to the door. "You find him?"

"Yes, ma'am. I'm afraid he's dead." The woman's face didn't change. She just nodded.

"Well, I wondered. I thought maybe." She paused for a couple of breaths. "Pity," she said.

"Could I ask you a few questions?" E said. "There'll be some people coming to help out, but maybe you can give me a bit more information about Mister Silverman."

"Okay. What I can, anyway."

E got out a small notebook. "Let's see. Can I have your name? And your husband's?"

"I'm Deirdre. Bullock. Husband's Tom Bullock. The girl is Sally. She's twelve."

"And your husband's a fisherman?"

"Well. He fishes." A pause. "We get the Support."

Sure. Like everybody here. No shame in it, but nobody's proud of it, either. "And ... did I ask you this before? Did you know Mister Silverman well?"

"Not really. Just to say hello."

"Can you show me where his truck is? I didn't see it coming in."

They walked together out to the road, and the woman pointed to where the gravel track turned right, away from the shore. Trees and a collapsed house or shed or something blocked the line of sight. "Behind there. Blue Ford truck." E looked. Nothing to see. She needed to hang on and keep the site unmolested, so she resisted the urge to make sure the truck was really there. *Later.*

"All right, thanks. We'll look at that when we get some more people here."

"Tom will be back for lunch pretty soon. I need to get it ready."

"That's fine, ma'am. There are other Security people coming. Just don't leave until they've had a chance to talk to you. And your husband, too."

"About four o'clock, I gotta go pick up the girl."

"Okay, I'll let them know that."

E got out some yellow tape and roped off Silverman's house and shed. It occurred to her that since the area had only four residents and one of them dead, the remaining three would be suspects until proven otherwise. There could be reasons why someone would shoot a neighbor. A twelve-year-old daughter might be one reason. *And if the husband's "out on his boat", maybe he's getting rid of something.* They would definitely want to talk to all three of them. Separately.

The taping took her back to the shed and around it. She took the opportunity to see what could be seen, both from the back of the house and toward it. No one close in along the shore could see the place where Silverman was lying. And from the sides, there was only a small pair of places, north and south, where the shooter could have been. *Had to have been right here, right behind him.* She turned back toward the water. Even somebody on a boat wouldn't have been able to get a line of sight in from the south side, and on the north, it was the same. All you could see was the lake and the little island. *Must have been here.* She made another circuit around the house and went back to her truck.

She opened the driver's side door, looked around once more, and slid in. She started the engine, partly out of habit and partly to keep the battery up. *I don't actually know if the radio uses much battery. I could look it up, I suppose.* She called Ed.

"Yeah, E. The Captain's coming over on the boat now."

"The Captain? "

"Yeah. The Lieutenant's off doing something, I guess. Or this's a bigger deal than I thought."

"So she's bringing the body team with her?" The body team meant the forensics people.

"Yeah. Probably be there in half an hour."

Okay. What can I do before that so I look like I know what I'm doing? "Ed, do we have any info on this guy's truck? License plate or anything?" *Might want to get that going, anyway.*

"Uh ... I don't think so. Did he have a truck?"

"Neighbor says he did. Parks it down the road where I can't see it without leaving the site."

"I can see if he ever got stopped or anything, I guess. You want to hang around there, though."

"Sure. I've got it taped off."

"Okay. Out"

"Out."

Depending on how many vehicles there were to load or unload, the time it took to get across to the island could vary. This time, Company Command must have gotten lucky. E heard traffic coming down the road in just under thirty minutes. Two trucks, one with the forensics people and one with the command personnel. Usually, there'd be a lieutenant in charge, one of the two at Company, but this time, the Company commander was in the front seat, just as Ed said. Captain Matthews. *Funny. But then, homicide isn't the run of the mill, up here. A little excitement, I guess.*

Captain Morgan Matthews was a year or two younger than E, but she'd started her career in the SB right after the Separation. She was a team lead in one of the Civil Security groups, and most of the people who were part of them moved right into SB when it formed. For her, that was all on the southwest side of the Lower Peninsula, in and around Grand Rapids. Now, she was out of her territory. A company command was one thing, but being out here in the woods and water as the saying went ... well, she still felt as though she was out of her natural habitat.

Dog Island, she thought. She'd asked somebody what the name meant, and got nowhere. "It's just what they call it." She looked a bit further into it and found out that it was an English settlers' transliteration of a French name, Isle aux Chien. And that was the French take on an Ojibwe name, Animosh-minis or something like that. Apparently, nobody knew what the name meant or who the dog was. It was just Dog Island. Or people would simply point in its direction and say "The island".

Publically, it was one of Security Branch's minor responsibilities. Publically, the only reason SB kept two sergeants and a pair of recruits on the place at all was that its eastern shore was in sight of Canada. That made it a border, and sometimes people brought things across borders. The hundred or so residents were almost all on public support. Kids grew up and got the hell out, so the population was short on that troublesome middle sector, the people who get drunk, raise hell, smuggle things, and so on. Teenagers, young adults, middle-aged folks –

all pretty well unrepresented. Young children being raised by grandparents or other old relatives; that was the basic household. For Matthews, it should have been a minor part of a bigger job, policing a large chunk of the eastern Upper Peninsula, from Saint Ignace up to the Sault. Should have been.

As Matthews got out of the truck, E walked up and saluted. "Good morning, Captain. Or ..." she looked at her watch, "... yes, still morning, technically."

"Good morning, Sergeant. You took the call, here?"

"Yes, sir." The word "Sir" had been officially de-gendered in the Army of the Republic. A superior was "Sir", regardless of any other distinctions, cultural or physical. "I got here an hour ago. Talked to the caller ..." E pointed at the neighbor's house, "... and then found the victim at the back, lying in the doorway. Shot in the back of the head, apparently. Deceased."

"Was there anyone else around?"

"Only the woman neighbor. She'd taken her daughter off to school, and she says her husband is out on the lake. Fishing. She says she hadn't seen the victim in a couple of days – we need to get that more specifically, but a couple of days, anyway."

"No one saw anything? Heard anything?"

"No, sir. Not according to ... " E glanced at her notebook, "... Mrs. Bullock." She looked at the Captain's expression. It was blank. "If that's true, sir, that narrows the times of the shooting down quite a bit. It would be really limited to when the woman is away, the man's fishing, and the girl's in school."

"Hm. And his vehicle?"

How did she know he had a vehicle? "It's supposed to be parked down there, sir. Out of sight. I haven't been able to leave here and check on it."

Matthews blinked hard. "All right. I think ... I think you and I should talk in the truck for a minute."

Really? "Yes, sir." The forensics team – all two of them – were out of their truck with their gear, and they seemed to be waiting for instructions. "Should I show the team where the victim is? And come back?"

"Yes, fine."

Why would we need to talk in the truck? E led the evidence guys to the back of the house. She noticed for the first time that the body was beginning to smell. *Hasn't been all that cold. Maybe shot yesterday evening?* She walked back up to the road.

They got into the cab of Matthews' vehicle. "Sergeant, do you agree that we're here by ourselves? That we can't be overheard by anyone else?"

"Um ... yes, sir. There's no one else around."

"So, I'm designating this a temporary classified information area. Given that, tell me what else you've observed about this ... incident."

What the hell? "Sir," E said, "I've ... told you, I think, all I really know."

"Again, this is a temporary secure area. I've been accessed to the Ice Rink program. You can provide me with any details that are ... relevant to it."

Oh, hell! Spook stuff! "Sir, I don't know about anything ... any information ... with that name. I don't think you ought to ... discuss it with me. Unless I'm really not understanding ..."

"Are you saying that you're not read in on ... anything ... regarding Mike Silverman?"

"That's right, sir. I don't know anything about him."

"Holy shit! Are you serious?"

"Yes, sir. Seriously."

"Oh, for ..." Matthews' face went blank again. "All right. I've made a mistake. I'll have to self-report it. We need to get you briefed on ... a secure program. Until then, assume that this conversation didn't ... happen. "

"Yes, sir." *This is a new one! Field Branch might screw up like this, but SB? Jesus!*

E and Matthews had a long talk with Deirdre Bullock and then another with her husband. He'd come in to within twenty meters or so of the shore, then stopped and watched the cops running around. Deirdre was encouraged to wave him in, and he complied. While she went to pick up the daughter, he had a long chat with the Security people. When Mom brought the girl home, they talked to her, too.

"I don't think it's impossible they were involved, but I really doubt it," Matthews said to E. None of her standard leading questions or little traps had turned anything up. The girl was almost neutral; she didn't seem happy that the grumpy neighbor was dead, but she was only conventionally sorry. The assertion that the family hardly knew him seemed convincing.

"I don't get any sour notes either," E said. "They seem pretty much like the rest of the people here. Just hanging on."

"Time of death will be important. As you said, there are only a few windows when none of them would have been here. To hear the shot, I mean."

"Right,"

The body was photographed, examined, bagged, and removed. The area where he was lying was examined and imaged. In fact, the whole house and its general area were recorded. Forensics found nothing to indicate that more than one shot had been fired. No cartridge case, no footprints, no tire tracks, at least any that could be distinguished from the neighbors' truck or the official vehicles. E walked down the road and reported that a pickup, probably Silverman's, was parked where it was supposed to be. She taped it off, and forensics planned on coming back the next day to go over it. E spent most of the rest of the day worrying. *What did I miss? Why was I supposed to know anything about this guy?* For Matthews, it was far worse.

First of all, she felt she'd been set up. The officer she replaced was gone when she got there. The Battalion commander ran through the few classified issues without emphasizing any of them particularly. Of course, there was the general concern with resistance groups, but he had nothing specific to say. He cautioned her to keep the pressure on drugs coming across from Canada, anywhere along the watery border. "Once in a while, people will try to get in. But not often. And usually just ordinary crime types. Nothing political."

Matthews knew that was bullshit. She knew very specifically about a political thing, and she knew the Major knew, and the Brigadier as well. And she'd been told that a sergeant in the company, a Sergeant Gorsky, knew. Now another person who knew was probably dead, and Gorsky seemed to be clueless. Gorsky, the person who was supposed to be looking after the victim.

And on top of that, who the hell *was* that, lying on his face in that cabin? Was it who Gorsky, at least, seemed to assume it was? Why did she seem to be sure about that? If she'd never seen him, never knew anything about him, why just assume it was him?

"If she really isn't read in on Ice Rink, well … yeah, why would she assume anything except that an old guy in a shack got shot? She's got enough experience to pick the most likely situation. His truck's there, the neighbors say he's been out of sight for a while. Sure, she thinks it's most likely him."

But Matthews wasn't going to make any such assumption. The age and general size of the victim were right, but forensics was going to have to do a lot more work before she'd buy in. "If it's him and he didn't get any protection, that's going to be very bad. If it isn't him, and he had to defend himself, and he's gone off on his own, that's worse."

She stopped herself. "Oh." A third possibility occurred to her. Much, much worse.

§

The former Les Cheneaux Schools complex was an uninspired piece of red brick governmental architecture. The population no longer needed anything like that much educational space, and a small part of it now housed the Republic's local Mail Service. The rest of it was the headquarters of Company B of the Nineteenth Battalion of the Twelfth Brigade of the Army of the Republic's Security Branch. It couldn't house all 220 members of the Company, but most of the rank and file were spread out over its area of responsibility. As Company Commander, Captain Matthews spent most of her time in town, in the old building.

She'd left E with instructions to report at Company – that was the usual way of referring to the building and the organization – in the morning. When E had been in Field Branch, she would have interpreted that as "first thing," but Security wasn't quite as rigorous a shop. At eight-thirty, then, E said hello to the Corporal who served as Matthews' admin support and asked if the Captain was available. Matthews was, and in fact heard E's question. "Come in, Gorsky," she called.

"Good morning, Captain."

"Good morning. I've got one quick message to send here, and then we need to go down the hall to the secure area. Hang on just a minute."

"Yes, sir." E watched in mild admiration as the Captain blasted out a message on her desktop computer. Her typing was blazingly fast and apparently without error – or else she didn't care about typos. She finished with a quick Ctrl-keystroke which E assumed was "send" – no time-consuming mouse clicks here – and got up.

"Let's go," she said.

Fifteen feet down the hall there was a blank door with only a room number sign. It did have a key card lock, and the Captain opened it with a card and PIN. Before going ahead, she asked to see E's ID. She looked at it perfunctorily, nodded, and they entered.

"This is a secure classified information area," she said, "and I've determined that you hold clearances that permit you to be here. Can you confirm that?"

"Yes, sir," E said. "I hold High Sensitivity clearances through Brigade Command."

"Yes." They were standing in a hallway with a number of doors leading off. All were closed except one, and E remembered that it was the conference room. They went in, and Matthews closed the door.

"I have approval to brief you on a High Sensitivity program. When we've finished, I'll need you to sign an SB110, agreeing to standard security conditions and prohibitions. Do you agree?"

"Yes, sir. I agree."

"All right. The program is named Ice Rink. For non-secure references, it's called P221, but you're unlikely to have reason to use that identification." E nodded. She'd heard this general formula before.

"Ice is an umbrella program with individual programs beneath it. Ice Rink is the only one for which you have need-to-know at this point." Matthews was clearly quoting from memory, and her voice sounded like it. E had seen quick indications that there was actually a human being under the Captain's façade. So far, they'd been infrequent.

"The scope of Ice programs is the relocation and protection of people with extensive, inside exposure to resistance organizations. These people may be individuals who were inserted into such groups by SB, or people who were members and have been recruited away." E nodded again. *This is going to be bad.*

"Ice Rink was initiated to manage a specific individual who was inserted into a rightist group in the southwestern region. He provided valuable information regarding the personnel who were active in that group, and many of them were arrested as a result. When the group was broken up, that individual was extracted. He was given a new identity, and he was placed ... here."

E had been looking directly at the Captain's eyes as she was speaking. Now she looked down at the table and said, "Here."

"Yes, here. Specifically, on Dog Island."

"I see. I see, um, the problem."

"When I took over the Company, I was briefed by higher levels of command. Specifically, by Brigade. My briefing included the ... statement that you had been briefed and were in touch with the person using the name Mike Silverman."

"And I was supposed to be protecting him?"

"Yes."

"And I wasn't briefed."

"There is no record that you were."

"What level of command ... Who was supposed to brief me?"

Matthews closed her eyes tightly for a moment. "That's

an awkward subject. I don't want to ... ah, let me just say that the same level of command that is now briefing you would have had that responsibility when Ice Rink was put in place."

"I see." *Captain Wright.*

Matthews drew a long breath. She looked around for a second or so and then breathed out. "I can say that neither Battalion nor Brigade was aware of this issue. And no one has suggested any concerns about your, well, your performance."

"Was I supposed to be reporting something? To someone?"

"Again, that would have been at the discretion of Company Command. The reports would have been classified at a high level. None were found. But again, the concern is with determining where in the chain of command the ... failure took place. No one is blaming you for not doing something you weren't told to do."

E nodded. She felt a bit less than one percent better. *Security screwed up, not me, personally. But a guy's still dead.*

"What I'm going to assign you to do is forget about protecting anybody ... obviously ... and assist me in investigating the death that took place on the island."

"Yes, sir."

"I've started some lines of inquiry myself, already. For example, I will try to determine what happened in the chain of command here. Why you weren't properly tasked. What I want you to do, first of all, is to confirm the identification of the victim."

E started to say one thing, changed her mind, and said "Yes, sir. I take it that the victim's name wasn't actually Mike Silverman?"

"I'm not sure yet who it was."

"You're not, sir?"

"Had you ever seen him, living?"

"Well, no. I hadn't."

"And we didn't show the body to the neighbors. So neither of us knows who that was on the ground, there."

Damn! We don't, do we? "I see. And we can't contact any family to confirm the ID?"

"No. The SB elements in charge of Ice Rink will have biometrics, though. Until we get that and get a positive result, we won't assume that we know who was killed."

"All right. I'll make sure Forensics knows what we want. Can I contact ... whoever is running the program? To get the bio data?"

"I'll give you a secure mail address. Were you set up with email on the secure network here?"

"Yes, sir. My password will have timed out by now, but otherwise I can use it."

"Good. Sign this ..." Matthews slid a form across the table "... and then I'll give you the link to what we know about Silverman. It's not very extensive."

"Yes, sir. It'll be good to know what's going on." Matthews looked up, started to say something, and then changed her mind.

"Work in here, of course. I'll get you a place to sit and a machine. And I'll check back with you before the end of the day."

E stood up. "One thing, sir. Do we know what his name really is?"

"You'll find it in the documents. Or, no, you'll find the name he used when he was undercover with the rightists. I don't know what his real name is or was, myself. Let's just go on calling him Silverman."

E sat in the conference room, waiting for Matthews to get her a desk and a PC. Her general state of mind was not pleasant. On one hand, the Captain apparently didn't consider her a complete fool. And having something more interesting to do? That was good, sort of. Policing the island hadn't been demanding ... kind of relaxing ... but except for being there to step in when old Ed retired or dropped dead or something, there wasn't much of a career path. So working on ... *Ice Rink?* ... would be better. *Possibly.*

Looking at it the other way, this whole thing could be a minefield. The big question, of course, was what the hell was up with Captain Wright? He'd been here one day and gone the next, as far as mere sergeants knew. At least E, anyway. And he'd had the whole two-plus years she'd been here to wake up and remember to brief her. Or did he? How long had Silverman been on the island? The whole time? She tried to recall that one other visit to Peters. Was anyone living in that house then? No idea. It was just a drunk and disorderly call, about someone in one of the other houses, one of the ones no longer ... viable. And the caller? She'd have to look it up. Probably anonymous. After all, if you wanted the police out there, you had to go find a phone or a cell signal.

Random. Stop that. Pay attention. She caught herself in one of her unproductive ways of thinking. She'd start jumping from detail to detail and lose track of a primary thread. She'd schooled herself to identify a core for anything important, the one or two central facts or issues. Pure reason wouldn't often produce an answer, but it could define the questions. Her education included dialectics, and her work and her general view of the world created something very much like it. Thesis, antithesis, synthesis; for E, it emerged as something like small questions, missing data, large question. It was iterative, and if it didn't point directly to a perpetrator or a damning piece of evidence, at least it gave her a way of going forward.

Right now, there seemed to be two big questions. One of them was formally her responsibility: *"Who was that lying dead on the cabin floor?"* The other one, not directly on her plate, but of great interest to her: *"why the hell wasn't I briefed?"*

§

Southeast of Grand Rapids, down Harperville Road, the countryside had been transforming from agriculture to individual homes, and along one of the mile-numbered side roads, a piece of ex-hayfield had become the Original Reformed Church. Neither the church nor its doctrine was "original" in any sense of the word. It was the old Dutch Reformed faith, pulled back from the small amounts of liberalization that the mainstream church had been undergoing since the Second World War. Its point of view wasn't technically Calvinist, but an outsider might have had trouble pointing out the difference.

The building was so obviously a church that its signage was just a small plastic display near the road. It had a long driveway and a modest parking lot behind the church itself. There'd been a hundred and twenty or so members of the congregation just a few years ago. Now, there were forty-eight names on the rolls. The cars in the lot were Fords and Chevys – pickup trucks, many of them – not the BMWs and big Chrysler sedans that used to show up. In the Republic, you could still take part, quietly, in religious activities, but conservative expressions of faith were distinctly unfashionable and potentially career-ending.

On this Sunday, services were over, and the congregation was leaving. People stopped to exchange a word or two, mostly about the weather or "How's your father?" pleasantries. Two men, though, paused by the edge of the lot and had a more serious discussion.

"Well," said one of them, "That was a nice little sermon, I guess."

"Nothing wrong about it, I suppose."

"Not quite what we used to hear. From Pastor Phil."

"Yeah."

"Did you ever say anything to him? About being, you know, more careful?"

"Nope."

"I wish I had. But ... you know, what would you say?"

"I don't know. He wouldn't have changed his mind, anyway."

"No. Seems kind of a waste, though."

"I try not to ... not to talk about all that. You know."

"I suppose. You hear anything about Alice?"

"She closed up the house and left. Probably went back to her folks. In Ohio."

"Shame. She was easier to talk to than Phil."

"Yeah."

They separated, collected their families, and drove off. A hound trotted along the edge of the church property, nose down, following some interesting scent. Three hundred and eighty kilometers northeast, a mild west wind was sending small waves against the shore of Canada's Cockburn Island. No one was around, but if someone had been standing on the beach, he might have noticed a red kayak, upside down and bobbing around offshore. If the viewer had turned his head to the right, he'd have been looking across the border into the Republic and along the forested west side of Dog Island.

§

Sergeant Wilbur Edmore, in common with E, had never liked his name. As soon as he could, he dropped Wilbur like an empty potato chip bag, and just grabbed the first syllable of his last name. Ed Edmore was just as easy to say, and (in his mind, anyway) didn't sound so much like a librarian or a bookkeeper. "Fah," with emphasis was one of his speech habits, meaning negation and distaste, and when he thought of "Wilbur" at all, "fah" was usually the next thought.

The ironic thing was now that he was in his late forties and losing his hair, he looked as much like a "Wilbur" as an "Ed". He'd started building a waist ten or twelve years ago, and he'd been moderately successful. It made him short of breath and red-faced, and if he wasn't in uniform, you might look at him and think "bartender". That he was a noncom in the Army of the Republic, Security Branch, Seventh Division, Twelfth Brigade, Nineteenth Battalion, B Company was really just a matter of the uniform.

The Dog Island post wasn't one he'd gone after, but he and the general situation sized each other up, and the more they did, the more it looked like a good fit. The island didn't offer much in the way of crime, and Ed wasn't a very enthusiastic crime fighter. The chances for promotion were slim, and Ed didn't have that kind of ambition. The social life was non-existent, but Ed was willing to relax in his apartment above the SB post five nights out of seven, and then drive up to the Soo for his days off.

When they told him he was getting another sergeant, it was mildly concerning. Maybe this was a step toward moving him somewhere else? Somewhere he'd have to work a lot harder? Somewhere away from the Soo? But after he met E, he began to relax. She didn't care about who was going to be in charge. And nothing came down from Company about any changes. After he got to know her, he realized that she was a very useful asset. She had serious experience. She could talk both "local" and "army". Ed never really got behind the whole meet-the-new-boss political frame of mind. By a tacit agreement, E got to deal with things in the realm of rights and entitlements, serving and protecting, being the friendly face of the new reality. And Ed wrote the traffic tickets and did the driving-drunk busts. And he did most of the supervising for the new kids that rotated in and out. They came with some small amount of training, but he gave them the real word, as he saw it, about keeping the back country safe for ... whoever it was they were keeping it safe for.

If he had any real concerns about E, it was that he knew the situation didn't call for another non-commissioned officer. The chain of command, all the way down from Division, was always agitating about waste. And yet, here she was. After a month or so had gone by and nothing bad happened, he shoved that worry off to the shelf where he kept his other four o'clock in the morning anxieties. The fact that she was some kind of a person of color made it slightly more concerning. He had lingering ideas about race that even the Republic hadn't been able to eradicate, but his prejudices were no longer about capability. He'd known all kinds of not-white people in the Army, and not-male, too, and they were as good at their jobs as anybody. That wasn't an issue for him. But it was harder to get rid of the sense that, somehow, his being a white boy might count against him. Still, there wasn't any evidence that Division was trying to ease him out, and that was a daily reassurance. Plus, this new sergeant was ... what? Easy to look at, he decided. Not ... say, cute. But still a pleasant face to see in the office. That thought led to another one, never too far from his attention. Tomorrow night there'd be another pleasant face to look at. Up at the Soo.

Initially, E bunked on the mainland at Company HQ, but when she said she wanted to live on the island, Ed offered to help her find some kind of place. They looked, and she came up with a house to rent, over on the east shore. There were four other households over there, gathered together in a non-official community. Naturally, it was called East Shore. Ten or fifteen minutes in good weather would get you into the office, twenty or thirty in the winter. Ed's commute was a lot shorter: down a flight of outside stairs, around the front of the building, and there you were. Another couple of minutes would get you over to the ferry dock. Or to the store and ferry office. Technically speaking, the dock was called The Ferry Landing, and so the little collection of buildings around it was called Landing. Or The Landing, interchangeably. Ed chose to call the community "Landing" and reserve the definite article for when he was talking about the specific concrete pier where the ferry landed. E picked that usage up from him, but it was an elective part of the training, not something that would be on an exam.

At Landing, the island's only paved road (Ferry Road, of course) began a complete circuit, following the shore, more or less, all the way around, passing East Shore and Peters, and coming back north to Landing again.

Where geographic names were concerned, Landing and East Shore accounted for fifty percent of the island's toponyms. The other two were Peters, where all the excitement and concern were focused right now, and Little Lake. Peters, like Landing and East Shore, was a collection of viable and non-viable, inhabited and uninhabited buildings. Little Lake, however, wasn't a town but, in fact, a little lake. Beginning about a kilometer south of Ed's office, down the eponymous Little Lake Road, it went south for about fifteen hundred meters, ending in an unnamed stream. Said stream ran to the west side of the island and emptied into Lake Huron. One of the island's three wooden bridges took Ferry Road over it and on down to Peters.

The island was pretty flat, and what ground relief it had ran in a low ridge, north-south down the center. On its eastern side, a spring-fed stream flowed southeast. It was called South Branch – the south branch of what was not specified – and it emptied into a small nameless bay on the south shore. A little gravel two-track ran along it (called, naturally, South Branch Trail), crossed it on another small bridge, and joined the southern side of Ferry Road. The third bridge took Ferry Road across the stream.

Along the official, winter-maintained roads, there were driveways or lanes, some leading out to the shore, more of them leading inland. Sometimes they ended in the woods with no sign of habitation. Sometimes they led to battered and creaky wooden houses, sometimes they ended at old rusting mobile homes. Sometimes there'd be people living there, sometimes not. Mostly, what you saw while driving these roads was trees. If you were close enough to the shore, you saw water on one side and trees on the other. But mostly, you saw trees. For variety, here and there along the roads there'd be clusters of mailboxes, usually as weathered as the dwellings.

There wasn't much actual paper mail these days. Your Support checks were direct-deposited for you. The government gave you a bank account, and your money just showed up there; your pay, too, if you had a job. Not many people on the island had anything more than the Support – that was the usual term for the Average Wage Act payments that evened up income across the Republic. Ed and E and the whole Army of the Republic got paid well enough; only the two-year National Service kiddies got Support because they were essentially paying off their educations. They got food and clothing and shelter free while they were serving, but no salary. Just the Support. "Keeps 'em humble," was Ed's opinion of that.

Sunday mornings, when Ed was off-duty, E was nominally in charge on the island. This particular Sunday, she was planning on working, anyway, Ed or no Ed. She had more looking and thinking to do around the shooting scene. She ate some toast and had a cup of coffee, put her boots on, and headed out. Just as she reached the Ferry road, the radio woke up.

"Gorsky. Go ahead," she said.

"Uh, Sergeant, this is Steve. At the Landing office." Steve was one of the two privates, doing his two years' service.

"Go ahead, Steve." *I know where you are.*

"We just a got a shots-fired call." *Oh, good.* "Uh, at one-twenty-one South Branch Trail. You know, west of the bridge, there?"

"They called from there?"

"Oh, uh, no. They drove up here. They didn't, I mean, really call. They came in."

"All right. Wake up Margie, and get her started down there. I'm closer, but if there's really anything going on, I'll wait until I see her show up."

"Okay, uh, you want me to stay here, right?"

Right, son. "You hang out there and stay on the radio."

"Uh, ten-four. Okay."

The address, "121", was a governmental fiction. As of the last time E'd been by the South Branch bridge, there were only two occupied homes nearby, and neither of them had numbers. One was a house, meaning frame construction, windows, roof, like that. A house. The other was an aging camp trailer, and if anybody down there was shooting, it was probably the jackass who lived in it. He wasn't supposed to have a gun, but somehow that didn't seem to matter.

She went south on Ferry Road, running around the east

shore, half a kilo or a kilo inland. This was the same way she'd have gone to get to Silverman's place. She picked up her microphone.

"Margie, are you on the way?" No response. "Hey, Margie?"

"Yes, Sergeant. I'm just getting into the truck now."

"Okay, well you come down South Branch Trail, and call me when you're at the split off. Where Little Lake Road goes off, you know?"

"Yes, Sergeant. Mrs. Bishop reported the shots. She said it was Mister Kriter again." *Thought so.*

"Did she see him with a weapon? Or what he was shooting at?"

"She said ..." There was a loud rattle, and Margie said, "Ow! Sorry. Potholes. No, she was just getting into her car, and she heard shots. She said it had to be him." *Well, probably it did.*

"All right. You just keep your eyes open. If you see him ... if you see anybody with a gun, you just back off, call me, and stay in your vehicle. And remember to tell me where you are."

"Yes, sir."

I'd love to catch this boy with a gun. E had met Dusty Kriter before, a silly little up-north guy, with a camo jacket and a flame orange deer cap. He was still a right-wing, American-flag, I-got-my-rights big mouth, even though his beer and whatever it was he ate were paid for by the Living Wage Act. As the road bent around west, she started watching the woods and brush on each side, just like checking for deer. If Dusty stumbled out into her way, she didn't want to hit him. *I haven't put a dent in this truck yet.*

"Sergeant Gorsky, this is Unit Two."

"Go ahead, Margie."

"I'm stopped a hundred yards short of the bridge. By the Bishop house."

"All right. I'm coming up to the bridge now. Let's go slow ahead until we can see each other. And Kriter's trailer."

"Okay.

The South Branch crossed the road named for it right where Kriter lived. It carried on a half mile due south, ducked under another bridge on the Ferry Road, and ran into a nameless bay on the south shore of the island. E drove across and stopped. Straight ahead was a white-and-rust-colored J-Ko trailer. There was a pickup truck beside it; the right front wheel was sitting on a cement block. Dusty Kriter was sitting in front of it, in a folding aluminum chair. There was an empty Molson can on the ground.

"Margie, Kriter's out in his yard. Just sitting there. Might be intoxicated ... Okay, I see you now." Unit two came into sight around a curve. "Hold there. I'm going to contact him."

"Yes, Sergeant. You don't want me to assist you?"

"I want you by your radio in case I have a problem with him." E opened the door of the truck and stepped out behind it. One reason the pot holes were so annoying was that the Army patrol vehicles – civilian model pickups with some extras – were heavier than their suspension was designed for. Part of that weight was some armor inside the doors, and it had saved a few lives. "Mister Kriter!" she yelled. He looked up.

"Mister Kriter! Are you okay?"

"What the hell you want?" he asked, not unreasonably. If a man couldn't have a couple of beers at eight-thirty in the morning and fall asleep in his front yard, what was the country coming to, anyway?

"We heard there was some shooting down here. Are you sure you're okay?" *I'm okay, you're okay. Where did that come from?*

"That damn dog. Getting into my garbage again." E couldn't see any sign of a weapon, so she stepped out from behind the door and walked up.

"So you were shooting at a dog?"

"That's what I said."

"Where is it? The dog?"

"Damned if I know. Missed him. He's back there, somewhere." Kriter pointed back over his head, toward the woods ten or twelve meters behind the trailer.

"Where's the gun?"

"What gun?"

Oh, come on. "The gun you shot. At the dog."

"Oh, that gun. In the house. By the stove." E gestured for Margie to come ahead, using her left hand, keeping the right in reserve, slack, a few centimeters from her holster. "Okay. Is it all right with you if my partner has a look in there for it?"

"Sure. Might as well. You're gonna arrest me anyway."

"We'll see. You scared people, shooting like that. You're not supposed to be doing that." *You useless little twit.*

Margie was in the trailer for about sixty seconds, and then she came out, holding a Marlin lever-action .22. E was pleased to note that she had the action open and the lever down – or Kriter had left it that way. *At least the Army teaches kids to clear a weapon. That's something.*

The arrest proceedings took a very short time. A couple of months before, Kriter had seen E deal with a much larger, very drunken friend of his, and he didn't want to be dealt with himself. His resistance was all verbal, mostly philosophical. They put him in the back of Margie's truck, and E let her inform him of his legal position. "Sir," the Private told him, "You are arrested on a class one offense, possessing a firearm, and on a class three offense, deliberately dangerous behavior. You'll be confined at Nineteenth Battalion Security Branch headquarters until the Judicial Department considers ..."

"Considers my case. I know how it goes. Well let me tell you something, sweetie. Both of you." He paused for a long breath. "Politics is nonsense. Profit is just stealin'. Religion is pure bullshit. What matters ... " another pause "... is whether people can just organize themselves. To survive."

I'll be damned. A closet anarchist. "All right, Margie," E said, "I'll follow you back to Landing and show you how to enter the arrest data. Then you can take him over to Company and they'll ship him off to Battalion." She looked Kriter in the eye. "Remember, sir. At the same time England stopped burning witches, it started hanging people who forged banknotes."

"What? Who said that?"

"Marx."

"Mark who?"

"Karl."

"Mark Carl. Huh. Never heard of him."

Margie drove off. E started her truck. When she looked up, a large black dog was watching from beside the trailer.

§

Meg was dropping out. Maybe it was the economics class that did it. Or the journalism department in general. Or it was just being, as she'd have put it, a decent, properly-raised, Christian young woman in an environment that didn't seem to care about that. Her mother had gone to this school, back when things were normal. Today, nothing was the way it was then. Nothing at all.

She had the conversation with the student affairs people. She had the final meeting with her advisor, and she signed the "Yes, I'm really withdrawing" papers. She acknowledged that she would not be graduating, would not do any two-year service, would not – and this was repeated several times – be eligible for citizenship. That they were so concerned about that just underlined her reasoning. "So I won't get to vote. I wouldn't anyway. Not for these ... people."

She was packed and waiting when Mom drove up. The car seemed a little out of place, larger than she remembered it. Oddly, her mother was thinking that the school seemed smaller. They greeted each other, put the luggage in the trunk, and left. "Well, Meg ..." said Mom. "What now?"

"I don't know. I ... maybe I'll talk to Uncle Philip. I could do something at the church. Or see if there's something I could do, oh, out of the ... out of this country."

Mom sighed. "I didn't want to upset you. While you were studying. But there's some bad news there. Really bad news. About your uncle and the church."

§

E gave Margie a quick refresher on the system for officially booking a miscreant. There was a small holding pen – nothing you'd really call a cell – in the Landing SB post, and they left Kriter there while they made his bad behavior official. Simple possession of a firearm and dangerous behavior. *A year in jail, son. Hope it was worth it.* The system confirmed his charges, and they bundled him off with Margie onto the ferry. E checked a few other office things, and then headed back off on her original trip.

The drive down to Peters was shorter from Landing than from East Shore. Without any delays, you could do it in 10 minutes, but there were always delays. The bridge over the tiny creek coming from Little Lake wasn't really designed for heavy vehicles, and you needed to take it very slowly. And again, there were deer. She used the time to ask herself questions, organizing the list of things she wanted to observe at the site. In the middle of that, though, something else occurred to her. *Why don't I connect Dusty Kriter with this?*

A fair enough question. Why not? He had a gun, after all. Not the right kind, just a measly little .22. But who says that was the only one he had? Margie had looked around the trailer, but hadn't done any real shake-down. And if you'd shot someone, you'd get rid of the gun, right? *If you were smart.*

And that was why, she realized, that she ruled him out. He wasn't smart. What spook in his right mind would recruit Dusty Kriter as an assassin? So, no. And he wasn't going anywhere, anytime soon, anyway. If something came up, he'd be where they could find him. No, something else happened. *Something, what? Sophisticated.*

When she stopped at Silverman's house, Peters was even more deserted than it had been. The Bullocks' truck was gone, and when E got out and walked down toward the water, the family boat was away, too. Actually, there was something way out on the water that might be it, but it was too far away to tell. She didn't want to talk to the neighbors, anyway. She just wanted to look.

The house wasn't worth any more attention, at least not now. It was taped off and nailed up, and threatening notices were stapled in place, warning people away. The collapsed garage had been rummaged through, the old car looked at carefully, the ground all over the area examined with both experienced eyes and metal detectors. All that turned up was an old screwdriver and a few bottle caps. E had no illusions about finding something new in the details. What she wanted to do was raise the sights, look out at the horizon and back up and down the road, try to find the larger constraints. What would the shooter have had to do? Or what would he have been unable to do? What kind of obstacles ... *wait.*

As she was turning things over, she was looking around, looking, in fact, at the horizon. But at one point, something got in the way. Between the back door where someone had been shot and that line segment where the lake and the sky met was a small spot of land. Peters Island. "Oh," she said, out loud.

She shifted her feet to approximately where Silverman had been standing. In between the shed and a tree, there was a clear sight line out to the south end of that island. *How far is that?* She thought back to basic infantry training. The marksman range was 100 meters, and some of the people in her squad could hit targets at that distance consistently. The island looked farther away than the range targets did, but still, it seemed possible. With a scope. The bullet was an older round, the forensics guys said; 7.62. Larger than an assault rifle would shoot, longer range. *I need to get out onto that island.*

Another twenty minutes convinced her that she couldn't just wade out. Even driving back to a point as close as she could get, then woods-walking down to the shore, it was at least fifty meters. With binoculars, there was nothing interesting along the shore line. She walked back out to the truck and called Steve, back at the office.

As a potential super-cop member of the Republic's Security Branch, Steve wasn't all that likely a candidate. He did, though, know how to get people on the phone, get them to phone someone else, and eventually make something happen. When he got back with E, fifteen minutes later, he told her that one of the forensics guys was coming over from Company, bringing some kind of boat with him.

"How long?"

"Well ... if he catches the ferry over on their side, you know, over ... there, um, and then, crossing time, and drive down to meet you ... you want him to meet you, right? It should be about ..."

"Okay, never mind. I'll come back up there and meet him."

"Oh. Okay.

On the way back to the ferry landing, E worked through the tactics. If the Corporal from Forensics brought something small and portable – a jon boat or something lightweight - they could try carrying it down to the water at the creek. *Some nasty brush in the way.* Or, they could go back to Peters, put the boat in there, and cross over. Naval Branch had the big, lake-going patrol craft and the City Class Corvettes, but inland waters were in SB's scope of responsibility, so there were boats for rivers and ponds and the smaller lakes. If the neighbor, Tom Bullock, was at home, maybe they could impose on him for some help launching and recovering. As she arrived, she set it aside. *It'll depend on what he's bringing.*

As it turned out, it did depend on it, and the answer was one she hadn't thought of. Instead of coming over on the ferry with a boat in a pickup bed, Corporal Musinski had signed out the Battalion's Zodiac inflatable and come over from their dock on it. "Showing some initiative there, Corporal," she said.

"Yes, sir. Nice day for a boat ride."

"It is. So here's what we're doing. I want to take a look around that little island, offshore from where the shooting was. Eight klicks or so, down the coast from here. Sound all right?"

"Okay. Uh, you expecting biological evidence? I didn't bring anything very high-tech."

"I wouldn't think so. Mostly, I want to rule out anything at all being out there."

"That we can do. I have the waterproof camera and so on, at least."

"Let's go."

The Zodiac could move fast when it was asked to, but E wanted to talk the situation over with Musinski as they went. Even so, they were coming in between the island and the shore in fifteen minutes. E had explained her idea in summary, telling him that it might have been possible to shoot Silverman from the small island, and that the task was to rule that in or out.

"I see," he said. "So maybe the first thing is to get a real good measurement of the range. I got a range finder in back, there."

"Yeah. And some good photos of the back of the house, as you could see it from the island."

"And of course we look for any obvious signs. Tracks, ejected brass, signed confessions."

"Like that, yeah."

The shore was coming closer. The summer's beach grass was about at its height, and that was all they could see, beyond the stretch of bare sand, sloping down to the water. When they were ten or so meters out, Musinski stood up behind the wheel. "You know, Sergeant, maybe you could watch the bows as we come in? So I don't beach this thing right on top of where somebody else beached theirs?"

"Right." E held on to the grab bar with one hand and kept her eyes on the shore as they crept in. "Nothing so far." They were on the inshore side of the island, and the water was as still as it ever would be. Musinski cut the motor off, and the boat drifted the last meter in. Just short of the beach, it ground to a stop.

"You want to carry that anchor," the Corporal said. "Don't toss it ... unless you can tell there's nothing interesting for it to land on." E stepped off into the ankle-high water, toting the mushroom anchor. She stopped just before the dry sand began, looked ahead, right, left. As far as she could see, no one had been here since the last storm.

"Looks clean," she said and threw the anchor up the beach.

Once the Corporal got his gear together and joined her, they walked up the sand to the edge of the grass. Straight ahead, looking west across the island toward the open lake, there was nothing sticking up above the grass. Off to the right, the little strip of beach curved gradually out of sight, around the island's north end. To the left – well, that was the interesting direction. Already, E knew that you could, in fact, see the Silverman house and the Bullocks' place next to it. That was obvious. Musinski brought up the handheld rangefinder. "So it's ... what the hell? Oh, wait." He did something to the adjusting wheels on the top. "It's ... two hundred and eleven meters from here."

"Okay. That's a long shot but not too long."

"Be closer from up ahead a bit. Might get down to, oh, a hundred ninety."

"We'll walk the whole shoreline. Shoot ranges from

everywhere we can see the house. And I'll tell you what, how about if I look at the house and the edge of the grass, and you watch the sand? So I don't stumble over something?"

"Yes, sir. Just tell me when you want a range measure."

They walked south down the shore. E counted steps, and every ten, she asked Musinski to take a range. The numbers came down steadily. He read, "One hundred ninety-four," took the rangefinder from his eyes, looked ahead, and said, "Whoa! Stand still!"

"What?!" E looked around reflexively, not down.

"Just in front of your right foot. Sticking up out of the sand." She looked down. A small brown cylinder was in fact sticking up out of the sand. "That's brass," he said.

It was. It was an empty cartridge case. A 7.62 by 51 millimeter NATO-spec casing. In the US, it'd be called a .308 Winchester. Either way, the better rifles that used it were capable of 750 meter shots. With a scope. In capable hands. And it hadn't been lying there for long. If it had, it wouldn't have been lying there, or at least it would have been covered with sand. Even on this lee shore, wave action would have taken care of that. Or just plain wind. The identification, of course, took some time, picking it up with a plastic bag, looking around to make sure nothing else was there, too. Labeling it with geocodes. But before any of that, within a second of Musinski's initial statement, E said, "Damn!"

Things got substantially more formal and official. Musinski had the sense to point out that they needed to make the island a crime scene, and E agreed. *How do you tape off a whole island?* Instead of doing that, they started making radio calls, notifying and requesting and suggesting, as the Corporal put it. The result was that his teammate from Forensics got to take a ferry ride in a truck with more gear and a security force, namely the first recruit who came to hand. That Private's job was to stand on the beach by the boat with his service weapon and make sure no unauthorized personnel interfered with anything. If it occurred to him to wonder who that might be, out here on this little chunk of sand, he kept the question to himself.

By the time Peters Island had been carefully examined by people who knew how to do that, another Zodiac had arrived, carrying more help and some "RESTRICTED AREA KEEP OUT" signs. The story, as E told it to Captain Matthews over the radio, was that there was one recently-fired cartridge, of the same type as the bullet in the victim's head. There was a place in the middle of the island where the grass was flattened out, suggesting that someone slept there. Or at least lay down. A wrapper from a kind of power food ... bar ... thing was nearby. And checking with a generic kind of rifle scope showed that, yes, the back of Silverman's house was clearly visible, in detail, from most parts of the little island's inner shore. She put all of this as generally as possible, since they were talking on an ordinary radio, not anything secure.

"So," she finished up, "Someone fired a 7.62 round from the island. Seventeen days ago, there was a pretty good blow out here, so the shot was probably after that. Otherwise, the cartridge would have been sanded over. Probably more recent, even. And the shooter would absolutely have been able to see the victim, standing in his back door."

Matthews sounded pleased. "All right. Good. I ... can't think of why anyone would be out there, shooting. I mean, any innocent reason. Can you?"

"Nothing's coming to mind, sir. Forensics says that's an old standard deer hunting cartridge, besides military, but why would you go out onto that island to shoot back at deer?"

"I wouldn't, for sure. Good stuff, Gorsky. This gives me something to tell Battalion, and they really want to hear something. What if you plan on coming over here tomorrow, early, and we call Major Vogel?"

"Yes, sir. That sounds like the next step. See if he has any directions for us. Oh, and for the record, Corporal Musinski is a good hand. Knows what he's doing."

"So I hear. I'll talk to you tomorrow."

As the forensic work on Peters Island finished up, E got Musinski to run her back to Landing. It was after 1900 hours, and there was nothing going on except the night duty at the SB post. She stopped in, saw Ed finishing up a couple of paperwork tasks, gave him a quick summary of the day's work, and walked back out. She stopped to breathe a little of the evening wind coming in from the west. There was a slight sound of footsteps, and a brown dog trotted by, heading toward the trees.

§

For Meg Cording, the rest of the drive back to Harperville was stormy. There was grief and denial, anger and some fear, and finally a feeling that, if she'd known the term, she'd have called righteous indignation. Uncle Philip, officially Pastor Philip Mikel, DD, was gone. Just gone. Arrested by the government police. Others too. No notice, nothing said, just gone. Meg's aunt had been left to clear up the house, and she'd done that and gone back to the US, back to her family. Just gone.

When she could think clearly enough to ask questions, among the first of them was about lawyers. Had the family done anything, well, legal about it?

"No, Meg. You can't do that sort of thing now." There wasn't any profession of law anymore. No private attorneys. If you were arrested, you got an Advocate. A government employee. And that was that.

This was hard for her mother. Meg recognized the short, precise phrases she was using as something she did when she was angry or very sad. Neither her family nor Uncle Philip's had been emotional people. They didn't kiss their children, and they expected them to listen and accept what their parents said. Meg had done that, and suddenly ... it wasn't there anymore. Behind Mom's stiff certainty, she could hear the worst of all devils, uncertainty. "What do I do now?" she thought.

East-southeast of Cockburn Island is the western tip of Manitoulin. The red kayak was making its way along, well offshore, and as night fell, it was due south, bobbing along, upside down, between Middle Duck and Great Duck. No one was there to see it.

§

In the morning, E drove onto the ferry. She was the only passenger. It was an old boat with an arch-supported bridge facing both ways. Sized for a dozen or more cars and pickups, it could hold a lesser number of greater vehicles, and that kept it in service. On the off chance that the AoR ever had to deploy more than a half dozen soldiers across the narrow water, they accepted the higher cost of running a bigger boat. The island was, after all, a border, a border with the Republic's largest and closest ally, but still a border.

From the boat, you could see either shore during the crossing. On the mainland side, you drove off and were instantly in the downtown of a very small village, De Tour. An immediate left, and you headed south and then west on Republic 134. Half an hour later, you'd be in Cedarville, parking behind Company HQ. Along the way, you'd have seen a lot of pine trees and the occasional side road or driveway. Sometimes, you'd be close enough to the shore to see the water. About half way, you'd drive past a blighted moonscape where dolomite used to be mined and shipped out. In general – assuming the wildlife stayed put in the woods – it wasn't an especially exciting drive.

E always packed for a two-day trip, whether or not she expected to need it. It was just old habit, started when she was travelling to symposia and on university business. Travel of any kind was spotty, inside the US, and air travel especially so. You never knew when you'd be stranded somewhere. The habit stayed with her when she joined the AoR, and uniform clothing and gear just made it easier. So although she expected to have her meeting with Matthews, go back to the ferry, and go home, she was also equipped for more than that, right down to a couple of energy bars.

She and Matthews met in the secure conference room again. "Before we call Major Vogel, I need to tell you that we got the biology report, and the victim was, in fact, Silverman. Or at least the person Ice Rink was set up to handle. So that's one more thing we know, besides your news."

Good. "Well, that helps, sir. Narrows things slightly."

"Another thing, though, is that I can't get a word about Captain Wright. Nothing. His records are all with Division now. Or so Personnel says. And I can't see them with my levels of access. So we just don't know what was up ... what went on with his transfer. If it was a transfer."

"Can we ask Major Vogel for some help with that?"

"I have. He's looking into it, and he said that if he got the same kind of ... nothing, he'd take it to Brigade. But let's call him, now, and see if he's gotten any further than I did."

Major Aditya Vogel hadn't gotten any further. He'd run up against the same obstacles The only difference was that he did learn, and probably shouldn't have, that there was another family of classified programs involved. There was the hint that if Brigade pushed on it, he and Matthews might get briefed.

"So that's where I am with it," he said. "But what have you got for me?" They told him, E doing most of the talking. His first question was whether E still felt there was something significant about the patrol boat hanging around off shore.

"Well, sir, nothing we've learned makes me any less sure. If it was a coincidence, I'd like to hear somebody in NB say it was. Or say that no, there wasn't any PB out there. I hope they don't say that, but still, I'd like to hear something about it, one way or another."

"Yeah, frankly, so would I. Matthews, what do you think about sending Sergeant Gorsky on a fishing expedition down to the Alpena base?"

"I'd be fine with that, sir. Do you have a contact down there?" said Matthews.

"I've had some interaction with their internal security people. They work through us, but they have to have staff that handle need-to-know. So, Gorsky, you could ask about who they have briefed on Ice Rink."

"All right, sir, I'll get Sergeant Gorsky a bunk here for tonight, and then she can go down there tomorrow. That all right, Sergeant?"

Glad I packed a bag. "Yes, sir. I haven't been below the bridge for a while. Who am I meeting with?"

"I'll get you a name by tomorrow morning," Vogel promised. "There are three or maybe four people who do this stuff, and I'll have to make a call to see who's on duty and knows the right things. But I'll get you that tomorrow AM."

"And, sir," said Matthews, "from my perspective, I do think we need to take this up the chain to Brigade. Is that your thinking, too?"

"Yes, it is, Captain. I'll be making those calls."

§

With the truck full of government gasoline and the name of a naval branch ensign to call on, E rolled out early the next morning. It was about as far to St. Ignace and the Mackinac Bridge as it had been from the ferry landing to Cedarville, but that was just the beginning of the drive. Once she was across the straits and down on the southern side, it was another couple of hours down along the Lake Huron shore – the "Sunrise Side" as the real estate ads used to call it. The road, now R23, was sometimes on the shore and sometimes inland, passing hundreds of what had been tourist cottages or residences. The lake levels had drowned or damaged many of them; unlike the west coast, the east side never had much in the way of cliffs or protective dunes. It was a lonely ride and with the exception, as always, of random wildlife, not an exciting one. Once across the bridge, she was close enough to get reasonable FM radio. The SB truck only had the scrambled satcom unit installed, but she could get national radio on her personal phone.

Republic FM 95, coming out of the capital, was a good choice, usually. No talk, no classics, just new music. *You can make a living out of it, now. At least.* She got the last few chords of somebody's guitar solo. The DJ said nothing except, "Now, this is Carol Awala, 'Lately I Find'." *Oh ... damn.* E turned the volume up a bit. Awala was a favorite. She appeared by herself, mostly, but for recording, her partner sat in with her, playing piano. Carol herself was a guitarist and a coloratura mezzo-soprano.

The song started with an intro on the keyboard, ta da, da DA, da-da; ta da, da DA da-da; ta da, da da. Then the guitar and the voice came in.

> Lately I find
> That I don't give one single flyin' damn
> For the things that keep you up at night
> And make you fly those banners on your car.

"Banners on your car..." E joined in.

> Katie, I knew
> You always drifted to the right
> And I just let it go.
> Now it's gone too far.

"... Too far ..."

> You talk of sin.
> Well, here's a sin for you:
> Telling and believing lies.
> Katie, on that score you're bound for hell.
> You are not well.
> There's a dead look in your eyes
> That's something new.

E felt a bit of moisture in the corner of her own eye. *So close to home.*

When we first met

There was no talk of hosts

Or holy ghosts.

No china angels on the shelf.

You could enjoy yourself.

The piano came in and played an echo of the last two verses. E knew the song well, and she sang the next lines almost in tune.

When I hear you talk

About the wicked left,

I'm never sure

What you think those people did to you.

Or is it just that they don't care,

And you so want them to.

You're old enough to know

There is no single Tao,

No gods, no heavens, and no hell

Except the ones you make yourself.

You used to do that well.

You didn't need the righteous boys

To tell you how.

The moisture became an actual tear. *Dammit.*

Now your friends are those
I do not nod to on the street.
I hate to be that way,
But I refuse to meet
Zealous bastards of the kind
Who lied the children into war
Twice before.
They're just not worth the time;
I might be indiscreet.

Zealous bastards. She wiped the tear away.

So, Katie, you must pick and choose
Which one you lose,
Those lies or me.
What you believe
Is not just false but wrong,
And you are no longer free.

Christ, I didn't really need all this today.

So you go on ahead.
Me, I'm headed for the bar.
Such a dark and quiet holy place
Where my old cronies are
And any lessons to be learned
Are not received but earned.

Da da, da DAH, da-da, da-da, da DUM went the piano. "Carol Awala. That was written twenty years ago by a man in Ann Arbor," the DJ said. "Now, we'll ..." *Jesus!* E turned the radio off.

§

Meg was no happier than she'd been on the ride home. The time slipped by, but nothing came of anything. The new pastor was bland and mildly sympathetic, but he had nothing in the way of volunteer work at the moment, let alone any kind of paid jobs. "We're just quite constrained, financially, right now, I'm afraid."

She found that her sleep suffered, and when she did sleep, there were frustrating dreams. She'd be away from home, getting ready to leave wherever it was, but unable to get her luggage together. The people with her would be no better, and in some undefined way, she was supposed to get them squared away as well as herself. She'd usually wake up, angry and resentful, just at the point where the chaos was reaching a peak.

It occurred to her that there might be something in the town's slowly-regenerating library, some book on psychology, maybe, or dreams, or even – she finally admitted it to herself – depression. So she borrowed her mother's car and dropped in. It was an unfamiliar scene. The libraries at the college had been large and obscurely organized. You were supposed to know what you needed. Here, shelves were labeled with topics instead of numbers, and people asked if you needed any assistance. With some help, she found a couple of books and sat down to see if they were something she'd want to borrow.

"Hi, Meg." She looked up, startled. Larry something.

"Hello, Larry."

"You were away at school, I thought." He wasn't a boy she'd known well. He came to church with his mother or by himself.

"I ..." She hadn't seen or talked to many people outside the family. There wasn't a prepared, public statement. "I didn't care for what they were teaching."

"Oh. Can I sit down for a minute?" Meg didn't really want company, but she couldn't think of a civilized way to say, "No, you can't". She fell back on, "Oh, yes, fine." At least he chose the opposite side of the table.

"Are you okay?"

"I'm ... I mean, what? Okay? How?"

"You know, about your uncle. And the church and all."

"Oh."

"If you don't want to talk about it, that's okay."

"Well." She came hard up against a breaking wave of emotion. She hadn't cried yet. Raged, yes, kicked against the injustice, banged her head, figuratively, against the walls of her parents' silence and reserve, but not wept. Now she did, softly and without making a scene. After a minute, she felt Larry pat her hand.

§

R23 comes into Alpena from the north, then bends east to run across the top of the city. It follows the Thunder Bay River down toward the shore, past what used to be an official wildlife area – now it was one by default – and keeps on past dead or dying strip developments, one after another. The store fronts that weren't boarded up were sometimes local stores, taking advantage of cheap rent, or they were government public service agencies. The north country was just about back to the sixties, economically.

Closer into downtown, she passed a functioning bar or two and the shell of what had been a large Catholic church. Then the highway turned sharp right, heading south and eventually out of town. E kept on straight, and in half a block drove up to the gate of NBBA: Naval Branch Base Alpena. It'd been a commercial marina, but now it hosted patrol boats, one of the big city class corvettes, and an ice breaker. As she stopped for the gate guards, she could see the corvette's seventy-six millimeter gun poking out from behind the main building. A large tan dog trotted across the road behind her.

The National Service kids at the gate took her ID, checked it against a list of expected visitors, and pointed her to visitor parking spaces outside the main building. She parked, shut the truck off, and started preparing for the visit. The truck had a welded-in lock box between the seats, and she took off her side arm and put it in. The general rule was to carry your side arm on your own turf, not on that of another AoR branch. Next, she followed some specific practices of her own. She shut her personal and official phones down, all the way to bare metal, not just restarted but actually turned off. She took another one, older and less capable, out of the box and turned it on. She dropped it into one of her cargo pockets and locked up the box.

E locked the truck and headed for the building. At the door, her badge let her in. She squared her shoulders and marched up to the welcome desk.

"I'm Sergeant Gorsky. I have a conference with Ensign Peterman."

"All right, Sergeant," said the Petty Officer behind the desk. "Let me just check, here ... yes, you're on the roster." He punched 3 keys on his phone. "Ensign Peterman, your eleven-thirty meeting is here." He handed E another badge and lanyard. "You'll wear this, if you please, Sergeant. While you're on the base. And Mister Peterman will be down in a minute."

Ensign Peterman was, in fact, down in a minute. He was young, but low-ranking officers tended to be. He didn't seem very comfortable with this particular event, but he put a good face on it. He made a point of checking E's badges – her permanent one and the temporary card she'd just been given – and took her back to their secure facility. As usual, there were two doors to go through, and between them a place to leave communication devices and other things prohibited inside. E put her old phone in one of the pigeon holes built into a wall, and she made sure Peterman noticed. He opened the inner door and led the way to the usual conference room. Nothing was said for the first twenty or thirty seconds, because somewhere right outside, a helicopter goosed its engines and took off. There was no window, and presumably the walls were shielded from electronic snooping, but even so, one of the big dual-rotor birds taking off was not a peaceful, quiet background noise. Fortunately, it was headed out over the harbor, and the sound died down.

"So, Ensign," E began, seizing the high ground, so to speak, "I'm investigating a homicide that occurred up in Seventh Division. A man named Silverman was shot in his home, and I'd like to see if Naval Branch has any coincidental information I can add to my report."

"I see. Yes, I was told that you'd ... um, want to talk about some patrol activities? Near the scene of your homicide ... scene?"

"Right. I was the initial SB contact to arrive, and while investigating, I noticed a Naval Branch patrol craft carrying out what appeared to be a search or a surveillance off shore. It was too distant for me to get a number, but the boat type was clearly a PC. Can you determine what boat of yours would have been patrolling off Peters, on Dog Island?"

"Well, I should be able to check on tasking for PCs in a general area. What date are we talking about?" E gave him the day. He turned on a desktop on a side table. "This will take a minute to come up. While it does, can I ask what the classified program is?"

"I've had verbal confirmation from our Battalion command that you're briefed for Ice programs. Can you confirm that for me?"

"Yes, in, um, superficial matters. I don't involve myself ... I don't actually work with the Ice programs. But I do have, ah, knowledge of them."

"The victim was involved in an Ice program. Ice Rink, specifically."

"I see. So you'd like to know ... ah, here we are." He turned back to the computer. "So on that date, in region L4, who would have been out there? That's funny. I don't see ... oh, yes. We did order a boat to that area. But it was Search and Rescue. Not ... criminal issues."

Search and Rescue? Of who? "That's interesting. Do you have any detail?"

"Let's bring that up. It's not classified at all." Peterman began to sound less tentative. "Let's see here ... all right, it says ... the general contact phone number here got a call ... from a sports equipment store, in Saint Ignace."

"Sports equipment?"

"Kay's Sports Rental, it says. The caller said she was the business owner. But ... odd ... she thought she was calling one of her customers, 'Caller stated that customer gave her this number ...' our number ... 'as his mobile phone. Customer did not return a rental kayak to the caller's business on time, and she called the number customer gave her'."

"So somebody rented a kayak, didn't return it, and the

contact number he left was Alpena NB?"

"That's how I read it. So ... let's see here ... we had a PC nearby, so it was tasked to look for anyone in distress."

"But ... why off Dog Island? That's a long paddle from Saint Ignace."

"Well, that's ... hard to say. The report just stops there. It doesn't say why, and it doesn't say if they found anything."

"Maybe the caller said something about the island? That's where the renter was going to take the kayak?"

"It doesn't say that. It just ends."

E and the Ensign looked at each other. He knew that she was thinking *sloppy reporting*; she was, and also was wondering what else he could turn up. "Well," she said, "can you tell which boat it was that did the searching? Maybe it was in the area? Or it sighted something like a kayak?"

"I can look ... um ... no. The boat was doing something classified. I'm not briefed on the details. It's border-related. And unless you're ..."

"I have access to summary levels of our border programs, but no specific ones. None of yours." That was not precisely true, but E had learned that people accepted 'I don't know' more readily than 'I can't tell you'. "But you can confirm that you had a PC out there at that time?"

"Ah ... yes, I ... can confirm that."

"How would I go about requesting access to the program in question? My command would probably put that request through."

"I ... hmm. I guess you'd have to ... go through your side first. I'm not really familiar with your secure program procedures. We handle the briefings for our people. On our classified programs. But, for you ..."

"All right," E said. "I can begin that process, up my chain of command. But you said the call about the missing kayak wasn't classified? Could I have the contact information for the caller? "

"Um, I don't see ... why not. How would that help you?"

"It might not. But it's something we'd follow up on. If the renter had left her our number, for example." *We take things like this seriously, boy.*

"Yes. Well, again, it's not classified, so ... I can send this to a printer here. I can't email it outside the closed ... ah, network."

"Thank you."

"Is there anything else I can ... help with?" His tone was a mildly amusing mixture of 'I have better things to do' and 'I don't really know anything, and I'm being useless.'

"Unless you have access to other activity around Dog Island in the timeframe I gave you, I don't think so. There isn't anything else you can see..." she gestured at the PC "... that you can share, by chance?"

"I don't ... well, there's one ... or two other things I can try." He wasn't all that keen on it, but somehow this Sergeant, combining a certain amount of physical attractiveness with a near-stereotypical aspect of squared-away military togetherheit, didn't seem like a person to be just brushed off. Ensign Peterman was, to be frank, something of a wimp. He typed this and that, clicked on things, and finally determined that there was little or nothing more he could share. At his badge level.

E knew, obviously, that the answer would be something polite but negative, but she asked anyway, "Are there other officers available today who might have wider access?" It was impolite, in a way, but she expected Matthews to ask if she'd asked.

"No, I'm sorry. There are only two ... I'm sorry, three ... officers here who deal with classified programs. I'm afraid I'm as good as it gets." E waited a second for the nervous laugh that should have accompanied this little attempt at informality. It came and went quickly. Peterman had just realized that he'd said "I'm sorry" twice in a few seconds. And "I'm afraid", too.

"Very well, then. I believe I'll collect that report you printed for me and be on my way." Peterman glanced at his watch.

"Have you, ah, had lunch yet? I was planning on going over to the dining ..." He waved a hand, pointlessly in the direction of the door.

"Thanks, Ensign, but I'll be stopping in one or two other places, off base. I'll get something on the road." *This kind of thing used to be annoying. Now it's just funny. I must be getting old.*

Peterman gave her the caller report, and he even found an envelope marked "unclassified" for it. E collected her phone from the entrance, and they went back to the lobby. She thanked him formally, turned in her temporary badge, and walked back out to the truck. She sat behind the wheel for a few seconds, just looking at the base HQ building. *Waste of time? Coin toss.*

She turned the engine on and hit an unlabeled toggle switch on the dash. A green light came on. She swapped the contents of the lock box with the phone she'd taken inside; she scooted up in the seat to put her side arm back on. She waved to the kids at the gate and went back the way she'd come. In a block, she turned right onto the highway. Another couple of blocks and she pulled into a gas and electric station. She parked at the side, left the engine running, and got out the old phone.

It came up slowly, and as it ran its boot up sequence, it began displaying a number of messages. Taken together, they indicated that the device had been infected with at least one piece of malware, probably more. As long as the green light on the dashboard was on, no electronic communication was going to come in or out. The truck was a little cyber-protected bubble, now, and the phone had been squeaky clean when she took it into the naval base.

§

The man in the green-walled office was quiet and cerebral, given to silences even in the middle of a conversation. Some people thought he was trying a cheap negotiating trick, doing a "Russian", just staring at you until you caved in or backed up on some point. But he wasn't consciously waiting for others to blink. He was exploring some new thread of the discussion, asking himself questions, looking for paths around some obstacle. Or remembering some line of verse, some lyric, some Latin tag. He was at best eccentric, perhaps slightly "off". He was also extremely valuable to the new little country.

He wasn't a soldier. He wasn't an elected official. He had an office in one of the government buildings in the Republic's capital, and there was a person at a desk outside it. To see the man himself, you had to get past the person at the desk. There was no title on the door or on a desk sign, although the man had one. It was so vague, though, that knowing it wouldn't have done you any good. Still, for all that vagary, he was an essential part of the Republic's government, a man you don't meet every day.

At the moment, he was thinking about a piece of conventional wisdom and how misleading it was in anything important. People were fond of paraphrasing the Tao, saying something about a long journey beginning with a single step. "No, it doesn't," he thought.

"Not if the journey involves more than a single person. It begins with many steps, in many directions. And some of the people don't know why they're moving. Or even if they're moving at all, until they suddenly realize that they've moved." Another text came to mind, one from W. S. Merwin. "... the whole mountain's been on fire for seven years, and you've just noticed."

Today, he'd spend time – several hours, at least – with some people who had only recently discovered that they were travelling. They represented many other people, only some of whom knew that the meeting would take place. Very few, actually. And not all of them would have approved, if they had known. The man's job, the thing he'd been politely asked to do, was listen to the visitors; be polite, himself; understand what they were saying and especially what they weren't saying. He wouldn't, of course, commit the Republic to anything. That was not his job. He wouldn't ask his guests to commit, either. There'd be time for that later, and other people would do it. The man was not a Godfather or a fixer or a diplomat. If a natural, never-really-gave-a-thought-to-it atheist could have been one, he'd have made a good Jesuit, capable of seeing an infinite number of sides to a question, believing in only one.

He looked quickly through a page of his own cryptic notes, in English but essentially incomprehensible to anyone else. He put the page back in a folder, put that back in a drawer, and locked it up. Late afternoon sun was lighting up the trees, but he had no outside view. "It would be nice to have a window," he thought. One story down, two dogs were lying in a planter bed, enjoying the building's shade along East University Street.

§

E drove well out of Alpena, then turned into a gravel lot in front of what had been a dealership of some kind.

Maybe landscaping equipment, maybe construction gear. It was abandoned now, anyway. She shut off the signal blocker and turned on her radio and the official phone. The number of the kayak shop was on the report she'd been given, and since it was only a bit after 1400 hours, she gave them a try. A young voice answered and said that Kay of Kay's Sports Rental was in the back. "I'll get her for you."

An older voice came to the phone rather quickly. "This is Kay Garner. You're the police?"

"Security Branch, yes, ma'am. This is Sergeant Gorsky. I'm calling about a kayak you rented to someone? And didn't get back? Is that still the case? You don't have it?"

"That's right. Took you people a while to get back to me."

"Actually, Ms. Garner, I'm not with the group you called. That was Naval Branch. I just heard about it from them today."

"Oh. Okay. Did they find the guy?"

"They did look, but they didn't turn anything up. Do you have time to answer a few questions for me? If I knew more about it, I might be able to help. And I'll be recording this call, if you don't mind."

The summary as E later transcribed it said that a young man came in on a date that turned out to be three days before the shooting was reported.

```
Subject rented a small river-style kayak;
one-seat; sit-in, not sit-on-top. Red. And
a paddle and life jacket. Term of the
rental was two days. Renter put kayak in
the back of what shop owner thought might
be a Chevrolet pickup, no markings or
damage, interviewee did not see the
license plate. Renter gave his name as Val
Mitchell, and left a phone number which he
claimed to be his cell phone. Renter was
described as a person of color, male,
```

clean-shaven, twenty to thirty years of age. Wearing "ordinary" clothes. Shop owner stated that renter did not speak with an accent.

Renter did not return property by close of business on the second day, and the next day, the rental company owner called the given phone number. Got Naval Branch, Alpena. According to the shop owner, the renter also left an address where he said he would be staying. That address was later determined to be a vacant parcel of land on Gorman Road, west of Saint Martin Bay. SB patrol dispatched from B Company reported no evidence that the property had been visited for months prior. No male person with the given name is known to SB, either in the 12th Brigade area or Republic-wide contact data sources.

Provided rental company owner with a report number for use with a business loss insurance claim. Assured owner that SB would inform her of any further developments.

So. E sat back from the terminal and looked at that summary. Somebody who knew the NB Alpena phone number rented a kayak, gave a bogus address, and vanished. Almost nothing connected it with Silverman except the patrol boat and the phone call. *This is probably a waste of time.*

Instead, there was that malware on E's decoy phone. That was more interesting and not at all a waste of time. Matthews had been briefly angry that phone hacking was going on at an NB base, and then quickly fascinated. "But," she said, "what suggested taking it along? Did you suspect ... what?"

"Sir, it's a thing I picked up when I was working down south. We worked with some cyber teams, and they showed us how to do it."

"Okay, but why this trip?"

"I didn't think anything would show up. But it's just a kind of ... self-defense, I guess. Any place with a budget and any kind of intelligence operation, you just have to assume there might be a threat."

"But do you do that all the time?"

"Oh, no. If all I want to do is keep threats off, then just having good defense software is enough. This is just when I want to find out what's out there, in some specific environment. And then, if I do get something, I don't have to hand over my own phones. Just the decoy."

"Nice. When will we know what's on it?"

"The cyber team is up at Battalion. I dropped it off with them on my way back. They'll either know what's up, or they'll go to Division."

"Too bad Major Vogel and I are talking to Battalion tomorrow. If you get anything back in time for that, get it to me. Otherwise ... hmm. Maybe we want to sit on it until we know what the bad stuff is. We'll be giving Colonel Macready enough to worry about as it is."

§

In the green-walled office, its owner had two visitors. One, a man, wore a naval uniform. The other person was dressed in the casually serious way that the republic's civilian leaders did; a woman's sport coat over a buttoned Oxford shirt, if you presented as a woman. Men didn't dress all that differently, except that the shirts might not be quite as tailored. No one wore anything even vaguely like a skirt or a dress. And no neckties, needless to add. In the academic world, some people were wearing turtlenecks again, but this was not the academic world.

The three of them were talking, talking about talking, actually. "How will we open the discussions?" the Naval Branch officer asked.

The other visitor frowned. "Do we want to open them? Or let the others open?" She was African-American, in her sixties, probably. She looked very fit.

"How would we like the talks to open?" asked the green-office man. "I would think a spirit of candor but not enthusiasm might be our theme."

"So, we're open but we're not forthcoming?"

"That might not be best. I personally would like to appear as a friend, but as a friend with commitments and concerns and cares of his own. Things that, as our visitors will understand, are compelling but are left unspecified."

The woman frowned again. "So it's 'happy to listen, nice to see you, but we're busy'?"

"Well, no. No. We mustn't close doors. I visualized it the other day as 'We understand your reasons, and we of course have had reasons of the same kind, ourselves. But we must bear in mind our own responsibilities in considering the extent to which we ...' If you see what I mean."

"What about the drugs?" said the Naval man.

"Oh, dear, no. Not at this point. What good could that do?"

"We're spending a lot of money on it, that's what. "

"But ..." the green office man spread his hands, "That's far, far down in the weeds. In the seaweed, so to speak. There are so many tactical things like that, things that will come up when there's even a suggestion of ... cooperation, let alone anything more binding. Certainly not at this point."

"Right," said the civilian. "They don't even know what they want to do, yet. If they want to do anything. We can't start right out talking about drugs. Or cheese either." Both men smiled.

§

In her shared room at the base, E was about to go out and find something for dinner. Her phone – her personal phone – went off; her ring tone was the first twenty seconds of a sixty-year-old synth-pop song, "Love is a Stranger". When she was still in academia, the Eurythmics and others from that era were briefly revived.

The number wasn't familiar, and despite the Republic's fierce laws against telemarketing, some unwanted calls still came through. *Oh, what the hell.* She answered. "Hello?"

"Hello, E! It's Kristin! Guess where I am?"

Well, well. "Kristin. Let's see. In a state of existential crisis?"

"Well ... actually, no. I'm in Saint Ignace."

"Really?! I was just there yesterday. Myself. What's up?"

The call lasted four or five minutes. The summary was that Kristin, an old friend, a woman she knew in academia, was in the area, if you considered fifty kilometers away to be "in the area". She was moving into town, looking for a place to live, starting a new job in the Republic's education department. She'd be driving "all the hell over" the Upper Peninsula, making things difficult for curriculum managers in the secondary schools. "We went to all that trouble to turn education upside down, and these people just can't manage to keep up. You'd think educators could let go of two hundred years' worth of dogma easily enough. They've had six years to do it."

"It's a sin and a shame," E had said. She told Kristin what she could of her own current job, and they agreed to a dinner the next time they were within at least a hundred K of each other. E hung up, and deliberately put it out of her mind until she'd gotten off the base and down the road a bit to a local bar. She ordered a plate of whitefish. And a beer. Canada was going through yet another craft brewing epicycle, and there was reasonably good product coming across at the Soo.

So, Kristin. Smart, cheerful Kristin. Kristin, the friend of Caroline. Caroline, the woman who always brought lyrics to mind.

> Although I bask in charming smiles
>
> All charms still fail to bind me.
>
> My heart turns back to Ireland's Isle
>
> And the girl I left behind me.

A vivid image presented itself: a campus bar, a bit more to drink than was really necessary, and the three of them, listening to a fiddle band playing Brighton Camp. It was the night they were bringing things to an end, E going away north to join the Separation, Kristin going out West to join yet another grad program, and Caroline, going nowhere. Staying there in Indiana, staying in a cruel and abusive department with dreadful little people in authority. Poor Caroline. She stayed and went down with the ship.

She couldn't let go. She had a place ... and so she had a place. And she stayed in it.

This was a train of thought E had identified long ago as pathological. It was a predictor of a sleepless night or at least a night of unpleasant dreams. She'd known that Kristin had come back from Seattle and gotten herself hired by the Republic, citizenship and all. But she was down south, working in the capital. E was on the west side, then, and frankly reluctant to open an old wound. But ... *well, hell, it was nice to hear from her.*

The dinner came, fresh if not remotely interesting. The bartender smiled as she set it down, but it was the kind of professional smile that comes with twenty years of tending bar. "Enjoy, honey," she said.

E finished up and paid her tab. On the way out to her truck, she nearly tripped over a golden retriever napping by the door.

§

Meg and Larry met again and then again, at the library and at a coffee shop. Strip developments were drying up and blowing away, but downtowns, even in small towns, were beginning to revive, and coffee wasn't one of the things her upbringing had defined as sinful.

To begin with, they talked about the closing off of paths and directions, the end of patterns that good people were supposed to follow. She hadn't found many people in school who were interested in virtue and doctrine – at least not in the forms she'd grown up with. Her ideas weren't well formed and easy to express, but Larry was good at listening. He was so good at it, she realized quite suddenly, that he nodded and smiled but never agreed. In particular, after she'd repeated her theory about the church people being targeted by the evil government, she stopped short. "I mean ... that's what I think." A pause. "Don't you?"

"Well," Larry said, "That's what a lot of the people here said."

"Yes. And so ..."

For almost the first time, he interrupted. "See, there's things that ... that not everybody knows."

"Are you saying you don't ..."

"I'm sayin' the whole truth didn't come out."

"The whole truth?"

"It didn't. I saw some things. In the church. So did some other people."

What followed took most of an afternoon, first at the café and then sitting in Larry's car. There were more tears and instead of comfort, some carefully worded advice. What she heard was a shock, and it wasn't anything she wanted to believe, but Larry was so candid and so unaffected, so real, that it was as hard to deny as it was to accept. But she couldn't imagine him concocting a tale like it or imagine him lying when he said he'd seen and heard things himself. There were guns in the church; he'd seen them. The small group around the pastor had been making lists of people, people who were "against them". There'd been money, Republic Dollars and US cash, kept in a cabinet. "Just in envelopes. Some from the offerings, some from I don't know where." And then the trips, Thursday nights when choir practice was missing a face or two, and nobody asked where Mister so-and-so was or Miss you-know-who. And then they'd be back on Sunday.

Meg went home, had dinner silently, and watched her parents' faces, trying to imagine them lying. Or even sinning by omission, keeping quiet, saying nothing. In the small hours, she reached a kind of conclusion. Larry's advice had been to keep quiet, keep her eyes open. Watch and wait.

§

Colonel Ellen Macready, like most of the SB's higher command, was a veteran of the Separation. If she was wearing her sleeves rolled, you'd be likely to notice a scar across her right forearm, received in the brief, confused fighting along the state line. Not many people were even wounded in the course of the Separation, let alone killed, and even though her injury was caused by a piece of flying debris, not directly by a projectile, it earned her a certain amount of respect. She didn't bank on it, though. She preferred to be respected for being respectful, for appearing to assume that her people were competent and dedicated, even if she privately thought they weren't. She'd observed first-hand just how little good screaming at subordinates did.

She greeted Matthews and Vogel, and she began by stating her assumptions. "You're here to tell me what you've got so far, and to ask me for help, right?"

"That's right, sir," said Vogel. "Captain Matthews and I have reached ... well, what feels like the edge of our area, and this case looks as though it extends farther. Maybe a lot farther."

"All right. Tell me where you're sitting with it now."

Vogel rehearsed the opening facts, stressing the closed-off nature of Captain Wright's transfer, the unexplained failure to brief Sergeant Gorsky on Ice Rink, and the unusual connection with Naval Branch. "We can't get any information on Captain Wright. It's all sealed at Division level. So that leaves us with a direction we can't go."

"I see. Let me ask, just for sake of asking, if you're sure that Gorsky isn't somehow involved."

"Matthews, will you talk about that?" Vogel asked.

"Yes, sir. For one thing, nothing in her record suggests that she'd be capable of taking the shot. She was just barely passing on marksmanship in training. More to the point, she's been full time in the AoR since the Separation, with no missing time or loaned-out assignments. Good appraisals from her command, but nothing to suggest that she has any clandestine mission chops. And of course, we looked at her background from before the Separation, and she had a background check when she got her clearance. She has an economics PhD."

"Economics? A PhD?"

"Yes. She essentially dropped out of academics, apparently."

"All right, so let's assume she's what she seems," said Macready. "What's your current theory about the shooting?"

Vogel handed her a single piece of paper. "We have two general ideas. One is that it was carried out by someone in or connected with the group Silverman was spying on. Either for revenge or to prevent him from providing any more information. Conceivably, there was something he didn't report, and the group needed to keep him from doing so. Or they just wanted him dead. That would be our number one idea."

"Okay."

"The second one, and we both" – he nodded at Matthews – "hope this is wrong, is that it was carried out by our own people, someone in the AoR, as some kind of counter-intelligence operation. We'd love to rule that out, but that would be way above our badge levels."

"Counter-intelligence? Why would you think that?"

"Well, there is this nebulous connection with Naval Branch. Ice Rink was a joint program between SB and the Naval people. As far as I've been able to find out, that's very unusual. The Ice programs are supposed to be just SB territory. And there's a sniff, nothing more, of NB having some interest in Dog Island's west shore, two days after Silverman was shot. Sergeant Gorsky observed a patrol craft moving back and forth off shore the day she initially responded to the shooting."

"That's pretty nebulous, I agree. But I see why you'd wonder about it. Have you checked with NB?"

"We tried. Gorsky visited them in Alpena, but she got nowhere. They did have a PB in the area, but it was supposed to be looking for a missing kayaker."

"Hmmm." Macready rubbed one hand with the other. "Arthritis," she said. "Can I ask you this? How about *Cherchez la femme*? Maybe not political at all?"

Vogel looked at Matthews. "Always possible," she said. "But there's nothing to point to in Silverman's personal life. No suggestion of a relationship."

"But if your sergeant wasn't briefed and didn't know she should be watching him, and therefore not reporting on him, how do you know?"

"The neighbors, the whole family, independently denied that he ever had any visitors at all. Or went anywhere, besides up to his mailbox or out for groceries. And in fact, the background we have on Silverman bears that out. It says he had no close family, no unusual travel, no unexplained gaps in his history. Classic undercover personality, as far as the records show. Again, sir, it's possible, but we have nothing to suggest it."

"So, if Gorsky wasn't briefed and wasn't even aware of Silverman, I think you said, how did you come to know that?"

"When I transferred in, I was briefed by Brigade security on Ice Rink and two other programs. That briefing categorically stated that Sergeant Gorsky's position was created to deal with Silverman, and it stated that she'd been briefed on it by Captain Wright. A couple of weeks after that, the shooting happened."

"Was there any reason why a sergeant had to be assigned from elsewhere in the Branch?"

Vogel took over. "There is another sergeant assigned to the Dog Island post already, but he doesn't hold a clearance. So evidently, Division decided there was a need to bring someone in."

"Why isn't he cleared?"

"He's in a relationship with a foreign national, a woman in Canada. She either can't or doesn't want to apply for residence over here, and that means he can't get a clearance."

"All right. And so what was Gorsky doing, then, for what, how long? If she wasn't watching Silverman?"

"Two years, nearly. According to her, as reported to Captain Matthews, she and the other sergeant split the work between them. He did the day-to-day policing, and she did community outreach and handled welfare calls. Things like the call about Silverman not being seen for days."

"And the one who would have been directly aware of that would have been ... Captain Wright?"

Vogel almost said "Right," and then changed it to, "Correct. He would have been the one to know that Gorsky had a classified assignment. And to know that she hadn't been briefed on it."

The Colonel didn't look especially pleased with this. "But ... didn't Wright's periodic reporting show any of this? No issues? No exception reports?"

This was a question Vogel had been expecting, and he had an accurate if not entirely satisfying answer. "Per the regulations for secure programs and specifically for the Ice series, reporting is required to limit itself to brief statements of status – "nominal" is typically all that has to be reported unless something, well, unless something isn't nominal. Unless there was an issue, nothing was supposed to be reported."

"Ah." Macready grasped the subtext of this discussion. "So now there's an issue, and you're reporting it."

"Yes, sir."

"It seems as though, somewhere, there's a problem with

that whole process. "

"I agree, sir. It's basically saying that if Sergeant Gorsky had been tasked, she would have been responsible for Silverman's safety, and she would, we hope, have noted suspicious events, reported them to Company, who would have ..."

Macready interrupted. "So, I'm guessing that your second theory has some level of focus on Captain Wright?"

"Yes, sir. It does."

"And you're asking me to see what I can shake loose?"

"Yes, sir. We asked the Auditor's Office, for example, if Ice Rink was ever examined, and they told us that they don't look at classified programs routinely. SB is supposed to audit its own classified work."

"Very well, Major. Give me a day or two to see what kind of trouble I can get into. I'll set up another discussion in ... let's see, two days. That ought to be enough time to make some enemies."

§

Larry had to be away "for work" for a few days. Meg realized that she had no idea what he did, other than sit with her and talk. She spent most of the time at the library. On the second day he was gone, she went there in the afternoon and read until evening. Her father had said, "Take my car. Your mother needs hers."

When Meg came into the house, her father was sitting by himself at the kitchen table. There was no indication that dinner was being prepared. "Where's Mom?"

"Meg," said her father, "She's gone. To see her sister. She'll be away for a while."

"What? Why?"

"She left this for you." He picked up an envelope and handed it to her. "I'm not very hungry. I'll see you later. In the evening. Or tomorrow." He left the room, and she heard his steps on the stairs, going up. The letter was sealed, and all it said on the envelope was "Meg".

When she opened and unfolded it, the message was at the same time as blank and impersonal as her mother always was and as personal a thing as she'd ever heard from her. "Dear Meg," it said. "I'm going away, down to Indiana to stay with Martha. I have discovered that your father has chosen to break his marriage vows to me, and I need to leave. You will have to make up your own mind, just as you did when you left college. If you choose to stay there, I will understand. If you want to join me here, we'll have to work it out. Martha doesn't have much room." There was an address at the bottom and a blot or smudge that might have been a tear or just a flaw in the paper. Meg had a sudden image of the dog they'd had. When he got old and partly blind, her mother had just put him in the car and taken him to the shelter. No one ever mentioned him again.

§

The Brigade's secure area was, reasonably, larger than Battalion's, but not really any more inviting. The conference room did have a coffee pot, but at three o'clock in the afternoon, it was empty. Major Vogel had been in the room any number of times, Matthews only twice before. Now, she and Vogel were to be read in on another program, one with a direct effect on their current case.

"Log Happen," the battalion classified programs officer explained, "was a program set up to examine and suppress a specific group of individuals operating in a suburban area south of Grand Rapids. This group, Group 41, as SB designated them – they had no name for themselves – was initially identified as a political resistance group. They were known to be accumulating military small arms, making public proclamations of opposition in a religious context, and redirecting funds from a church to these activities. The Log Happen Program succeeded in inserting an individual into the group. He used the name Erik Hollandisch, and he was able to document the group's overt and covert intentions. They were not the intentions that were originally suspected, but a kind of triple-mask scheme."

"Triple mask?" asked Matthews.

"In a sense, yes. Their public face was a more or less fundamentalist Christian church. Beneath that, they appeared to a smaller group of people as a political resistance group with military intentions. But in reality, they were a criminal enterprise, dedicated to obtaining pharmaceuticals internally, at Republic-mandated pricing, and exporting them to the United States. Where they sold, illegally, for much higher prices."

"They were smuggling medications out of here and into the US?"

"Yes. The informant, Hollandisch, documented their activities, and SB raided the church and arrested nine people. It was reported publically as suppression of a resistance group. The decision was made at a high level not to report the smuggling activity, publically."

"I'll ask why, although I can probably guess," said Major Vogel.

"The reasons for that decision were not documented in anything I've been shown."

"If people are going to be sent to jail, we'd rather have it be for resistance and guns than economic crime. And of course, we don't want to give people any ideas about drug export, either."

"You may or may not be correct, there. As I say, I wasn't

briefed on the rationale. But to continue, the informant was arrested along with the others, but was then taken into the Ice series of programs and relocated. His relocation program at that time was Ice Way."

"Ice Way?" Matthews said. "What about Ice Rink?"

"Ice Way operated for approximately three months. It was then shut down and its records sealed. I have not seen any information concerning the reasons. The informant was given a new identity, Ice Rink was initiated, and it was assigned to this Brigade."

Vogel made a sour face. "Something went wrong. Somebody leaked something, or they didn't arrest everybody they should have."

"The briefing I've just given you is all the information I have," said the classified program officer. "If you'll sign these ..." he pushed a couple of SB110 forms across the table ... "I'll let Colonel Macready know you're ready for your meeting. She'll join you here." Matthews licked her lips. She had a vaguely bad taste in her mouth.

§

When Larry came back, Meg didn't answer her phone. He gave it an hour, and was about to try again when she called him. She asked him if he could pick her up. There was an issue with cars.

He'd never seen her house, in person. He knew it from satellite imagery and maps, though, and it and its neighborhood were as represented. Suburban but not recent. Dug partly back into a slope so that the garage was level with the road and bedrooms were above it. One car outside in the driveway, both garage doors closed. In the summer heat, what lawn was left looked patchy and undernourished. Meg met him at the door, and it was apparent that she was further down, more obviously unhappy. A rim of red under her eyes hadn't been there before.

At her suggestion, they went to a park. They walked a few meters away to a picnic table. They looked at each other. "What?" Larry said.

Meg looked down. "I ... I think I need help."

"Okay. How? Like help, how?"

She told him what had happened. Her father was basically catatonic. He got up, drank a cup of coffee, and went to work. He came home, said nothing, and watched TV. If he was eating, it must have been out of the house. There was food, and she offered to cook, but he just said he wasn't hungry.

"And do you want help for him? Or ... for you?"

Meg looked at him, straight in the eyes. "Me. I want to get out of here."

"All right. I know somebody. A woman who'd talk to you, at least. Maybe find something. But we'd have to go to the capital. She's there."

"Why don't ... why don't we go back to the house. So I can get some things. And then go."

"Right now?"

"Can you? I mean, can you go now?"

"Sure. Yes, I can. While you're getting your things, I'll call my friend. It's a couple of hours' drive. Got to get gas, too."

"Let's go."

§

Back at Company, Matthews found E at her cube in the secure area. She gave the Sergeant a synopsis of the conversation with Macready. The gist of it was that the Colonel was on board with escalating the whole thing up the chain, and that they'd probably be hearing about the results in a day or so. It was the end of a long day, but E had some news of her own.

"I heard from Battalion IT about the phone, sir." she said. "It's got a rootkit, they say. "

"Really?"

"I had to ask what that meant ... not my area of specialization ... They said it's malware that hides in the operating system core. They kept saying 'Colonel'. They said they just shut the phone off, hook it to something else, and start it up from there."

"That's 'kernel', with a K. I know a certain amount about malware. It sounds right, I mean, about how you detect a rootkit."

"What they said it was doing was monitoring voice communication. Listening to phone calls. Converting the words to text and uploading them somewhere."

"Uh-huh. That's not too uncommon, I guess."

"And they said it was coding each one, marking it if it had certain words or parts of words. She said it was looking for 'ite', with a long I. And 'vermin'. And 'ink'.""

"Weird. What the hell would that be about ... oh! "

"Yes. Ite as in Wright. Vermin as in Silverman. And ink as in Ice Rink."

"Oh, Lord."

"And by the way, I told the IT lady that it didn't mean anything to me."

Matthews looked at E, and she looked back. "I see."

"Battalion IT isn't cleared for anything to do with that, as far as I know."

"No. No, they aren't."

"The way this is going, Captain, I kind of wish I wasn't,

either."

"It is getting a bit spooky. In both senses of the word. I'll make sure Battalion knows – in fact, send me a paragraph on what you heard from IT. Or do you have a document?"

"Just word of mouth at this point. But they said they'd send a formal doc. I asked them to copy you."

"Great. Major Vogel will want that to go up to Brigade, for sure. But, unrelated topic: when I was reading your file – you know, for briefing you on the program – I saw you have a doctorate?"

"Yes. Nineteenth Century Economic Theory. It's been very useful in my career." *Rein it in. Don't get sarcastic with the boss.*

That was what Matthews had seen in the personnel record. She'd been curious about E beforehand, and this adjustment in her perception of the taciturn Sergeant boosted the curiosity.

"I don't … there are four or five things I could ask, but they all sound like 'That's funny, you don't look academic'. Did you … leave it behind?"

"I discovered that I didn't get to just read and study and think. I had to teach, too. And I got tired of that."

"Teaching undergraduates?"

"Yes. And having to explain that nobody was 'right'. There wasn't any one, correct view of money."

"Where were you teaching?"

"A university in Indiana. Before Separation. Ninety percent of the kids in the econ classes were there to get business degrees and get rich. Because that's how you get rich."

Matthews smiled. "I thought it was studying law that did that."

"That, too. A lot of them wanted to become 'skilled in circumventing the law'." E cocked her head slightly in a way that indicated a quotation.

"Ambrose Bierce," said Matthews. "Our schools teach him now. My nephew's son quoted something of his, the last time I visited."

That's my cue to say something about family. "I don't tend to get home a lot." She paused. The Captain made a "say more" expression. "My father's in the US, and the rest of them are overseas."

That slight clue made sense to Matthews. There was clearly some African or Asian element in Gorsky's genome. South Asian, she guessed. But North American, culturally. Just a Midwestern US accent, for one thing. At this point, her left brain gave the right half a dope slap. None of this curiosity was in the least bit proper. Officially, everybody was just human protoplasm, but with the increasing diversity of the government, business, education, society ... there were so many fascinating things to wonder about when you became acquainted with a new person. This Midwest-sounding woman with a sharp, straight nose; dark eyebrows and eyes, too, for that matter; a PhD and Sergeant's stripes; who *was* she? The other Sergeant on the island, the Lieutenant in charge of the Company office: just ordinary white guys. No real curiosity there. But Gorsky; who *was* she?

The Captain shifted back to business. "There's another thing I want bring up. Willy," – she gestured generally in the direction of the Lieutenant's office – "brought me a spreadsheet of everybody's HR data. Time in grade, salary, ratings, like that. This is something he came up with on his own. He likes that kind of work." E nodded. She had no opinion of the Lieutenant at all, one way or the other. *Harmless, anyway.*

"And what it says about you is that you're eligible for

Lieutenant school, yourself."

"I am? I knew I was getting along in that direction, but I thought there were a couple of years to go?"

"Willy spent some time looking into the regulations when he wrote his ... file. The thing he uses. And you've got a couple of boxes checked already. Your clearances, for example. And your Field Branch reviews were very high, you know, before you transferred. And you've got some command experience, too."

Commanding truck drivers, yeah. "I see."

"Now I don't want to put any kind of kink into the Silverman investigation, and bluntly, I don't want to see you go off for officer training and then get assigned somewhere else. But Willy pointed out that with your qualifications, you wouldn't have to go through the training. You could study on your own and just take the test."

That PhD is finally paying off. "That's very interesting, sir. I had no idea."

"We need to get through this current business, but my thought was that if we can retain you here, I'd give Willy some local experience, up at the Soo. The Lieutenant up there wants to transfer back down south, she says, and we could put Willy in her place. We'd keep you here at Company and give you, for example, the crime prevention program to run. Or working with Brigade Intelligence on the satellite imagery. For the border, you know. That's a hot item with Brigade right now."

"I see. That sounds very exciting, sir. If that's something you feel we can pursue, I'd be happy to take part."

§

The sun was out from behind cloud cover for the first time in two days. It was time for E to go back over to the island, pick up some clean clothes, and see what might still be unspoiled in the refrigerator. It was a good plan, and it lasted almost twenty kilometers. At that point, the radio stifled the usual mutter of going-to, arriving-at, clearing-from background. It demanded the attention of all units in the Nineteenth Battalion. Everybody operating south of Gogomain Road was ordered to respond to a barricaded gunman situation up in a place called Traber, up on the Saint Marys shore.

Traber. E hadn't been to that little crossroads since being shown around, her first month in the north. She remembered it as being basically a small bar where Traber Road turned northeast, away from the water. Just that one small bar and a few houses. She checked her mirrors and carried out a two-point turn. The road up to Traber was just a hundred meters back.

With the lights going and given its size, E's truck was not something other traffic argued with. On Traber Road, it was irrelevant, since there really wasn't any. Two cars went the other way, but in general it was just on and on and on, between pine trees, all by herself. Two paved lanes, a few small houses or mobile homes; by Dog Island standards, it was a superhighway, but by any other measure, it was out-in-the-woods. The land was flat, and the only engineering other than the road itself was an occasional run of guard rail where one side or the other dropped down a few feet.

The radio was being both interesting and frustrating. E gathered that experienced staff were working the command and coordination duties, back at Battalion, and the troopers on scene were all National Service kids. Their reporting skills weren't particularly good. Somebody would probably get a ding for allowing the recruits to charge in without at least a corporal on hand. It dawned on her that she might well be the senior NCO when she got there. *I should probably say something.* She picked up the microphone. "This is 43, Gorsky. I'm on route to the emergency."

"Battalion. Is that Sergeant Gorsky?"

How many Gorskies do we have, son? "Affirmative. Probably five minutes out, riding single. Who's in command?"

"Um, wait one." A pause. Then a different voice. "You are, Sergeant. This is Lieutenant Mecklin."

Thought so. "Ten-four. What's going on?" The road took a long right bend and pointed off toward the river and the town. At a driveway ahead, two large dogs were sitting by a mailbox. They watched as E went by, their bodies still, just their heads turning to follow her on down the road.

"Ah, apparently a person ... a Mister Finn was assaulted by his son. No name there, yet. Son is intoxicated to some degree. Mother has been contacted, and she's on her way."

"Do we know if there's a gun? That's how the call came out."

"Confirmed. Subject is firing randomly. Two units are on scene, have not been able to contact anyone in the house."

"Ten-four." *Fabulous.* E came around a bend and there was the situation. Two SB trucks, all lit up. Four National Service privates standing behind them, on the side away from a small, single-story cottage. One of the kids saw E coming and pointed at the house. "43, arriving," E said to the radio.

She parked the truck with its nose toward the house, not side-on, as the others were. A bullet has to go through more metal that way. She left the driver's door open and moved quickly back to the rear. One of the kids started to run over, but she waved him back. "Stay put! I'm Sergeant Gorsky. What kind of a gun do we have?"

"I don't know for sure!" he yelled back. "It's a long gun, anyway!"

"It's a shotgun," shouted another one. At that point, the subject in the house ended the debate by firing a twelve-gauge round in the general direction of the trucks. Bird shot plinked off the side of one of them. The shooter followed this up with a short and incomprehensible string of loud words.

"What's he been saying?" E yelled.

"We can't understand most of it." This was the one recruit who was nearest to E, a young woman with her helmet on. None of the three boys had thought to grab theirs. "I think he's saying something about cops. Or maybe crops."

"Intoxicated?" There was another shot from the house, this time hitting nothing at all.

"That's what the caller said. His father's in the house with him. Says he's been assaulted."

"All right. I'm getting into the bed of my truck. I have a bull horn. Any of you got one?" No one did. E dropped the tailgate and climbed cautiously up. She kept her head down below the roof of the cab. As long as the loony in the house didn't have any slugs, she was probably safe enough, but why take chances? And her own helmet was in the same locker as the bull horn.

As she grabbed her serious gear, the radio on her belt said something about backup. She got what she came for and climbed back down. Once she had the whole truck between her and the shooter again, she got out the radio.

"This is 43. Last caller, repeat your transmission."

"43, this is 51, Corporal Henry. I'm nearly at your 20. Minute or so out. What do you need?"

Another adult. That'll help. "Ten-four, 51. I'm on site, we've got a shooter, intoxicated. Which way are you arriving?"

"I'm coming in from the east, from the lake side. I can see your lights now."

"Okay, come in and set up at that end of the line. I'm parked on the west. You set up down there on the east end."

"Ten-four. I'm ... ah, I'm arriving."

E had met Corporal Henry once, and he seemed steady. *So we've got a battle line, but we've got the heavy forces on the ends. I'd rather we were in the middle. Can't have everything.*

She turned the bullhorn on, pointed it at the front door, and began the negotiations. "In the house! Come on, stop shooting at us! We just want to talk to you!" There was a second's pause as if the subject wasn't expecting amplified communication. Then he responded.

"BULLSHIT!" he screamed, and fired again. This time he hit a patch of the gravel driveway.

"Come on, now! That's not nice! We're here to help you!" There was no response at all to this. *Probably reloading.*

E glanced to her right, toward the east end of her phalanx. She saw Corporal Henry positioned as she was, behind his truck. And beyond Henry, coming down the road, was a car. *Oh, hell! No time for the radio.* She pointed the bullhorn at both the car and Henry. "Henry, stop that car!" She saw his head jerk around, and he started to wave his hands at the vehicle. It slowed, all right, but it came right on in behind the SB trucks and stopped.

What happened then made E's report of the incident substantially more amusing than any she'd written before, at least to those who weren't there, getting shot at.

> Subject in the civilian vehicle was a white female, fifty plus or minus years of age, heavy set. Female subject ignored instructions from SB personnel, exited the vehicle and approached the house. Subject in the house did not fire any further shots. Female subject entered the house via the front door. SB personnel followed, exercising caution and keeping windows under close watch. Loud voices were heard from within the house. Female subject then exited the house, with a younger white male, subsequently identified as the shooter, under control. In the presence of SB personnel, female subject began to assault the shooter with hands and feet. An older male subject exited the house, and the female subject handed the shooter over to SB personnel, then proceeded to assault the older male subject, using hands and feet. Female subject directed loud abuse toward both male subjects in the course of these assaults.

E later provided Ed Edmore with a less formal description. "So, Junior gets drunk – he's had some issues with alcohol before, I found out – and beats his father up. The father calls us and tells the kid the cops are coming. Kid gets this old shotgun and a box of shells – number 6 birdshot, thank God – and starts shooting. Two of our trooper units arrive, he shoots at them. I show up, he shoots. Corporal Henry shows up, the kid's still yelling, but now he's out of ammo. Then, all hell breaks loose."

"Yeah, I heard a little about that."

"Mom comes home. She ignores us, goes right in the house and kicks the kid's ass. Drags him out, kicks his ass again, and hands him to us. Dad comes out, says something, and she kicks his ass, just because."

"How'd it end up?"

"Well, we booked the kid, for sure. We seized the gun, naturally, and gave Dad a real talking to about having it. And then ... well, I decided to spin it with Lieutenant Mecklin that Mom helped us out. We cautioned her, but we didn't end up charging her. Frankly, I liked her style."

Ed cracked up. "E," he said, "You've got this place figured out. "

"Well, some of it, anyway."

§

Colonel Macready greeted Matthews and Vogel. The coffee pot was as empty as it had been earlier, but Matthews brought a glass of water. She noticed that her officers were unsupplied. "Do you want coffee? Or some water? This time of the afternoon, I've had enough caffeine, myself." Matthews declined, and Vogel excused himself to the bathroom.

"So until Aditya gets back, let me ask if anything's come up."

"No, not really. Sergeant Gorsky got pulled into a domestic assault response yesterday, and that chewed up most of her time."

"A domestic? I thought she was dedicated to Silverman?"

"She is, but there was an all-hands because there was a firearm involved, and she happened to be the only Sergeant who could respond. She was on her way back to the island, and she just happened to be close to the action."

"Ah. Anybody hurt? I think I saw a report go by, but I was dealing with something else."

"The shooter didn't hurt anybody. But his mother came

home and disciplined him. Severely."

"Oh, good. I like to see initiative and responsibility among the citizenry ... oh, here's Vogel." The Major came in and closed the door.

"Here's where I got to with Division," Macready started. "Division Intel didn't have a clue about Wright. But they called in Personnel. And to both our surprise – Intel and me – HR admitted to having at least heard of him."

"Do they know where he went, at least?" asked Major Vogel.

"No."

"No? They don't?"

"They say not. What they do know is that he was transferred to another command, urgently and under classified conditions."

Vogel turned his head slightly to one side, making a kind of "what the hell?" expression. "HR doesn't know any more than that? One of our people just got plucked out and sent somewhere, and ...?" He made a hands spreading gesture.

"Yes and no. I went around with them a bit, poking at things and so on. By then, I had my appointment with Division, himself." Matthews looked blank. "General Dichtmann. And he was not an especially happy officer."

"He wasn't?" Vogel asked.

"No. He had only, it turns out, heard of Captain Wright's disappearance ... wait for it ... the day before."

"What?"

"That was what I said. In the normal run of things, it seems, the transfer of one of his officers wouldn't come across his desk unless there was a vacant-slot problem. Since your" ... she nodded at Matthews ..." transfer in was immediately approved by Division HR, and since it was immediately filled ... the whole thing flew under his radar."

"So, how ...?"

"My request for a meeting with him. Naturally, he had his admin find out what I wanted to talk about, and she put down 'Captain Wright Transfer Issues'. Since he hadn't heard of a transfer, period, let alone any 'issues', he asked some questions, and got nothing much more substantial than I did. So he called up to SB headquarters, and ..."

"And?"

"He got stonewalled, too. He got a hint from the adjutant general's office that there were some 'legal concerns', but they couldn't be specific. He talked to a major who used to report to him, and he still didn't get anywhere. Then he remembered a sergeant he knew, and ... you guessed it. The Sergeant had some intel. He wouldn't swear to it, but the word is that there were some sexual harassment allegations."

"About Wright?"

"About Wright."

"But," Matthews started, "shouldn't that have come to Major Vogel? Or you?"

"Yes. It should have. And it's almost certainly bogus. In my opinion. And the General's."

"For the record, I never saw anything about him that would suggest ... anything. Like that." Vogel looked distinctly unhappy. The "Report it to Your Commanding Officer" message was hammered home every time his officers were together, along with a direct command to pass the word on down. Anything, from dirty jokes to butt pinching to rape, you report it.

"I believe that," said Macready. "I never even met Wright, but I know as well as I know much of anything that harassment doesn't get handled that way in SB."

"So ..." said the Major, "Where did you and General Dichtmann leave it? If I can ask."

"He was mad enough that he bumped two other meetings in order to talk to me as soon as possible. I have a direct order to find out what the hell is going on, and if I get blocked, Dichtmann will go up through Branch Command and sic them on Naval."

"Why Naval, specifically?"

"Because when you get transferred somewhere SB can't find you, it's either going to be Naval or Field. And the General asked some people in Field – people he trusts – and they're as clueless as we are. So it's got to be Naval."

"Colonel, I heard something about Naval from Sergeant Gorsky that is ... might be ... relevant," said Matthews.

"What?"

"When she visited Alpena Naval Base as we discussed? A phone she took with her came away infected with malware."

"Explain."

"On her own initiative, she took a decoy phone along. And somewhere during the time she was at the base, it got hacked."

"Are you ... kidding me? On an AoR base?"

"Yes, sir."

"Mother of God! What the hell is going on here?"

"Well ... we don't know. But the malware? It seems to have been trying to identify phone calls about Captain Wright."

"Okay, then." Macready's face was a blank mask. "Will you get me a copy of that report?"

"Yes, sir. As soon as ... No, I'll call Battalion IT from here and get it to you through them."

"Good. As quickly as you can. There's a General who needs to know about it."

§

At 0420 hours, the PRS Detroit cast off her lines and began nosing out of the harbor. Two of the NB's patrol craft were already outside and waiting. The ship's diesel engines brought her out slowly, keeping the departure as quiet and unobtrusive as possible. The only thing that appeared to notice was a grayish dog, trotting slowly down the dock. It turned, watched briefly, and trotted on.

As modern corvettes went, she wasn't as large or as heavily armed. But she was fast, fast as a thief, almost as fast as the patrol boats. And where they had reasonably good radar and communications, the Detroit had outstanding electronics. When necessary and with approval, she could hijack one of the Republic's geosynchronous satellites and have its near-real-time imaging all to herself.

The Republic hadn't set out to be a miniature sea power; originally the Naval Branch didn't exist. Field Branch had a collection of small boats, and SB called on them when necessary. But as things got friendlier and friendlier with Canada, the people in Ottawa came up with a remarkable idea. "It occurs to us," they said, "We've got all this shared water between us. You know, lakes. And we've got other things on our minds, right now. Like Asia, for one thing. And Europe. How about if we kind of outsource the lakes to you?"

For an international agreement, it didn't take long. The Army of the Republic spun up a whole new branch on Canada's nickel, bought patrol boats, borrowed ice breakers from Canada and helicopters from the Field Branch, and – taking a deep breath – bought three ex-

Indian Navy corvettes. In modern navies, "frigate" meant "small destroyer", and a "corvette" was a small frigate. All three of the new Naval Branch ships were stripped of their missile and torpedo gear, given some beefing up to deal with Great Lakes storms, and named after lake cities: Detroit, Traverse City, and Marquette. On this dark and early morning, the Detroit and the patrol craft had an assignment.

One hundred and sixty kilometers southeast of Alpena, there's a town on the shore of Ontario's Bruce Peninsula. Two boats, fishing craft in theory, were going to be putting out to sea. When they did, the Detroit and the PCs wanted to have a word with them. There were some questions to be asked, questions about guns and ammunition. Questions about coming over the international boundary unannounced. Questions about passports and visas and names on lists. They were known to be fast boats, and there was reason to think they might not hang around to chat. And since the intelligence received indicated guns being transported, it was possible that not all of those guns would necessarily be packaged up. Some of them might be ready to hand. Consequently, the officer in charge of "Force A" – so called because it was the only non-routine group operating at the moment – developed a plan slightly more sophisticated than just barging in on the target.

The patrol craft were faster but lightly armed. The Detroit could out-gun anything else on the lakes, but the target boats could run away from her. So the tactical plan, not unlike some of Marlborough's concepts, was to confront the opposition with the heavy main force and send the cavalry to one or the other of the enemy's flanks. Instead of seven or eight thousand infantry, the main line was the corvette. Instead of horsemen, the patrol craft would get around behind and cut off the other side's retreat. Captain Satya Greene explained it that way to her officers and to the intelligence guy that

NB headquarters had sent aboard. He nodded and looked wise. Greene's private assessment was that he no idea what was going on, tactically. He had an NB uniform with Commander's insignia, but nothing about him suggested any experience at sea. "A spook of some kind," was her thought. His ID tag said his name was Thomas Derecha.

For half an hour, the three boats sailed together southeastward, straight out across the lake. When they were well out of sight of land, the PCs carried on, and the Detroit turned southwest, back toward the Republic shore, aiming at Oscoda. As she closed in on the land, satellite intel showed three targets moving away from the Canadian side, coming out of Kincardine. "Captain, we're tracking three vessels, not just two."

"All right, Chief. Copy Lieutenant Ng."

"Done, sir. And he acknowledged." Charley Ng was the officer in charge of the patrol craft.

"Very good. Let me know if they separate."

"Yes, sir."

Derecha, standing close by, noted this exchange. "What's going on?" he asked.

"The satellite's tracking three boats together, not the two we expected. If they all keep on the same course, we're fine as-is. If they separate, we'll react depending on what they do."

"Have we got the ships for it?"

"Another tell," Greene thought. A naval officer wouldn't call the patrol craft "ships".

"I have air support on call," she said. "If I have to deal with separate targets, we stick to our plan, and a helo from Alpena goes after whatever gets away from us."

"How would a helicopter search a boat?"

"It wouldn't. It'd stand off out of small arms range, order the target to steer toward us, and destroy it if it didn't comply."

"Oh," said Derecha.

Once the corvette had coasted south to the mouth of Saginaw Bay, she turned east again and steered to cross the targets' course. The PCs were now at a point where they could turn south and come in behind the subjects. There was beginning to be some light in the east. "Seventeen kilometers to the lead target, sir. Targets are in line astern."

"Understood." She switched to local loudspeakers. "Action stations. Hands to intercept and detain."

Most of the crew were already in position, but there was a certain amount of scurrying around. The 76 millimeter gun on the foredeck rotated slightly and aimed its long barrel a few points to port. In five other positions around the ship, crews loaded rifle-caliber automatic weapons. A flare gun team set up just below the bridge. Derecha was staring out ahead into the dark. "Where are they?"

"Out of sight still. In this light. But over there. Where the gun's pointed."

The range came down. Detroit turned slightly to starboard, and moved in across the targets' course.

"Twelve kilometers. Target speed eleven point five knots."

"Gunnery radar on." There was no visible change, but for the first time, Detroit was radiating. And it didn't go unnoticed.

"Captain, target is changing course. Speed increasing."

"What?" said Derecha.

"They saw our radar signal." Greene said, "Warning shot," into her microphone and pressed the gunfire authorization button. The gun aimed off a half a degree ahead of the lead target's track and fired.

"Captain, targets are separating. Lead boat turning toward. Other two turning away."

"Starboard twenty. Gun action port." Greene switched to the PC group channel. "Ng, we're in contact. Targets are separating. Take the trailing two." She switched to the loudhailer. "Unidentified craft! Heave to at once, or you will be taken under fire!"

"Target one is closing at speed!"

"Weapons free to ... " She didn't get to "port" before someone on the approaching boat opened up with a rifle. Two rounds went overhead, then two more hit the bridge. "Weapons free to port! Open fire!" Three of the ship's pintle-mounted AK-74s let go. Without any kind of automatic targeting, they were simply firing over the sights at the oncoming boat's bow wave. The shooter on the boat fired again. Then the corvette's main gun fired, and that was the end of that. Flames appeared on the target's stern. It veered north, then back west, and then stopped.

"Cease fire!" Greene was looking hard at the burning boat. In the light from the fire, she could see figures jumping overboard. "All back full. Stand by boats!" She looked over the edge of the bridge. No visible damage. She switched communication back to the PCs. "Ng, target one neutralized. Shots fired. Report." As she turned back, she saw the casualty team coming up the ladder. Then she saw Commander Derecha lying on the deck.

§

In the green office, the man was meeting with the woman from the External Relations Department. He enjoyed dealing with her; she could be blunt and colloquial in one sentence and diplomatic-formal in the next. "And never without a reason," he thought. Like most of the people he saw frequently, he knew her background. He reviewed it mentally, taking only half his attention away from what she was saying. US Army. Police work. Law degree – US law, naturally. Separation veteran. In her early sixties. Expert on our North American peer nations. PhD from the National University. Very high clearances. Doctor Jerilynn Klein.

As usual, the man gave no indication that he was thinking about anything at all except what his colleague was saying. Klein only occasionally spotted a moment of multi-tasking on his part. Right now, she was focused on her own narrative, giving him information as clearly as she could. "The basic theme is that Naval Branch is not playing by the rules." The man nodded.

"They kicked off an operation based on intelligence they got on their own. SB knew nothing about it. Three boats coming in from Canada, guns and ammunition, two people to insert illegally. Naval heard about it, and they sent out two of their small craft and one of the corvettes. When they lit up the targets, two ran, and one started shooting. The corvette sank it, and the patrol boats caught one of the others. A helicopter shot up the last of them." She paused.

"I see."

"But ... that's bad enough. It gets worse. Naval lost an officer. A man named Derecha was hit, on board the corvette. Right on the bridge, right beside the officer in command."

"Oh, dear."

"And it still gets worse. The casualty is supposed to have been a Naval Branch officer, a Commander. He was ordered aboard half an hour before the group sailed. Special assignment." She paused. "SB is, of course, investigating. They're required to, and Naval is required to cooperate. And ... Derecha has a personnel file that goes back a little less than thirty days."

"That's quite a short career."

"It is. There's nothing on this Thomas Derecha, anywhere. No citizenship, no legal, no taxes, nothing. And NB isn't coming up with answers, yet. They say they can't understand it. They're researching it."

"Like Athena, he seems to have sprung fully formed from the brow of Zeus. How did the Naval people learn of the smuggling attempt?"

"Canada."

"Do we know that?"

"We do. We have ways of knowing."

"Well, well. I have a thought or two, if you've got time."

Klein smiled. "I do," she said.

"Naval is doing something both proper and improper, simultaneously, it seems to me. Looked at one way, they're stopping an illegal act. Looked at another way, they're doing something that one really shouldn't be doing at the level of a national organization. I think the term is freelancing."

"Indeed. But a freelancer gets paid, typically. Who are they freelancing for?"

"Now there, I'm afraid, I can't speculate. Not without a bit more background. I have an idea, and given your areas of responsibility, I wonder if you have it, too."

"Canada."

"Doctor Klein, I'm always gratified at the way your mind and mine work along similar lines. I think what I ought to do is speak with General Casanuova."

"Who? You mean Newhouse?"

"Yes, the Commander in Chief's name is more pleasant to say in Italian, don't you think? And of course, Derecha in Spanish is 'right'."

§

It was a big house on West Liberty, well out of the downtown and capital areas. Meg had asked, when it occurred to her, if they should call ahead. Larry said, "I did. She's expecting us." Well down below her very personal troubles and uncertainties, Meg had a brief thought about Larry, about the fact that she knew almost nothing about him. At least since high school. But that wasn't anywhere near the top of her concerns.

The front of the place seemed like a cross between a living room and a waiting room. There was one other person, a young man, sitting on a couch. He nodded to Larry. They went down a hall, and Larry knocked on its wooden paneled door. "Come in," someone said.

"Meg," Larry said, "this is Karen. Karen Mather. She's a friend of mine. She helps people, when she can. Karen, this is Meg Cordell."

"Hello, Meg. Larry says you need a place to stay for a while. That right?" Karen was a large woman, probably in her forties. African-American. Her smile came and went, depending on context.

"I'd like ... I need to be away from home right now. "

"Okay. We can help with that. You mind sharing a room with another girl?"

"Oh, no, that would be ... fine. I shared rooms, I mean, I had roommates in college."

"All right, then." She slipped a sheet of paper across the desk that was between them. "How about if you give me some of this basic stuff, and I'll go see about the room."

The form was extremely basic. It just asked for a name,

a phone number if there was one, and a contact person. She listed Larry. There were one or two other items, all health topics. She could truthfully say that she had none of the issues listed. For the one that said "Is there a chance that you could be pregnant?" she wrote "No."

Karen came back, bringing a young Asian woman with her. "All right, dear. We got you in with Una, here. She'll help you get settled, tell you a little about how the days go, here. When meals are, like that."

Meg brought her suitcase and a backpack in from Larry's car. Una helped her get things put away, and Larry vanished. When she had a minute to think, Meg asked Una where he'd gone. "Don't worry about him," she said. "He comes and goes when he's in town."

"Do we pay something? For living here?"

"No. Karen's very generous. After a day or so, you'll get some chores assigned. I'm helping with dinner, myself. You'll get to do some of that, or, you know, feed the dog. Or water the gardens."

"Gardens?"

"Oh, yeah. Karen grows a lot of veggies out back. The corn is great, and we make a corn and tomato salad that's a treat."

"Why … I guess I should ask… why are people here?"

"Different reasons. Mostly school. I would say, oh, eighty – ninety percent. People like me who couldn't settle down. You know. Couldn't dig in to it. One girl had home problems. Oh, and Alan. He's our only guy, right now."

"I sound clueless, but who runs it?"

"Oh, Karen does. She gets donations."

"And are we … can we leave? If we want to?"

"Oh, sure. We can. I'm here 'cause I want to be. But we

can leave. Give it a day or two, though. I bet you won't want to." The door opened slightly, and a brown nose pushed its way in. "Hi, Ginger. Come on in, sweetie." A medium-sized dog shouldered the door open farther and came in. "Ginger's one of the best things about bein' here."

§

E was spending a day at Company, working in the secure area, poking into corners on the classified net. She'd given up on Captain Wright for the moment. Matthews had given her a summary of the gathering storm up the chain of command, and E's thought was to let that boil for a day. *I didn't reach this high position of power and authority by interfering with angry officers.*

Instead, she went looking for information on malware, and among it there was an internal paper on the varieties of it and the kinds of people who enjoyed fussing with it. It was harder to do than it used to be, the author asserted, with governments running their processes on internally-built, unique, proprietary operating systems. E already knew that. In the Republic, everything even remotely official ran on the deliberately obscure PR Information, Quantification, and Leverage Environment, PRIQLE. *Good old Prickly. Four years in general release and no intrusions yet. That they admit, anyway.*

PRIQLE was from-scratch code, with a fixed kernel. It included inherent mode-of-use security, also known as what you do is what you get. An admin user was hardware-firewalled into office automation applications; the further into the code you got, the further into the system you were allowed to go. Prickly was a "Hotel California" system, from the standpoint of security – malware could check in anytime it liked, but it could never leave. The architecture for capturing intruders was a single chip. No user storage was anywhere near it, and anything unauthenticated landed there, essentially jailed, unable to modify or delete itself. Legitimate updates to anything came in as firmware, carrying hard-coded credentials. All of this chip-swap maintenance was feasible because the systems weren't for-profit products. They didn't have to be easy, convenient, and sexy, and there were no competitors.

The author of E's article went on to draw a distinction between the random, unsupported hackers and professional, state-supported cyber intelligence organizations. The kids built traps and scams for the notoriously insecure commercial operating systems in civilian phones. *Insecure all right. As I just demonstrated.* The sophisticated groups who were largely locked out of governmental systems focused either on commercial targets for economic warfare, or on widely-cast nets of individual devices, getting what was being called demographic intelligence. They looked for data to aggregate and turn into conclusions, suggesting what entire populations were thinking or could be led to believe. And on another tack completely, they wrote code to run through billions of records, looking for isolated topics. *That's what the thing on my phone is about, I guess.*

The report said that states known to be sponsoring this last sort of malware were usually wealthy and centralized and faced with specific external and internal threats. Obviously, as the author noted, there was no good way to list all of the governments involved, but likely examples included the United States, the European Union and some of its individual members, and Japan and Canada. *Really? Canada?*

The author cited classified intelligence generated by the Security Branch. Three separate programs had examined sources of malware, ruling out lower-impact nuisances and individual efforts, and they found that the nation-states the public generally assumed to be bad actors were surprisingly impotent. As the data indicated, countries east of the Austrian border and west of Japan and those south of the Mediterranean were so consumed with internal economic, environmental, and social crises that they were no longer serious cyber threats, externally. Even Australia didn't appear as a major threat source, at least outside its own borders.

I had all those same misconceptions. But Canada? That's very strange. Her secure desktop made a small sound, and a popup appeared: "Lunch". Especially in the closed area, she was prone to losing track of important things. She closed down the machine, locked up her work space, and went back out into the normal world.

As usual, the first thing she did was check her open-network and personal messages. Right at the top of the list was a call from Kristin. It was in Kristin's usual, slightly non-linear style; the summary was that she was coming down from the Soo, heading back to Saint Ignace, and it would be pleasant to have dinner. Did E have a favorite place for dinner, somewhere in the general area?

After a series of calls and messages, structured by Kristin's in-transit state, there was a plan. The least complex option turned out to be the one interesting restaurant anywhere along the shoreline road, a place called George's. It was a bit west of E's location, along the road to the straits and near a north/south road that Kristin could take, after she left the highway south from the Soo. In fact, along all of R134, it was the only place with a bar and a wine list, let alone adult food.

E ate something forgettable in the base chow hall, went back into the secure area, and spent the next three hours poking around among various documents on hacking and hackers. She came out of it with a reasonably accurate idea of what a rootkit was and not much more than that. There was nothing she was able to access that expanded on Canada as a cyberthreat. She shut things down, went back to her open area desk, and sent Matthews a brief summary. It was time to go and meet Kristin.

Ten minutes out of town most works of man vanished. The land along the road had been a nature preserve, and it still was. The only changes were that the Republic was allowing individuals to grow small crops – potatoes, typically – in one-quarter-hectare plots. Otherwise, it was all pine trees on the right and occasional glimpses of Lake Huron on the left. This went on and on until the road curved back away from the water and crossed the Pine River. Suddenly a few houses appeared, and with them, George's.

The parking lot was not full. There were five trucks, one of them with Field Branch markings, and close to the door there were two of the small utility vehicles that government organizations issued to their travelling personnel. Either of those could be Kristin, E thought, but as it turned out, she was driving one of the trucks. "Like my hot ride?" she asked, as almost the first thing she said.

"Which?"

"The blue pickup. We're trying to standardize on the same things you guys drive. But we insist on our own colors."

"I didn't know the Department of Education was blue."

"Can you keep a secret?"

"In the Security Branch? Of course not. We don't know the meaning of the word."

The hostess looked at them closely. The two new guests who'd just entered were exchanging all this light banter by the door, and they weren't paying any attention to her. One of them was even in uniform, but still. Kristin leaned closer to E and stage-whispered that the head of DoE was a University of Michigan grad, and the department's blue fixation was her idea. "I wanted green." The hostess had heard enough.

"Would you ladies like to have dinner?" she said, in a tone that included the unspoken thought "Or are you just going to stand here and chat?"

The menu featured things that could be built around local materiél: fish, pork, venison, potatoes, and sweetcorn. The salad for the evening was a dish of corn and chopped tomatoes, tossed with shreds of basil. Kristin and E found things to order, and then the question of wine came up. E recalled that wine meant more to Kristin, and she deferred to her judgement; the list was just a page in the general menu, but Kristin went through it carefully.

"Oh, hey. Look at this. Did you know they were growing wine grapes up in the Keweenaw, now?" She pointed at a two-year-old bottle of Pinot Gris.

"Wine up there? Huh. It must be that climate change thing I keep hearing about."

"Yeah. This is a nice one. Kind of acidic, but it won't clash with anything we're eating."

"What does the name mean?"

"Na Carraigeacha Dubha is 'The Black Rocks'. The winery's just up the east coast from Marquette. The shore line through there is all black rock."

"What is that, though? Gaelic?"

"Irish, technically. I guess there are some people up there with roots in the auld sod. But you have some languages, don't you?"

"I do all right in French. My mother's side of the family are from Mauritius. And German ... well, *ein bisschen.*

Ich kann es besser lesen."

"What?"

"I read German better than I speak it. And I've got no Spanish at all."

"Oh, I can do Spanish pretty well. We have to. But it's not really more than conversation."

"I've got no Spanish. Well, I can sing 'Viva la quince Brigada' in a Christy Moore voice, but that's all."

Kristin looked away. "I remember hearing that with you and Caroline."

The salads arrived and Kristin ordered the wine. As they ate and sipped the pinkish pinot grey, the slightly nervous edges and the banter began to wear off. Over the entrées, Kristin told stories about the school administrators she had to deal with. The Republic's regulations for education were deliberately specific, full of thou shalt and thou shalt nots, and still the unconvinced and unconverted found ways to deliberately misunderstand them.

E said, "I remember when we were in college we had all kinds of great ideas. Simple, straightforward principles. And then somebody would say, 'yeah, but there'll always be assholes.' That got to be kind of a saying of ours, didn't it?"

"Yes. We were ... young, weren't we?"

"You, maybe. I was born forty years old. I've just grown into it."

"Oh my God! We are that old, aren't we?" The conversation stopped. Kristin looked down at her plate.

"Look, I think ...," E said, "... we ought to raise a glass to the unhappy elephant in the room."

"To Caroline?"

"Yes. And then ... we're done with that."

"Are you done with it?"

"I ... came to be. We left her down there. And I heard that she overdosed. That she died. But I didn't poke into it, not for a couple of years."

"But then you did? I never heard any more than that she was gone."

"I did. She took some prescription meds. Who knows why she had them. But what was worse? I got ahold of the coroner's report. She was pregnant."

"Oh, hell. Who?"

"Who knows? I can think of three people, at least. That it might have been. And with any of them, it wouldn't have been ... intentional."

"So there she was, all alone."

"All alone, in that little apartment, looking out on a parking lot. And with nothing to look forward to but another day with the faculty from hell."

Kristin raised her glass. "Caroline."

"Caroline," said E. They drank. "And now, we admit that we tried and she didn't want our help. And we go on."

Kristin raised the glass again. "Going on." E joined her. They both declined dessert.

"My instincts say that another glass of something would be good, but my older mind says no." They stood up together. Kristin insisted on picking up the check. "Your turn next time." In the parking lot, E held out her hand. "This was fun. Let's make sure there's a next time."

"You bet your ass, baby," said Kristin. She took the hand, then pulled E into a bear hug. "Next time."

§

The meeting room at Karen's house was just two rooms that had obviously been combined. The signs of a wall having been removed were only painted over. There were a dozen folding chairs, plus a desk at the front, not unlike a classroom. The desk had a laptop, and there was a screen behind it.

There were eight people sitting down or standing up, talking. All but one were young women; the odd man out was a young man, not odd looking at all. He was just a white boy, late teens or early twenties. Karen came in, and the ones standing quickly sat down.

"Hello," Karen said. "Or hello again, if I already seen you today. Like always, I'm gonna talk, an' then I'm gonna see if you want to talk, all right?" It wasn't a question, it was an agenda. "What we're gonna talk about is three things, and I'll get to 'em in a minute here. But write this down." She hit a key, and the screen showed a list of three underlined words: Sensible, Sensitive, Harmful.

"Look at each other," Karen said. "Look at what y'all wearin'." The class – that's what it obviously was – looked around. "Now, why you wearin' those clothes? You don't have to. You know what the law is about that? Anybody know?" Nobody did, apparently, and most of them knew enough about Karen to recognize the opening stages of a simile.

"The law says, out in public the genitalia, the perineum, an' the anus gotta be covered. And that's all. If I wanted to, I could come in here topless. So could you. You could go to work in just your underwear. And nobody can say you can't unless you're military, or a doctor, or something dangerous or sanitary. Like a cook." She looked around, making eye contact.

"But I don't run around half-dressed, and you don't, either. Or at least not that I've noticed." There were a few chuckles. "An' why not? Anybody?"

A girl in front said, "Does it have something to do with 'sensible' and all?"

"That's right. Here's the deal." She waved a hand at the screen. "Half the time, it's too damn cold here for that stuff. You'd freeze yourself. And the other half, you'd get sunburned. It wouldn't be *sensible*. And you know what else? I bet there's people here who wouldn't appreciate it, at least if I did it. Anyone here really want to see me without a shirt on? Don' answer that." More chuckling. "So I'm not gonna go bare naked and offend people. I'd respect their sensibilities. I'd be *sensitive*."

"And now, here's number three. Suppose I did offend some of y'all. What might happen? Remember, I'm not breakin' the law. I got a right to go bare. But if you really didn't like it, what would you do? Alan?" She looked at the young man.

"Um ... I guess ... I might leave?'

"Yeah. And since you're here to get over some bad times and get yourself back together, that wouldn't be good, would it?"

"Well, no."

"So, there's number three. *Harmful.* I could do something legal that'd still be harmful for some people. And me, too. Because I don't want y'all to leave." She paused, looked back at the screen, looked around the class. "Sensible, Sensitive, Harmful, right?" Another pause. "Okay, show me hands, anybody think I'm really talkin' about nudity?" Nobody did.

"That's right. Take a long breath, folks. I'm talkin' about religion."

Only the young man and Meg reacted. He looked unhappy; her expression was astonishment. "Now, I know," Karen went on, "Religion is one of those things for some of y'all. You got brought up in it, maybe, or maybe you got into it later on. And I'm gonna try not to be harmful. Like I said, I don't want to lose anybody. But we gotta have this discussion."

She touched the keyboard, and a new slide appeared. It said Keep Your Hands to Yourself. "See that? Anybody ever hear that before?" Meg's roommate, Una, raised her hand.

"That was a rule when I was in grade school."

"Yeah, I bet it was. And it meant don't touch people, don't hit people, like that. Right now, everybody who gets a job gets that message. On their first day and over and over again. It means hands off, right?" Una nodded.

"And it's our sensible, sensitive, harmful thing, all over again. You touch somebody wrong, and you lose your job. It's not sensible. People don't want you touchin' them. It's not bein' sensitive. And harmful, I don't even have to talk about that, right? Well, that's what I mean about faith. The law says you can believe whatever you believe, but you can't push it out onto anybody else. You make your own decision, and you keep your hands to yourself."

The young man raised his hand. "I'm sorry ... but 'harmful'? I'm not understanding ... I mean, I don't see the similarity."

"Well, because I want to be sensitive, I know there's people who've been through this question before. Can we hold it 'til afterwards, and I'll talk about it with just you an' me?"

"Okay ... yes, that's fine."

Meg raised her hand. "Can I be part of that talk, too?"

"Alan, you all right with that?"

"Oh, yes. Fine"

"Okay, then. Now. Anybody got anything general to talk about, here?"

There weren't really any topics. "What's the next session?" "Is the chores list posted yet?" Most of the class had been at Karen's house for some time. Alan and Meg were the new people. It wound down, and Karen was left alone with them.

Alan started off. He couldn't see that evangelism could be harmful. "Fair enough," Karen said. "But what about this? Did you get that faith easy? Did it just come to you?"

"No. Not at all."

"You had to work at it? Think about it hard? Did it keep you awake at night?"

"Yes."

"Real atheism's just like that. It's not careless. It takes work. If somebody just says 'I don't know', that's something else. Fancy word is agnosticism. Benefit of the doubt, it's bein' a seeker. Or lazy. Or afraid. I don't call somebody an atheist if they have any doubts about it."

Alan was increasingly unhappy. "I don't see what ..."

"What I'm sayin' is that one point of view's as strong as the other. You think you've got the knowledge, so does the person you're preachin' to. If you say, 'Son, you're goin' to hell,' you got no right to object if he says 'You're wastin' your life'."

"But if I believe in ... heaven ..." He almost whispered the word.

"Then, you believe in it. And if he doesn't, then he doesn't."

"But I have a duty to try ..."

"Nope. That's where you go off the track. He's found something that's sensible. To him. And if he's not trying to pitch it to you, that's sensitive. He knows you'll be unhappy. And if you don't give him the same space, you're bein' harmful."

"Can I say ... can I ask a question?" said Meg.

"Sure you can."

"Alan, did you ever feel ... betrayed? By anybody?"

"I don't know ... I guess, yes. I thought the university was trying to ... undermine ... me. Somehow."

"I think ... " She stopped. There were a lot of gaps in this discussion. Karen knew when to push and when to shut up. "I feel like I was left ... left holding a ... a misconception."

"A misconception?" Karen asked.

"A wrong idea. They ... People let me go on thinking something. When they knew ... it was harmful."

"I'm sorry."

"But ..."

"Go on, Alan."

"If there's no belief ... what keeps a person from ... killing and stealing?"

"Some people, nothing does. Maybe you've noticed, some people do kill and steal. Atheists. Christians. Muslims. Some people do that. What lets some of those people do those things? What keeps the others from doing it? I say, sensible, sensitive, harmful. Thinking about the world like that."

Alan stood up. "I have to go and think. And I'm supposed to be helping in the kitchen."

As he left, Karen looked Meg hard between the eyes. "You hold on to that, honey. About people hurting you. But don't let the holdin' on hurt you, itself. Be sensible."

Off the south end of Manitoulin Island, there was a lively southeast breeze. On one of the many little islets off shore, a red kayak was lying on a patch of sand. A wave came in, lifted it up, and sucked it out into the water. The next waves pushed it back, but now there was a rock in the way. It bounced off two or three times, then missed the rock and was driven away, through a gap between the bits of land. In ten minutes, it was moving steadily over blue water. On the main island, some five hundred meters away, two large dogs chased each other down the beach.

§

Jeri Klein had spent twenty minutes talking to her management – if you could call it that. In fact, she and her formal superior treated each other with great informality. Their opinions were very similar, but Jeri was the one who got to run around meeting with strange people and communicating with foreign officials. She didn't see heads of state or even senior diplomats; rather, she dealt with the next tier down, the ones who did real work.

She finished up the discussion with a mention that the green office man planned on speaking with the head of the AoR.

"You know him better than I do," her colleague said. "What do you think of him?"

"People ask that, I notice. More than usual. Sometimes I have to pretend I've never heard of him, sometimes I can be a little more forthcoming. Depends on clearance levels."

"But really, what's your take on him?"

"He's a unique figure, in my experience. I don't think other governments really have someone like him. Or even realize the need. I see him as both the conscience and the subconscious of Council and the Administration. He's the voice that keeps you awake, worrying at four AM. And he's the dreams that come afterward, if you get back to sleep. One thing for sure: I never ignore anything he says."

§

"I thought the capital would be, you know, intense." Meg was talking with her roommate, Una. "Living here, I mean."

"I guess it is. If you're doing stuff. Working, I mean."

"How long are you going to stay? Here at Karen's?"

"Until fall. Then I'm going back to school."

"You are? I thought you didn't want to."

"I changed my mind. I want to go back."

"Oh. How did you … how?"

"Karen helped. We get … there's a program for people who quit. If they want to go back."

"They said I wouldn't get in. If I left."

"You know that's what Karen's place is about, right? Getting us back into school? Or into something, anyway?"

"I guess. That's what Larry said."

"Just ask Karen. She doesn't make a big deal out of it. But if you ask, she'll tell you. Do you think you want to go back?"

"You know, right up to now I didn't think so. But maybe I just changed my mind."

"Just talk to Karen. She knows all about it."

Larry, meanwhile, rapped on the frame of Karen's open door.

"Good mornin', Larry," Karen said. "You been out in the field, so to speak?"

"Here and there, Karen. How's Meg?" Larry looked tired.

"Meg's doing pretty well. Pretty well. But we lost Alan."

"Oh, damn. I thought he was salvageable. "

"We tried. All we can do."

"Did he leave any contact information? "

"He just packed and left."

"Okay. I'll get him re-listed. Make sure you let me know if he comes back or calls."

"Of course I will. About Meg, though? I heard some things from her about that church out there. And then I called Peter, and he told me things, too. Things he probably shouldn't have."

"Yeah?"

"Meg don't know the half of it."

"I know."

"You do? Peter said you didn't. "

"I've got my own ways of knowing things."

"You know best, honey. Just stay out of trouble. Now, you need some breakfast? You look tired, boy."

"Thanks, K. I ate, but I wouldn't say no to some coffee. I have to go down the street, next, and see what they've got planned for me."

"Let's go back in the kitchen. I'm about due for a cup, myself."

§

In the Field Branch of the AoR, each Company included a reconnaissance team. Initially, these small groups were classic recon: sneaky people who went out, looked around, and came back with their findings. A year or so into the post-Separation period, high command noticed that the skills involved in recon work were also applicable to long-range concealed attack operations, that is to say, sniper work. There was, obviously, no call for hundreds of snipers, but still, a few of them might be useful. And so recon teams were ordered to train one recon trooper in distance shooting, along with developing his or her clandestine movement and information seeking skills.

The FB's Fifth Division was centered on Saginaw, and it had responsibility for an eastern chunk of the Republic, running in from the Huron shore and Saginaw bay to a point about half way west. One of the Fifth's company commanders, in his headquarters at Bay Port, was dealing with a personnel problem. He was missing his sniper.

Two weeks before, he'd received an order from Battalion, endorsed by the Brigade commander. It directed him to provide his "Long-range small arms specialist" on a temporary basis to Naval Branch. This was not any kind of a problem – FB loaned out everything from truck drivers to entire infantry companies .Security Branch was the usual customer, but Naval also made requests. The problem this time was that his sniper hadn't been returned.

The young man in question was picked up, gear included, by a Naval Branch ensign, driving an NB truck, and driven away. After that, silence. A look at the regulations covering inter-branch assignments showed the Captain that anything longer than ten days required a request for extension. Nothing like that had arrived. He looked back at the initial set of orders, and he noted that there was no specific NB command or contact information. That was worrisome. He tried contacting NB in general, and got nowhere. They said they'd look into it. So, despite his usual reluctance to stir up trouble, he prepared to report the missing person to Battalion. As part of that, he had to note that along with the human asset, he was also missing the soldier's long-range personal weapon and its telescopic sight. As he always did with potentially unpleasant communications, he carefully checked his sources – in this case, nothing besides the order he'd received from Battalion – for security levels. There were no classification markings, and it made no mention of security in reference to the operation, whatever it might be. He saved the message and hit 'send'. He didn't like it. He had a lifelong aversion to causing trouble, to "petting the tiger" as one of his superior officers had called it, but there really wasn't an alternative. "I need my damn sniper back."

Among the things Security Branch taught its non-commissioned officers were methods of making investigations take less manual labor. E learned, for example, ways of using the government's information technology to watch the flow of documents the AoR generated. To do this with classified material, she had to have access to a specific group of documents, and she had to set up her alerts on a secure machine. But just to watch the run of the mill torrent of unclassified reports and orders, her standard office computer was sufficient.

When she'd gone out this particular morning, headed for the ferry and a trip to Company headquarters, she'd locked her machine at the Dog Island office, but she left her watchdog applications running. This was routine; it could run on its own and let her know if it found something. When the Silverman case kicked off, she'd tried to imagine what search terms might be productive, and when she discovered how the shooting had been done, she added '#long.range#' to her search items. All that meant was 'look for any document that contains 'long', a single other character, and 'range'. Her other search terms hadn't yet produced anything interesting, and this one hadn't, either, so far. But tonight when she got back from Company and logged in, there was a hit. She found herself looking at a report of Naval Branch borrowing a sniper from Field Branch Fifth Division and losing him. And he went off to NB two days before the Silverman shooting. *Holy shit!*

§

Clairette and Dean were happy together. She was a quarter Ojibwe and he was a full-blood Canadian white boy, but neither of them cared much about anything except having tolerable employment, food on the table, and each other's company. She taught youngsters at an elementary school, and he did anything the ministry of transportation said to do. In the winter, that was mostly driving salt trucks and plows; in the summer, it was mostly driving asphalt and gravel around.

When neither of them was working, their favorite recreation involved a picnic somewhere on the shore. They'd drive out as close as a road would take them, then load lunch and sundries in a backpack and hike another half a klick or so to a place where the beach was nice and the view was due south, straight down the length of Lake Huron. Unless there was a boat going by close inshore, there was just no one around. They'd eat, walk up and down the sand, and sometimes get naughty.

This particular Sunday, they walked out of the woods and onto the beach around 11:30. Dean set the pack down and dug out the blue tarp they used for a picnic rug. Clairette stretched her arms up over her head and took a long breath of lake air. She was staring out onto the water when Dean said, "Look down there." She turned back, and saw he was pointing west. There was something red lying in the sand.

They walked down toward it, and it was clearly a boat; a little closer, and it was obviously a small kayak, upside down. "That's the biggest thing, I think, we ever found out here," Dean observed as they reached it. "Bigger'n that wood box last month."

"Yeah, but we can carry it ... or drag it back," said his wife. "Looks like there's something on this side." She pushed it partially over, exposing letters melted into the plastic. They were upside down from her point of view, but Dean was already on the other side of the boat, and he was able to read the text.

"Kay's Sports Rental, St Ignace. It's come a long way down to get here."

"Let's turn it all the way over. Easier to drag it back to the lunch," Clairette said. She got a better grip on her side and rolled it over toward Dean. Something inside it slid down against his side. "What's that?" she asked.

"Don't know. It's long. Gotta shove it down and angle it out ... oh, oh."

"What?"

"I think it's a case. A bag. For a gun." He pulled the object out lengthwise. "Sure is." The zipper was Delrin, not metal. Its time in the lake hadn't damaged it. Dean got it part way open, then pulled the contents half out until the attached scope caught on the case. It was sufficiently exposed, though, that he could see the Peninsular Republic property disk on the stock. Clairette was now on his side of the kayak, looking over his shoulder.

"Oh, Jeez," she said.

"Hey!" Dean shouted. Back down the beach, a large gray dog was nosing around in the backpack. It looked up at him, picked up one of their paper-wrapped sandwiches, and walked casually back into the woods.

§

The man from the green office had an appointment with General Alexiana Newhouse, PhD, Commander in Chief,

Army of the Republic. An academic transitioning into high office wasn't uncommon at all, at least in the PR, nor was a woman unusual in AoR Command. "The thing about her," the man thought "that I find surprising is that someone with her intelligence wants to deal with all these soldiers." Although he knew perfectly well the steps in her career that had led her to the job, he still wondered why she'd accepted it.

He used one of his several electronic credentials to enter a parking ramp at the main government complex, built on the site of what had been a large sports stadium. He left his small gray car, and, using another badge, went up six floors. Immediately out of the elevator hallway, he greeted a sergeant who smiled, returned the greeting, and led him through to the General's office. He wasn't a frequent visitor, but he was known.

Newhouse waved him to a seat, shut off her phone, and took the buds out of her ears. "Nice to see you," she said.

"My dear General, you always say that, and I'm afraid it seldom works out that way for you. One day, I'll ask to meet with you, and just to salve my conscience, I'll bring some good news. "

"So I can assume that you're not bringing me any, this time?"

"Sadly, no. What I have is a series of perplexing things to go over. I initially thought it was just one or two, but in the event, it turns out to be more. "

"Very well. Make my day."

"I think I will begin, if you're willing, by presenting things in the order I discovered them or had them reported to me. Then perhaps I'll try to bring them into some sort of coherent order. First, though, let me present the component parts of this situation." Newhouse leaned back in her chair, assuming a position that she'd assumed many times before, the I'm-listening posture that she'd adopted years ago with nervous young doctoral candidates. It was a habit deeply ingrained in her way of being.

"First," he said, "I had a situation described to me by someone high in External Relations. She told me and I confirmed it from other sources that our friends in the Naval Branch carried out an arms interdiction effort without telling anyone else."

"What do you mean, anyone else?"

"I mean that they did not involve Security, and that the effort wasn't based on intelligence developed by Security or by any other internal source. As my contact and I put it, they were 'freelancing.' The effort went badly, in the sense that several of the subjects died or were injured, much of the physical evidence was lost in the process, and one of their own officers was killed."

"Yes, I saw reports on that incident. Security is involved now, though. They're investigating, as required."

"They are, and it's not clear how forthcoming Naval is being. But there is an investigation. That alone wouldn't concern either you or me, except in a routine sense. But there are additional aspects. Next, it appears that some weeks ago, Naval somehow got a Security Branch Captain transferred to themselves. Or at any rate, he was transferred somewhere, and that action is masked by a screen of classification and general silence."

"Good old General Silence. I know him well."

"Yes. So that's two of my little items. Now, the third is both more and less obscure. On the surface, it's as simple as a homicide with no suspect yet, being investigated as always by the responsible Security Division. But there are troubling undercurrents."

"Okay."

"For one thing, the victim was a man being kept clandestinely out of sight, since he had been a Security Branch operative, informing on some antisocial elements. For another, he was killed, so Security asserts, by someone skilled in long-range shooting. And although there were Security assets tasked with keeping the victim safe, they appear not to have actually been tasked."

"No?"

"No. They do not seem to have known anything about him until he turned up dead. And the really interesting thing about it is that the officer directly responsible for the man's protection was the now-missing Security Branch Captain, the one who Security believes was strangely transferred to Naval. That happened very shortly before the shooting took place."

"I was thinking that this wasn't up to your usual standards of bad news. Now, finally, you're beginning to make me nervous."

"I'm sorry. This story does develop slowly. The pace picks up soon, though. The next interesting little event involves yet another missing person, a Field Branch Corporal. He was a member of a reconnaissance team, one of the people that Field trains as long-range marksmen." The General betrayed a slight reaction, just an upward twitch of her eyebrows. "Naval requested such a person, Field supplied him, and now he's just ... missing. Field wants him back, and Naval isn't really responding."

"Oh, my. And can I assume that Security is beginning to put these pieces together?"

"Well, no, I don't think you should assume that yet. But I've been led to believe that very shortly there will be connections made and conclusions drawn and reports written. And that you will be involved, as others will be.

The reason I say that is that there are still more little tales to tell."

"Oh, fantastic."

"Yes. The next part involves, oddly, a kayak." This time Newhouse kept a poker face. "Yes, a kayak. The small boats that people like to paddle around on. It seems that Naval did admit to Security that they had a patrol boat in the general vicinity where the shooting took place ..."

"Which shooting? The undercover guy, or the drug arrest?"

"Oh, I'm sorry. The shooting of the unfortunate clandestine informant. What Naval told Security is that the boat was there, but it had been detailed to look for a missing kayak. And presumably the person in it. And now, just this morning, I'm told that a kayak has, in fact, been found, somewhere on the Canadian shore. And it had no boater associated with it, but it did have a Field Branch rifle inside."

Newhouse kept her poker face on. "You said, I believe, that you'd be able to bring all this together? Is this a good time to do that?"

"Well, yes, at least phase one of doing that. You see, all of these relatively small things do seem to draw together into some sort of larger whole, but with just these elements, there's a problem of causality, if you see what I mean. They exist, but is there a larger implication?"

"I'll be happy to hear the answer to that."

"I don't know if you'll be happy, but let's move on and see how it all comes out. We have a dead man, shot, probably, by someone with long-range shooting skills. Naval borrowed such a person from Field, and now he's missing. Security had a Captain who was responsible for keeping the shooting victim from being shot, and he's missing. Naval apparently has some connection with that. Naval explains the presence of a patrol craft near the shooting as a search and rescue effort for a missing kayaker. And a kayak has turned up, with a long-range weapon in it."

"Ugly," said Newhouse.

"And there is a hint, nothing more, that the Naval Branch officer who was killed during their home-made arms interdiction effort was not who he seemed to be."

"Explain."

"There is no believable paper trail on him. Nothing, at least that has been turned up yet, from further back than a month. The name in use, at the time he died, was a Spanish word meaning "right". And ..." He paused.

"And what?"

"The missing Security Branch officer's name is Wright, with a 'W'."

"Oh, come on."

"Those are both facts, I'm afraid. Conclusions are another matter."

Newhouse leaned back and stretched her arms over her head. "Things like this make me wish I had a window. So I could stand up, join my hands behind my back, and stare out of it. Like perplexed generals do in bad fiction."

"From my standpoint, what all of this suggests," said the man, "is that Naval Branch is doing something or some set of things that are related to a very diverse set of really quite unfortunate occurrences. People going missing, poorly managed fights on the high seas, deaths, and this mysterious kayak. The obvious question at least to me, is why? What force or set of forces would produce this strange apparent behavior?"

"You took the word right out of my mouth. I can't wait to find out. Can I assume it's not as trivial as, say, the head of Naval Branch is an idiot?" That was an idea

Newhouse had been turning over in her mind for several months already.

"I really don't have any data related to that hypothesis. Not at this time. But what I do have suggests something that might lead you to draw another conclusion about Admiral Petronas. As I said, that first set of topics was a small collection of difficult but not very wide-ranging problems. But having applied some reasoning and some additional information, I find that there are larger issues."

"I think ... if we're going to move into those issues, I'd like another cup of tea. Would you like anything?"

"Why, yes, tea would be exactly the right thing, thank you. Without milk, please."

§

"What would I have to do if I wanted to get back into college?" It had taken Meg a day of pondering, but gradually the emerging adult in her head got the upper hand. An idea developed, the idea that a plan – any kind of a plan – was better than just hanging around. And a hint or two from outside became clearer; with a completed degree and some National Service might come a chance to ... fix ... some of the things that clearly needed fixing.

"So you want to?"

"Yes. I think I do. It's nice here, and ... it's great, what you're doing. But I think I want to jump back in."

Karen smiled. "You been talkin' to Una. That's what she wants. Wants to jump back in. And maybe kick some tails, too."

"Yes. I don't know about kicking anything. But I'd like to be doing something. "

"Good. But don't forget, you already did. You made up

your mind to get out of a bad thing. Now, you gotta build on that. You know what you might want to study?"

"Not really. I was just getting ... through school, before. I hadn't declared anything."

"What does it feel like now? Anything that seems more interestin' than it used to?"

"What did you study?"

"Me? Oh, Lord, that was a while ago. Ready for this? I was an accountant."

"I don't ... I don't think that would be best for me."

"No use to anyone, now. Laws are all changed. But I did take a couple of psych classes."

"Psychology?"

"Right. You might want to look that way. And you know what Larry's doin'? He's takin' a mix. Psych and theatre. He told me he can't decide which one is comin' in more handy." She chuckled.

"Oh. Oh, that makes sense. That explains a lot. About him, I mean."

"You know what he does, right? Besides school?"

"I didn't, at first. But I guess he works with you?"

"Not just me. He's in school. But he's doin' his National at the same time. Helpin' people. Department of Education pays him, a little bit, anyway. He's why you're here, girl."

"I ... wondered about that. But we knew each other, before. We were in high school together."

"Just luck. Your good luck. He brought Alan in here. Maybe we'll get him back. And Larry tipped off the guy who brought Una. She tell you that?"

"No. But I can see it. I can see him doing that ... finding people. And people trust him."

"Yeah. Part of that's the psych and theatre, and part of it's just Larry. So, you want me to get you started down the path? Get you into National, here or up in Mount Pleasant, say? Let you look at some program descriptions, so you know what's available?"

"I think ... yes. Let's start. I think that's the best thing for me to do, right now."

§

The general's aide and doorkeeper brought hot drinks quickly. It wasn't surprising to him that meetings with this particular visitor would generate a call for tea.

General Newhouse picked up her cup and concluded it was still too hot to drink. "I think you were about tell me what all of this Naval malfeasance added up to. If you'll forgive the stranded preposition."

"Well," the man said, "I'm able to explain the things it suggests to me, taken together with hints and whispers from other sources. Your mileage, as some industry or other used to say, may vary. I think the center of it all may be Pilot Ruby."

"I wondered if that might come up."

"It is on people's minds right now. Some people's, of course. Speaking frankly, the suggestion that another Separation by another chunk of the United States might happen has not been greeted with enthusiasm among most of the people with whom I discuss it. That is, to the extent that the Republic might involve itself."

"So your group isn't going to recommend ...?"

"Let's get to that at the end of all this. Pilot Ruby isn't ... I'm sure you know this ... the code name for a possible Separation off to the west of us, but rather the term for my little group. Our task is to evaluate the possibility and to recommend our public and private responses."

"Yes."

"We have become, the more we learn about it, increasingly skeptical that a Separation in the west can succeed. The people involved have done none of the things we did here in terms of paving the way. They're still undercover, they've leaked nothing at all. And they have a large, lower middle class, conservative population about which they've done nothing. We regard their chances of a unilateral Separation as no better than twenty-five percent. And that's the high estimate." He took a sip of tea.

"The proposition as they tendered it to us at first, that they should join the Republic in some manner, is almost unanimously rejected among our group. First of all, we would require that they accept our constitution. That would be impossible to impose on any but a minority of their people. The issue, alone, of nationalizing public services would create a large and well-funded opposition. And to their credit, the Naval Branch representative in our efforts was among the first to point all that out."

"What exactly was pointed out?"

"He was very cogent. He reminded us that our friends to the east are funding the bulk of Naval's operations. And he pointed out that an addition to our responsibilities of the kind we're talking about would do little or nothing for Canada. They have no land border with the potential new area. And only a small border in Lake Superior. But there we would be, having to deal with a whole new range of responsibilities, and they would get nothing from it at all."

"Canada has their own set of problems," said Newhouse. "And we solve one of them. Or Naval does."

"And therefore, they have reason to – let's be polite and call it exert influence on our policies. And Naval is really the only place where they have leverage."

"So tie this back to all the earlier things. I don't see the connections, yet."

"I didn't either. But just recently, I learned a few facts and heard a few opinions that let me reach a conclusion or two. One is that Canada sees certain kinds of Great Lakes security in a different light than we do. When we hear of something dangerous happening, something like a shipment of arms coming into the Republic or the insertion of undesirable people, Security Branch likes to make a trap out of it. They like to let the bad actors get here, and then they pounce on them, capturing both contraband and dangerous individuals. Security's view, and I happen to agree with it, is that a live terrorist facing life in prison is more valuable than a dead one. Canada, however, simply wants the whole thing suppressed. They don't want people to see the lakes as any kind of criminal highway, either into or out of their territory. If anyone is going to smuggle anything, they'd rather it came by land where they have their borders well secured. And so, they'd rather raise an alarm directly with Naval, than go through Security."

"Really? Why wouldn't they try to get Security's tactics changed?"

"I don't know. But I wonder if their perception of that approach may have been colored. By Naval, if you see what I'm suggesting."

"Naval says Security won't change its ways, so you should deal directly with us?"

"That's one hypothesis, yes."

"That isn't simply untrue, you know. It's illegal. Specifically."

"Yes. Individual branches aren't supposed to act independently in that way. And yet, Naval seems to be."

§

The Radio E liked was being annoying, playing light and fluffy music for people's morning trips into work. She switched to National FM 50, the general news and opinion station. It was in the middle of an arts program, interviewing people in and out of the Republic. She heard the last sentence from an author in Dubai, and then the host turned (figuratively; it was radio, of course, and the interviewees might be physically in a studio or just electronically connected) to a man who taught photography in the National University System.

E listened through the introduction and the usual greeting formalities. There were a few quick "tell us about your own work" questions, and then the host brought up the issue of careers. The guest denied all knowledge.

"First of all, I teach photography as an expression of the individual behind the camera. If someone's trying to 'to do art' to achieve some kind of goal or to become something – to become an 'artist' – then we really don't have a lot to talk about. I don't have anything to say to that person or about him."

The host tried to push back gently, but the guest wasn't having any. "What I just said a minute ago is all I can say." This went on for another few sentences, and then the host referred to the previous guest. She'd mentioned post-modernism in reference to her writing. That got a reaction.

"The great point of the post-modernists – their great insight – is that viewers of art react differently to it than the artist did. And the thing the theorists miss, sometimes deliberately, I think, is that it's a staggeringly obvious observation. One that a child could make. Of course the audience isn't the artist. But it shouldn't make the slightest difference to the person who is actually creating the work. It does seem to make a great deal of difference to a writer *about* art, though. It gives him something to say in a time when most of the artists I respect think of talking about art as a useless distraction. The thing to do is just to do something – anything at all – except talk."

"So you're saying that people's reaction to your work doesn't matter to you?'

"I like an occasional pat on the back. I admit it. But I go on doing things, regardless. Even if someone stages a show of my pictures and absolutely no one comes, it doesn't make me stop shooting. I know when I've done something that pleases me, and if it doesn't please anyone else at all, I'm still pleased. What else is there?"

"Of course, I do have to point out: you have a teaching post. A – forgive me – a job."

"Right, I do. And when I'm doing that, that's when I worry about the audience – the students and their interaction with me, when I'm teaching. Because as you suggest, I get paid to do that. I teach people how to create things, and I show them examples of what other people have done. But that's the teaching part. I'll say it again; when I'm shooting my own stuff or showing it, I'm not talking to anyone but myself."

"Well, thank you for being with us. Since we're not talking to ourselves here, we have to break for some news headlines, and then we'll be back with a man who ..." E switched back to the music station. *I wish I'd been allowed to talk that way, back when I was teaching.*

§

"It's been a long thirty minutes. Do you have any more good news?" asked General Newhouse.

"I do, and if you've gotten the sense that our little

advisory group is leaning toward some sort of armed neutrality with reference to our western neighbors, the last phase of this conversation will reinforce that idea. We do have more reasons than I've presented so far."

"Oh, good."

"We believe, as I said earlier, that there is little chance of a Separation over there. And we feel that if we were to go any farther than wishing them a guarded 'good luck', we would be grasping what an old colleague of mine called an opportunity to fail."

"I can see the logic behind that."

"And if so, congratulations, because you don't have all the reasons, yet, the final set of things that drive us to that opinion." He glanced at his watch. "I'll be brief, since I know you have other demands on your time. When we've finished here, I suspect you'll set yourself some additional tasks, as well."

"That's always the way with our little meetings, I notice."

"With great office comes great responsibility. Here is my last little insight. The United States is not a friend of ours, given our divorce. The wounds there are still raw. At first sight, then, you'd think they wouldn't welcome another such abandonment by one of their states. Or even an attempt at it. And yet ..." He paused.

"And yet?"

"What if there were a neighbor of ours, not a very tractable part of the US, politically, or very wealthy, either, that might offer the US a stick with which to beat us?"

"I don't ... are you suggesting that the government down there ..." She gestured southward with her thumb. "... is setting us up?"

"I am suggesting it. Us or the state in question or both of us. And I'm doing so because some knowledgeable people and some interesting facts suggest it to me. One doesn't have to just rush out and find an opportunity to fail. It can be offered to you. And we think that this whole situation may be encouraged or even manufactured by the US government."

"Well, well, well. All of the objections that have been raised now seem quite … inspired. We'd have to spend money, we'd have to expand our government services, we'd have to cope with a disaffected majority of the new population."

"And we'd be seen in a very Cold-War, 1950s-Soviet-style-exporter-of-revolution light. That is, by the international community. In many capitals, we're still seen as a kind of junior America, with the same drawbacks and much less money. No matter what it did to us internally, it would be damning, internationally."

"Proxy war. Despite everybody's best efforts, it's still a favorite thing. 'Let's you and him fight' as my grandfather used to call it."

The man smiled. "I'm always confident that you will, but it's still pleasant when you grasp my little explanations so clearly. Of course, we'll still have to plan for some troublesome events. Perhaps you'll recommend a set of mild and mostly unpublished expansions in the AoR. We'll have to keep a sharp eye on what, if anything, really happens on the far shore. Intelligence will be critical, and I wonder if some expansion in the Security Branch might not be necessary."

"Do you think we'll have anything formal to say to the US? Nation to nation?"

"Of course, that's for the External Relations people to ponder. I hear quiet voices suggesting that, no, we won't have a thing to say unless there really is a revolt, and it spills over into our areas of responsibility. The lake, for example. And our message would be along the lines of

'Can't you keep your people in better order?' I think Canada would be willing to chime in on that, in harmony with us."

"And by God, if we take that approach, we turn the game around. If Washington really is playing games, we've given them back their opportunity. To fail, I mean."

"Yes. Well, General, I believe I've done enough harm for one day. But let me just finish with a question for you. Do you have any thoughts about Naval Branch? Is there anything, for example, I could help you implement?"

"Oh, I'll be dealing with that. And I'll let you know before I have anyone shot or anything."

"Splendid. And I'm sure you won't use that particular phrase with anyone more sensitive than myself. Two people have already been shot, after all, and I think Council won't want to see any more of that."

§

The front of the classroom was as unadorned as most of them. There were no flags, no religious icons, no political slogans. Just a desk and a big screen. There were thirty-plus student desks, and most of them were occupied. As the last one or two kids came in, so did the instructor. He was in his mid-thirties, and his class members were all in the nine- or ten-year-old range.

"All right," he said. "Sit down and let's get started." He clicked a remote, and the projector hanging from the ceiling lit up. The screen displayed "HS&R 100".

"I've learned to start these classes off with a quick story. You're here to learn things, but now and then, I do too. This is a story about something I learned." The students were at least watching him, whether or not they were actually paying attention. It was the first class period of the day, after all, and not many of them had yet discovered the magic of coffee.

"The first time I taught this class, I set things up like this." He waved his hand at the screen. "Just the course number. And then I jumped right into the topics. The things we'd be covering. It looked like this." He clicked a remote, and the screen showed a dozen bullet points. As the class read down through them, there was at least one audible snicker.

"Now, most of the class, like you, read down the list and didn't seem startled. But one young man looked very confused, and he raised his hand. 'Sir,' he said, 'Isn't this Beginning Economics?'" There was some nervous laughter.

"That taught me two things. One, always spell out the full name of the class." Another click, and the screen said HS&R 100: Human Sexuality and Reproduction. "So, is there anyone here who's in the wrong class? As you can see, this isn't Beginning Economics." Nobody moved.

"Good. But here's the second lesson I learned. In a way, this *is* economics. You can't have an economy – not for long, anyway – without human reproduction." He let that sink in. "But – but! – you can destroy your economy by being too enthusiastic about reproduction." There was a general silence. Some students looked around at their neighbors. Some looked mildly shocked. The instructor clicked again. The screen said BIG IDEAS.

"Most of your classes are built around big ideas, and here's the first one for this course." Another click.

Reproduction Can't be Random.

Again, there were a few looks around. "If humans don't watch out, they'll reproduce themselves out of the game. But that doesn't mean what everybody thinks it does." Click.

Sexuality and Reproduction Are Not The Same.

"Reproduction – making baby humans – was originally,

way back in human history, the reason for sex. That's a very simple way of saying it, and when I say human history, I mean our ancestors – the living things that evolved into us. But by the time we became what we are now – look around, look at all the people in this room – reproduction became a side effect. Who knows what 'side effect' means?"

A girl raised her hand. "It happens by accident?"

"Okay. Some side effects do. But sometimes, we know about side effects of something, and if we do that thing, and the side effect happens, that's not an accident, is it?" He looked around. Another hand up.

"It's like drugs. Having side effects."

"Yup. And not all side effects are bad or dangerous. But you should know about them. And know what to do if they happen. And how to keep them from happening. And here's the good news." Click.

Sexuality Doesn't Mean Reproduction.

"Sexuality is a combination of who someone is and what kinds of other people they like. That's about as simply as I can say it. Now who knows what I mean when I say subset?"

"It's math, I think."

"Math uses that word, but it's all over the place. If I call this class ..." He waved an arm at the whole room. "... a set of people, then you over there ... " He waved at the right side." ... are a subset of the people in the set. And if all the things people do because of their sexuality are a set, reproduction is a subset. And not a very big one." He paused; the room was quiet.

"So I'll say it again and in a different way. Sexuality is a big, complicated subject. Reproduction isn't. At least when you think about its relationship to Sexuality." Click. The screen showed a large circle in gray, with just a small part at the bottom covered with a darker circle. The large one said "Sexuality"; the small one couldn't hold the entire word, so there was an arrow linking it to a label: "Reproduction".

"Does everyone see the difference? Sexuality is the big circle, reproduction is just a small part of it. That's how this class is designed. We're going to talk about what sexuality is and why people spend so much time thinking about it. Reproduction is going to be a small part. Okay?" Heads nodded.

In the back of the room, Kristin made a note on a form, checked several boxes, and quietly left. "Pretty good," she thought. "Now ..." She looked down at her schedule. "Let's see how the economics classes are starting off." She remembered the previous inspector's notes. "Keep an eye on Mister Clark. He's a closeted Friedman fan."

§

E would rather hold meetings and discussions in the morning. Then the rest of the day would be available for taking action on things. This morning, she and Captain Matthews were among the first people in the office; they were the first ones in the secure area.

"So I have some things for you, but let's start with anything you've got for me," said Matthews. "That'll give me time to absorb the coffee."

"Fine, sir. I'm actually one cup ahead, I think. It makes the ferry ride go faster. I have two things to report, and I'll start with the less ... interesting of them. Based on what we have so far, I don't think we have any more useful work to do on the island." Matthews nodded slightly.

"We have absolutely no indication that anyone there had any connection with Silverman at all, leaving out the neighbors for the moment. He bought a few things at the

Landing store, used an ATM there occasionally, and went across to the mainland for any other shopping he had to do. Nobody at Landing or anywhere else on the island knew him by name or any other way except 'the guy who's living at Peters now.' The only exceptions I could identify were the neighbors."

"Okay."

"We've been back to talk to them twice, both times trying to make the point that they weren't suspects, we just have to get all the data we can get... that approach. The last time, I asked Brigade to send one of their people along, one of their psych experts. He and I chatted with all three of them, and while that was going on, I had one of our recruits attach a tracker to the husband's boat."

"Really? The recruits know how to do that, now?"

"No, but I taught her. She did a good job of it. It's still transmitting, and it shows that Mr. Bullock never takes his boat anywhere near Peters Island. In fact, he never goes anywhere in it except a mile or a little more out into the lake. He motors slowly around in a way consistent with fishing, then comes back. And his trips never coincide with bad weather, poor visibility ... essentially, he's just fishing."

"And the wife and daughter? I think we both wondered if there was anything sketchy there?"

"Mrs. Bullock moves around a bit more than her husband, but it's almost exclusively up to the ferry at Landing. And weekends, all three go over to De Tour for shopping. There's no indication their patterns have changed, either recently or when Silverman moved in."

"How about the girl?"

E handed over a document, labeled as a Brigade Psychological Officer Assessment. "The Psych guy talked to her for twenty minutes, and she kept that same flat affect that you and I observed. His take is that she's perhaps a bit underdeveloped. The homicide, our people running around, being talked to by scary police ... none of it seems to really hit home. Whatever she is, she's certainly not traumatized by it all."

"Any possibility that they're thinking about leaving? "

"I don't think so. That little house and the lake are all they have. Both of the adults state that they have no living family elsewhere, and we checked, and they don't. Unless someone's done a really professional job of hiding things."

Matthews nodded. "And you know, I'm not all that sold on the overall professionality of this particular crime."

"I agree, sir. Especially in light of the second issue I have to report." She slid a document across the table. "I picked this up on the Army open records site. Not classified at all. The summary is, Naval Branch borrowed a sniper-qualified corporal and his rifle from Field Branch, and then apparently lost him."

Matthews was in the middle of a sip, and with some difficulty avoided spilling any of it. "What?"

"They requested a temporary personnel assignment, long-range shooting qualified and with a weapon, from an FB company in Fifth Division. There wasn't any detail about where he was going or what he'd be doing, and I guess his command assumed it was something classified. As of yesterday, it had been two weeks and nothing heard of him, so his command sent that report ..." she gestured at the document ..." to their Brigade. Essentially, they want their property back."

"Oh ... my. That's ... Sergeant, we're involved with something very, very strange here. Is that all you have?"

"Yes, sir."

"Well, then, let me give you something more. I was just notified, all the way down from Division, that a red kayak was found, washed up on Manitoulin Island. Marked as property of that St. Ignace rental shop you talked to." E was doing a very creditable job of keeping her eyebrows under control, but her eyes were wide. "And ... well, see if you can guess what was in it."

"A signed confession?"

"No. An AoR-issue sniper rifle and scope."

"I see. Sir, do we have any f... flaming ... idea what's going on?"

"I think ... an idea is beginning to emerge, at least at higher levels of command, and ... the next topic I have is specific to you. Because you're going to be involved in ..." She ran out of military-sounding terminology. "... figuring it the hell out."

"All right, sir. I do have a request, though. I think it would be a good idea if I were to locate over here, at the base, for the duration of this ... effort. "

"Okay with me. You've been staying over here some nights, already, right?"

"Yes, sir. To be frank, I'm not sure that being out on the shore of that island or anywhere else that's at all isolated is especially secure, right now. From a personal standpoint."

"Oh, I see what you mean. Yes, let's get you over here for the duration. I'll let Lieutenant Mecklin know. "

"Thank you, sir. I have everything I'll need with me now. For at least the next week. And I'll let Sergeant Edmore know that he's got his island back."

§

General Newhouse had several small, more or less trivial things to deal with while she recovered from the green office man and his little narrative. She asked her aide to order a sandwich "or something", and she started in on her list. She'd gotten through one and half items when the aide opened the door. "General," he said," you have a call. From Councilmember Felix."

"Oh. All right, I'll take it." Few of the council members had any reason to talk to her directly, but Alistair Felix was an old, steady political hand, finishing his term in office. He was always worth talking to – and listening to, even more so. The secure phone buzzed.

"Well, General, how nice to speak with you again." Felix had a practiced foxy-old-guy tone that he used, and he even cultivated a kind of comedic, Hal Holbrook accent to go along with it. "I hope things are well with you over there in your Vauban fortification."

"Yes, we're tolerably well over here, Mister Felix. How are you?"

"Oh, I can't complain. And if I did, what good would it do? But I do have a question for you, if you have a moment to spare."

"Of course. What can I tell you?"

"It has to do with chains of command and how rigorously you and your people like to observe them. For example if you were considering any kind of important change, say, in your personal status or your organization, should I take it for granted that Council would hear it from you or from your office?"

"What on earth?" Newhouse wondered. "Why, yes. That's policy … and just common courtesy."

"Now, that's what I thought. But you know, I had a young man in here just a few minutes ago. And he led me to understand that perhaps the Army was thinking of some fairly high-level changes in organization and command structure."

"No, nothing at all like that."

"That's good. That's very good. I think things are quite well structured over there, and I believe that most of my colleagues do, too."

Newhouse was beginning to feel a twinge in her stomach. "Can I ask what ... what made this person think that things were changing?"

"I'm afraid I anticipated you there, General. I asked this fellow that, myself. He didn't really explain it all that well, but he seemed to think the Naval people would be assuming something, shall I say, higher of a role in the command structure and the strategic thinking of our Republic."

"The Naval people?"

"Yes. That was the uniform he was wearing."

"Did he have any ... basis for his ideas?"

"No. When I expressed skepticism, he asked my pardon and went away."

"Can I ask you who the person was?"

"You may. I thought you'd want to know. It was Admiral Petronas." There was a pause. "Are you still there, General?"

"Yes. Yes, I am. I was just planning a discussion with the Admiral. I'll be sure to mention your call."

"You go right ahead. I probably misunderstood him. My hearing isn't what it used to be. But thank you for your time."

"Thank you."

Newhouse cut off the call. She didn't bother to get up and stare pensively out the window she didn't have. If the United States or Venezuela or someplace had declared war, she might have done that. Of course, she didn't have such a window, but even if she had, this was different. She touched her aide's call button. "Michael, ask General Hallstatt to come and see me. ASAP."

§

"Sit down, Phil," Newhouse said to Hallstatt when he arrived. "This might take a few minutes." Newhouse gestured at her visitor's chair. "We've got a problem." The commanding officer of the Security Branch followed orders and sat down.

"General," he said, "on the way down here, I wondered if that was what you were going to say. I'd just come to that conclusion, myself. If we're talking about Naval Branch, that is."

"We are. And you have some concerns there, too?"

"Yes. But, please, you start, you probably have a longer list than I do."

Newhouse gave the head of Security Branch a summary of what she'd heard from the green office man. "How much of that has come by you?"

"Not all of it," Hallstatt said. I've heard about the missing Captain. And about a homicide up in Seventh Division. And just now, about the missing Corporal from Field Branch. But as I thought, you have a bigger picture."

"Here's something else you haven't heard. Admiral Petronas has been lobbying Council members for a change in command over here. Meaning me."

Hallstatt opened his mouth, closed it, and then said, "He's doing what?" Newhouse summarized the call from Councilmember Felix.

"That's ... that's not acceptable."

"It's not. I'm going to have him in here tomorrow, and here's the outline of what I'm going to tell him." She passed a single sheet of paper over the desk. "I'll be giving this to your colleague in Field in ... what? half an hour. And tomorrow, when I'm finished with the Admiral, I'm going to fire his ass. And I will ask you to initiate an investigation of the whole thing. So, you might want to start thinking about how you'll do that."

"I will. May I have a quick look at your agenda? To see if I have any questions?"

"Please do. Every bit of it is straight from the Constitution or AoR General Regulations." The paper was a list of points.

> Branches of the Army of the Republic are collegial, not adversarial.
>
> Outside a state of war, interactions with other nations are the sole responsibility of the Republic's Department of External Affairs.
>
> The Army of the Republic interacts with the Council of the Republic as a unified whole, under the direction of Army command. Individual commands have neither the right nor the responsibility to do so unilaterally.
>
> All members of the Army of the Republic are subject to the laws of the Republic, regardless of circumstances.

"Thank you, sir. Do you intend to distribute this? I'd like to share it, at some point. With my people."

"Oh, I'll be distributing it, all right. But hold on to it until I have a chance to brief Admiral Petronas on its finer points and implications. I wouldn't want him to misunderstand any of it."

§

Matthews wrapped up a status call with Battalion. Vogel was as unhappy as she was, and he, poor fellow, would have to make Colonel Macready unhappy, too.

"Oh, one more thing, sir," Matthews said. "I want to get Gorsky on the path for a bump up in grade. She's eligible for the Lieutenant exam, when we can spare her."

"She's qualified?"

"Yes, sir. She has time in grade, command experience, the whole thing."

"Well, how about this? I have two acting lieutenant slots I don't need up here. We can give her one with just my signature and yours. And then when – I hope it's when and not if – this business gets sorted out, she'll have that on her personnel sheet, and we can probably waive the exam."

"We can do that?"

"Yes. Do you want to?"

"Yes, absolutely."

"All right ... hold on a minute and I'll send you the form." There were keystrokes in the background. "Okay, it's on its way. Just hit the signature block, send it back, and give her a set of bars. Personnel up here will deal with the records and pay and so on."

Matthews noted a new file in her mailbox. "Got it. Thank you, sir. That lets me knock one thing, at least, off my to-do list."

§

Ed Edmore kissed his wife goodbye. His weekend bag was on the passenger's seat of his truck, he was back in his SB uniform, and he was ready to head back to Dog Island. It was longer than just a run down from the Soo.

From her house – their house, in fact – back to Landing was a hundred and seven kilometers by road, with a border to cross at one end and a ferry ride at the other. The place they owned was east of the bridge, on the river, looking back at the Republic. From their patio, that was just half a K southwest across the Saint Marys. There was nothing much but woods to see over there – one or two houses and a dock. And of course, the freighters up bound and down bound. If you drew a line due south-southeast, it would cross the border three times back and forth before reaching Ed's apartment above the Landing SB post, and it would take nearly 70 K to do it. He was very clear which end of that vector he preferred. "Three more years, baby," his wife said as he got in the truck.

"Don't let those guys out of your sight," he answered. "They don't know one end of a beer truck from the other."

"I won't. Three more years!"

He backed the truck out onto the street and headed for the bridge. "Three more years," he thought.

Out of the neighborhood, he turned onto Queen Street. It was like a drive through the Detroit suburbs had been, back, oh, even in the nineties. The pavement was in good shape. Things seemed reasonably affluent. But there were trees. That was the main difference. Where the foliage was cleared away, you could see the river, and that would have been a feature of at least Detroit's northern neighbors.

As he came into the city proper, the look and feel became older, but not in the way cities of his experience had aged. The buildings were elderly, two-story, and brick, but they were still in use, not standing empty. Coming out the other side of downtown, things opened up, and the road became slightly more highway-like. Then it was just a quick right-left and past Canadian

Customs. He went out onto the bridge, over the river, over the locks, and down into the Republic's border check.

At the window, he showed his SB credentials, got a salute from the National Service private, and carried on. In keeping with his personal ritual for these trips, he started singing, "Back in the USSR".

§

In the few minutes left before the head of the Field Branch was due, General Newhouse looked at her message queue. There was nothing exciting, a thing for which she was grateful. "Just one flaming disaster at a time, Lord," she thought.

General Kydo was on time, as usual. Somehow, her parents anticipated her career, naming her Sekhmet. "Punctual, our goddess of war," Newhouse thought. "Not really lion-headed, though. Hearted, maybe. "We'll see. This might call for a lion-heart." The Commander in Chief was not as familiar with Kydo as she was with the Security chief. The head of Field Branch was new in the post, after a medical issue sidelined her predecessor.

"Good afternoon, General. Thanks for coming over on short notice. I need to make you aware of an organizational change." Kydo nodded. "That's not a phrase people usually like to hear, myself included. But this is a necessary step. Possibly overdue. Maybe an emergency. I intend to relieve Admiral Petronas, with effect tomorrow." She looked Kydo straight in the eyes, and the look was returned, steadily. "Good reaction," she thought.

"Naval Branch will report to me while the three of us – you and I and General Hallstatt – redesign the high command structure. I don't have a finished concept in mind, but I will say that I expect it to be somewhat different from its current ... state."

"I see. Thank you for advising me. I was considering a conversation with you on the subject of Naval. This will subsume that, I believe."

"Was it about your missing soldier?"

"Yes. You've been made aware of that situation?"

"As part of a general report on Naval, yes. It's not my only reason for taking action. But I do find it concerning."

"What action do you need from us?"

"Read this." She handed over her summary of points. "Once the change in command is complete, I will want this run down through the entire chain of command. But hold up on it until you hear from me. "

"I believe you said 'tomorrow' for the changes?"

"Yes. By end of day, at most. And if there's some reason why not, I'll be informing you and Phil Hallstatt immediately. But I don't think that will happen."

Kydo took the four points document and the General's summary of the situation. "Steady," Newhouse thought. "Not a twitch, even though this is a damned ugly mess." On the far wall of her office, she had a framed map of Ireland, with a small stick-on dot in the northeast. "A Niús townland," she thought. "My people should have stayed there. All things taken together ..." She remembered a character from the Irish folklore book she was reading. "... the Morrigan gets a bad rap."

Seven hundred and thirty kilometers north-northwest, just before the shore of Lake Superior makes its big bend west, the Pic River empties into the lake. There's a scattering of houses on the north side of the river, but on the south, it's wooded, part of Canadian national land. Back from the water, twenty-four men were camping, sheltering in small, camouflaged tents. Somewhere out in the woods, a coyote howled.

§

E was at her desk in the secure area. The volume of open, unclassified Naval Branch documents was, unsurprisingly, large. She'd nearly run out of ideas for searches; there were only so many terms you could try if you were looking for things on vanishing personnel. Her next move, if nothing else came up, would be to try similar snooping in Field Branch and Security Branch files.

She'd just kicked off a query on "boat" and "rental", thinking that perhaps the NB had policies or records relating to temporary kayak acquisition, when Matthews knocked on the door jamb. "Got a minute?" she asked.

"Of course, sir. I'm just fishing in the sea of bureaucracy, here."

"As good a place as any, right now. I have one piece of good news, anyway." She held out her hand. "You can put these on." They were a pair of hook-and-loop-backed lieutenant's badges.

"Oh, that's ... um, a surprise. I thought we were going to work on that later on."

"I mentioned bumping you up, and it turns out Major Vogel has a pair of temporary acting lieutenant slots on his roster. His idea was that we give you one of them now, and when things calm down a little, we work on the full-blown move. You get paid at LT rates while this is in effect."

"Thank you, sir. I appreciate it."

"Don't be too grateful. We hope this helps you rattle cages with a bit more rank behind you. Not that you haven't upset any apple carts already."

"To a certain extent, that's our mission, isn't it? If we do a good job, somebody's unhappy."

"Exactly. Well, anyway, get these on – save your sergeant's patches, just in case – and Willy will get your new rate info up to Human Resources. Oh, and congratulations. I think ... yes?" Her Admin Corporal was standing behind her.

"Excuse me, sir. Major Vogel wants to speak with you. Can you call him from your secure line?"

"All right." She turned back to E. "Here we go again."

§

Admiral Malcom "Mal" Petronas had just turned forty-nine. When he was employed in the marine engine business, back before the separation, he'd been known among his clients for his long, hyperbolic proposals and contracts. Privately, they were referred to as "Malware". Now, he restricted his long-windedness to verbal communication, since in the area of written material, he had people to do that for him.

Physically, he was below middle height, just starting to put on some weight and just beginning to lose his hair. In a more traditional military uniform, he might have looked better, but in the casual, utilitarian dress that even ranking AoR officers wore, he looked unconvincing. If Ed Edmore looked like a bartender, Mal Petronas looked like a boat salesman. He was one of the few people you'd meet in the Republic who actually regretted the death of the necktie.

"Good morning, General!" he said as he walked into Newhouse's office. "Always a pleasure. I'm glad you set this up. I have a few ideas I want to share with you."

"Really? Well, can we hold those while I share some of mine?"

"Of course, of course. What's on your mind?"

"You are. By the way, do you know Mister Douglas?" She

gestured to a man in her other guest chair. "He's from the Legal Department." Petronas lost a portion of his bonhomie.

"Ah, no, I don't think so. Not that I recall."

Douglas got up and handed over an envelope. "General Newhouse asked me to examine a statement of certain allegations, backed up with supporting material, and I've given her my assessment of them. My opinion and that of my department is that the course of action she's taking is appropriate and in accordance with law and regulations."

"What ... exactly what are we talking about, here?" he said.

Newhouse leaned forward. "Effective immediately, you are relieved of your command. Your accesses and clearances are suspended, and you will have a workspace in building two while investigations into your conduct and into the actions and personnel of Naval Branch take place."

"What ... do you think you're doing? How can you imagine that ..."

"That what?"

"That Council will allow you to relieve me? Do you understand who ..." She slid another piece of paper across the desk.

"Council's liaison office sent this to me an hour ago. It confirms my authority to structure the command of the Army of the Republic as I determine necessary, in the interests of the Republic and its people. And here's another, from the Director of the External Relations Department. It instructs me to investigate and correct any case of unauthorized international contacts and negotiations that may come to my attention."

"Do you know what you're doing!?"

"I do. The facts I've been shown convince me that you don't. You're relieved, sir, for incompetence at least, and depending on investigations I've just ordered, for potential violations of the law. For a summary, read this." She gave him her four points document. Then she touched her call button. "Because you no longer hold clearances, I'll ask these gentlemen ..." the door had just opened, and two Security Branch non-coms came in "... to confiscate your badge and escort you out of this secure area. They'll show you to your temporary facility. Or, if you prefer, you can take the day off. That's up to you."

§

In his green office, the man was speaking with Jeri Klein. "So, Doctor, as I noted, Naval Branch has been decapitated. But since the investigation of the rest of its body is just now starting, I wonder if we've really closed off its inappropriate contacts with our eastern neighbor."

"I can't guess," Klein said. "From what little I know of the Admiral's style, I'd imagine it was at least partly delegated. But maybe it was all him."

"I have the same uncertainty. Security will, of course, be looking into that. But I think a preemptive strike by your people might be the best thing. And General Newhouse agrees, I might say."

"You're right. I said that to my next level up, and they want to close that door right away. Like this evening, yet, if we can. Do you have any thoughts about what to say?"

"If it were I, I'd start with loving assurances that their interests on the lakes are our highest priority and concern, and we wish to ensure that those interests are being looked after by the Republic as a single, unified body. To achieve that, we've taken some administrative steps, etc., etc., and still, as it always has been, your point of contact with us is through the ambassador's organization, which stands ready etc. etc. If you follow that."

"Remarkably like the text I suggested to my boss. Shall I press the button?"

"Please do. I support that completely. Ambassador Morgen will initiate the discussion?"

"Right. And we'll let you know how it goes, as soon as ... well, as soon as it has."

"Good. I'll be reachable throughout the evening. Call anytime."

At a little after 2300 hours, Klein called him. "Done," she said. "The Ambassador said he wasn't sure his opposite number really knew what it all meant, but that person said he'd let their national police know – the Mounties – and their Department of National Defense. So I think the message has been sent."

"Very good. The message has been sent here as well. All three branches have been notified. Security is initiating one or more programs of their own. And Admiral Newhouse is pondering how long she can do two jobs before she decides what to do with the newly orphaned sailormen and women."

"I think I'll get some sleep. Before the next wave of chaos hits."

"Oh, Doctor, you're so refreshingly optimistic. I find myself thinking, as the lamented Louis Armstrong sang, nobody knows the trouble I've seen."

"Nobody knows the sorrow. Well, goodnight."

"Goodnight, Doctor. Sweet dreams."

At the mouth of the Pic River, a man was going from tent to tent, waking the sleepers up. One of them said, "What? What time is it?"

"Eleven-forty. Get packed up. It's off."

"It's off? What the hell?"

"They don't tell me anything. Just pack up. We're going back up to the road. Trucks'll be there by one o'clock."

"But where're we goin'?"

"Back to Parry Sound. Like I said, it's off."

"Son of a bitch."

§

There wasn't a space large enough for all the SB personnel in B Company to gather, but most of them were in small, local offices, and could take part remotely. So the gymnasium – a hold-over from the building's days as a school – was adequate. There weren't enough chairs, but Matthews and Vogel intended to keep the meeting short.

"Let's get this going," said Vogel, speaking into a microphone. "First of all, nothing we're going to say is classified, but you are not to talk about it with civilians, even the press, without authorization. It's not secret, but we'd prefer not to just walk out the door and drop our pants, if you'll excuse the metaphor. When we've described the situation, we'll provide a couple of ways you can describe it to friends and family." The room was quiet; this was not an approach they'd heard before. Usually, things were secret or they weren't.

"Here's what I heard, in summary, from Battalion and Division last night. I was instructed to present it to our Companies as soon as I could, and I'll be tearing around the UP today, doing that. You, on the other hand, many of you, will be digging into a large new investigation. If you find that exciting, great. If not, sorry, but I can't help." This time, he got a chuckle or two.

"Captain Matthews and I heard the same message from

above, and she's your source here. She's the one to talk to, because as I said, I'm going to be hard to reach for a day or so. All right?" Silence.

"So here's the summary. Very high level work – way up the chain of command – found some very concerning things going on, things involving, for example, the homicide that's being worked here, in B Company." Vogel's speaking style became somewhat run-on when he was under pressure.

"High level investigation determined that some of these concerns were specific to Naval Branch." People exchanged looks. "As a result, the commanding officer of NB has been relieved." Concern. Even a whisper or two.

"There is a new program, some of which is open, and some of it classified. The open portions are referred to as River Slide. That's slide with an l, not 'side'. The objective of both the open and closed programs is to determine where things went off the track, who should have done what about it, and whether the issues were only operational, or if laws were broken. We've done work like this before – it's in our charter – but we have not worked on things like this within AoR, not at this ... scale." He had the group's attention.

"I can't take the time to be specific about what ... went wrong. Was done or not done. But I want to show you this set of points. It comes down all the way from AoR. I was told General Newhouse herself wrote it." The viewing screen had been blank, but now it lit up and showed a simplified version of the document Newhouse had shown to her Branch commanders.

Branches work together, not against each other.

AoR branches work internally, within the Republic.

```
Council   and   the   AoR   interact   at   the   top.
Period.

AoR obeys the law.
```

"If that gives you some idea of the seriousness of this ... situation, well, um, it should. Those aren't things anyone here should have be, ah, reminded of. Told. And the programs I mentioned, River Slide and the closed one, are designed to work on those... those principles. And whether they were followed." It seemed that the message was getting through. People were obviously reading and re-reading the screen, and again there was some whispering.

"That, I'm afraid, is what I have time for. I'll leave Captain Matthews to handle your questions. I have to go and do this again in two other Companies. Thank you." He looked relieved. One down.

§

E very seldom watched video news. She preferred it in text summaries, without any personalities and experts getting in the way. In the small hours, she sometimes wondered if this wasn't simply egotism, a kind of just-give-me-the-facts-and-I'll-decide mentality, but she usually managed to suppress those voices. Today, though, she and two of her colleagues were watching a broadcast from the capital. The National News Channel's government affairs reporter was on the corner of Main and Capital Avenues, standing in front of the still-oval-shaped set of buildings that housed most of the Republic's leadership. Privately it was known as the Quiz Castle, a play on "Puzzle Palace," a now-obsolete nickname for an American agency.

"Today, as we reported earlier, the government announced organizational changes in the Army of the Republic. Details were few, and we don't know a lot more now than we did then, but NNC has learned that the changes focus on the Army's Naval Branch, and there is an as-yet unconfirmed rumor of a command change there." A young man walked across the shot behind her and in passing gave the reporter rabbit ears.

"Political statement?" said Lieutenant Mecklin.

"Or he's a media critic," E said. "If it was political, he'd have used just one finger." *I can get used to this being-an-officer thing. Yesterday, I wouldn't have said that.*

Editorial comments from the public were routine enough, and the camera kept going. "I'm fortunate to have with me the Council's Press Officer, Mister Douglas Fitch. Mister Fitch, thanks for joining me."

"You're welcome, Marta. It's nice to get outside, especially on a day like this." Fitch was forty-odd years old, an African-American with a political journalism background. "I know that people are anxious to hear what's happened and what's going on now, and I can summarize it, at least as it's been explained to me."

What Fitch was able to say was nothing more, in fact, than Marta herself had already said. There was no current precedent for crises on this scale, and neither Council nor the government departments were used to internal turmoil, not the kind the public wanted to hear about, anyway. Behind the camera, across Capital Avenue and off to the south, people were taking down tents and displays, clearing away an arts festival and making the ex-golf course available for tomorrow's huge weekly farmer's market. Up north, E and her colleagues clicked off the video feed and dug into their new world. There was muck to be raked.

§

The green office wasn't in the capital oval, and General Newhouse felt mildly nervous leaving that womb of security for even a short trip. Of course, this other building was as secure as any, but out there on the street ... well, anything could be lurking, right? She stifled her inner person. "Time for that later."

"Thank you all," said the man, "for braving the angry universe to come over here. I do somehow think that meeting personally is just the slightest bit more secure. And certainly more pleasant." People nodded. Besides Newhouse, Jeri Klein was there, General Kydo had sent a representative from Field Branch, and the Seventh Division's head, General Dichtmann, was representing Security.

"The composition of this little group has changed somewhat, you will all note, and in particular, we welcome General Newhouse. She's wearing her new Naval Branch persona, and I welcome her participation. She comes on the stage, I admit, in the last act, but regardless ... " He gestured in her direction "... this is surely the right time for an important contribution."

"Thank you," said Newhouse. "When you say last act, I assume you mean that the group is prepared to issue its recommendation to Council?"

"I do mean that, General. I believe that both in committee here and individually, we've reached a consensus on Pilot Ruby, although if I'm mistaken, please, anyone, correct me."

"From External Relations' point of view, we're in agreement." Klein opened her briefcase. "But just for drill, here's our formal position." It was a single page, with four points. She had exactly the right number of copies to go around.

The Department of External Relations regards any support of any party in a separation attempt on the part of any current US state as dangerous and offering little advantage to the Republic.

The Department joins with other groups in recognizing the unlikelihood of any further successful separations from the US, unless there is evidence of the long-term preparation and development that took place prior to the Republic's formal withdrawal. In the case in question, that evidence is not apparent.

The Department agrees with the assessment by this advisory group that the specific separation in question may be clandestinely supported, in part or in whole, by the US, and as such may be an attempt to damage or discredit the Republic.

The Department's recommendation to the group is that the Republic adopt a completely neutral attitude toward any separation initiatives from any external party, and that it should take any steps its military organizations consider necessary to mitigate negative implications for the Republic and its allies of such separations should they actually occur.

Dichtmann looked quickly at the bullet points. "I've heard this already, verbally, but to make sure I understand, we stay out of anything that may go on over there, except for covering ourselves? Right?"

"That's right."

"I'm good."

"Captain Clarke? Does Field Branch accept this position?"

"My instructions from General Kydo are to support the group's consensus recommendation."

"Very well. And General Newhouse?"

"Well, since you and I and Doctor Klein essentially wrote them ... in somewhat more terse language, I must say ... it would be strange if I didn't agree."

"Stranger things have happened, General, but with that, I believe we've come to a conclusion. Can I ask, just once more to make sure: shall I submit Doctor Klein's points to our Council Committee?" He looked around, making eye contact with each person in turn. Some said "yes," some just nodded. "I will let you all know when I've done that. My friends, we have done what we were chartered to do. We are adjourned. Thank you all."

"Thank you," said Klein.

"Right," said Newhouse. "This was the least time I've had to spend on a working group in my career. One meeting, say 'yes', and go home. That should be a standard."

"We do our best," said the man. "On to the next little challenge."

§

"What do you think of this?" Una held out her notebook, turned back to a page.

Meg took it and read aloud. "Just on the cusp of too hot to touch. I used to love it so very, very much." She handed the book back. "It's nice. Did you just think of that?"

"It just popped up. It might be part of a song. But it's just a fragment, still." They were in their shared room, getting ready for the evening's entertainment. Karen played an acceptably skillful blues guitar, and Una had a clear, precise soprano voice. Meg had some choir experience, and she was acquiring a taste for the currently popular jazz-blues form the media was offering. The three of them had worked up a few songs, and they were going to be the household's after dinner music.

"Let's try Leanin' again. I keep coming in too soon," Meg said. She set her phone down and tapped the Play icon. There were some opening chords, and then the three of them, Una, Meg, and the phone, came in.

Leanin', leanin, lea-nin'

You know they say (they used to say)

The East ... the Eee-eee-east is red.

Everything I see (all that I can see),

Is surely, slowly-ee-ee, turnin' green.

And I'm leanin', gir-ir-rlllll, I'm leanin'

Harder to the left (ha-aaa-arrrder to the left).

"Soundin' good, ladies." Karen stuck her head in. "It's gonna be fun tonight." With a kind of wonder, it came to Meg that she was, in fact, having fun. And on the heels of that, she realized how very long it had been.

§

E's first set of tasks was to call a list of Naval Branch officers, down at the lower end of the command chain, and see what they might be willing to admit. The theory was that with the Admiral out of the picture, there might be an increased level of candor among the rank and file. Or, if there wasn't, if the walls were still up, that might point to an additional layer of command that needed to be removed. Either way, it was as much progress as could be expected, on the first day of the program.

She had no deep conviction that she'd turn up anything, but just the release of doing things was a motivation of a kind. Rosters and phone numbers were easy to come by, and on her own initiative, she chose to begin with the Alpena base. *Their big drug operation came out of there. And the patrol boat off Peters. And their malware, too, now that I think of it.*

She'd asked Matthews how much the NB rank and file had been told. "Can I expect them to know what's up, or will I have to explain it?" Sadly, the Captain didn't know. *So I wing it. If they just hang up on me, that at least answers the question.*

By 1400 hours, E had her answer. She knocked on Matthews' door frame. "Excuse me, sir. I have a request."

"All leave cancelled. Sorry."

"Actually, I was going to ask about travel. Not for pleasure, though. I want to pack a bag, grab a couple of recruits for assistance, and go back down to Alpena. Get bunks at the FB base or our post, and show up at the Naval base at the crack of dawn. They're holding out on us."

"Oh ... wonderful. You'll need some covering fire, though. I can get Brigade to cut the orders, I imagine. Major Vogel is away from his order-writing desk, but I'm sure Colonel Macready will jump in. Her boss is ... oh, did I tell you? General Dichtmann was tapped to represent SB in the overall spanking ... investigation of Naval."

"Good. I'll get my gear together. I'll ask Lieutenant Mecklin for some volunteers, then?"

"Right. Do you have another decoy phone?"

"No, sir. I don't think this calls for that level of subtlety, anyway."

"Give 'em hell."

§

Right in the middle of the nineteenth century, iron

mining and export – especially export – called into being a small village on the shore of Lake Superior. Marquette survived the ups and downs of mining and shipping, and it became the largest city in the Upper Peninsula. That wasn't, of course, saying much. By the time of the Separation, it had just under thirty thousand people, and although it was still the biggest, it now reported fewer than twenty K.

Naturally, its relative size and its location on a good shipping bay recommended it to all three branches of the AoR. Its civilian airport was a valuable hand-me-down from the US Airforce, and there was a railroad rehabilitation project underway, one that would eventually link the city to the north shore of Lake Michigan. It was the best-connected place north of the Straits of Mackinac, and Field, Security, and Naval all had bases. Security's Eighth Division was there, Field had its whole northern presence on a base outside of town, and, obviously, Naval took up a large part of the port.

At the moment, it was dark out and beginning to show the onset of fall temperatures. It had touched fifty degrees the night before, and now – 0400 hours, four AM to civilians – it was below that by a hair. At the SB Divisional headquarters, there was only the usual handful of recruits and non-coms, plus a single lieutenant, minding the store. Things were quiet. One of their Companies was dealing with a domestic assault, off to the Southeast near Harvey. In Marquette itself, the bars were closed, and the Naval recruits and merchant sailors had stumbled home hours ago. The Lieutenant was getting through her paperwork, performance assessments, and so on. Then, a Corporal stuck his head into her workspace.

"Excuse me, sir. I just forwarded you a message. I think we need to jump on it."

Forty kilometers northwest, a young woman put her phone back in her jacket pocket. "I hope you're listening, down there," she thought.

They were. It took a few minutes of calling and waking officers, but by a quarter after, things were moving, and conversations were taking place. One of them involved a Battalion commander and his local post chief, a Corporal Samuels, forty-five klicks up Republic Highway 550, in a town called Big Bay. Samuels listened carefully, took one or two quick notes, said, "Understood, sir," and hung up.

"Christ on a crutch," she thought, "This had better not be a drill! Wait ... no, I hope it is!"

There were exactly eight people in the Big Bay SB post. Samuels had five troopers, all National Service boys and girls. The local man who cleaned the place – Phil – was working somewhere around the building. And there was a visitor, one of those Department of Education people who sometimes needed a place to spend the night. Against that, according to the call she'd just received, there were fourteen or fifteen resistance fighters coming to take over the post.

It took ten minutes just to get people up and together. The troopers, at least, fell in armed and theoretically ready. The DoE lady was sleepy and confused. The janitor seemed mildly excited. "I know some first aid!" he said. That didn't make Samuels or anyone else happier.

"All right, Phil. You don't have to stay, though. Or you either, ma'am. Although, Command recommends that all civilians stay inside. So it might actually be safer here."

"I'm good, right here. Happy to help out any way I can, we got a whole first aid cabinet down in the basement," Phil said.

"Okay. Let's make your – your workspace, downstairs, I

mean, a first aid point. Everybody know where I mean?"

"I don't," said their visitor. "But more to the point, if I left, where would I go that's any safer than here?"

"I don't know, ma'am. You're probably better off with us. But you should go downstairs with Phil. I don't know whether there'll be any, um, combat. Shooting."

"I hope not, anyway. Mister..." She turned to Phil. "Phil, is it? I'll try to help you out. Let's go see where you'll set up."

"All right. Questions?"

One of the troopers raised her hand. "Corporal, who's warning the rest of the people? The town, I mean."

"Battalion is doing that. They say. But nobody gets in here. We're keeping the doors closed. No matter what. Let's get this place secured, people."

The SB post was in a large brick building, originally the elementary school for the town and nearby. Now, the classes took place next door, in what had been a church. The old school building was SB and, when needed, barracks for any other AoR people who happened to be in town. It was a standard old-school school, red brick and with only a gesture toward accessibility. The formal front door on the north side had two sets of steps. There was another, smaller, door on that side, and a third one in the back. Neither the east nor west had doors at all. And on all the sides, the walls per se were solid enough to withstand small arms fire, but the bad news was, all four sides had large runs of nearly full-height classroom windows.

"Here's what we do," Samuels began. "One of you," – gesturing at the troopers – "to each wall. One, two, three, four, north, east, south, west." She poked each of four of them in the chest while counting. "Got it?"

"Yes, sir," in chorus.

"You," – she tapped the fifth one, "With me. We'll move around as we have to, provide fire support, relieve anybody who's hurt, watch for hostiles, plug holes. Right?"

"Sir!"

They were in what had been a large lecture room – larger, anyway, than the classrooms, and located in the middle of the building. "We got no windows here, and good solid fire doors. This is our first fallback. The basement stairs are right over there" – she pointed at the corner – "and down there is our first aid station. Right? And our civilians. Right?"

"Sir!"

"So if we get breached from any side, we come in here, and we hold the doors. And if we have to fall back again, we go down there, and we hold the stairs." She looked them up and down. "Any questions?"

"Sir," said one of the boys, "Are we getting any help?"

"We are. Battalion's putting it together. Anything they send will have friendly-unit ID transmitters, but more use to us, there's a password. Anybody who yells "muskox," don't shoot 'em. Right?"

"Right!"

"Let's … oh, wait. I forgot. It's weapons-free on anything out there that fires at us. Any help we get will know that. So don't be shy. And also, anybody who attacks this place is breaking the law. When they surrender, handcuffs and ankle ties and leave 'em for later. Now, let's go."

Troopers North and West ran out together. "You notice she said 'when' they surrender?" said North.

"Yup. I hope it works out that way."

§

In the capital, General Newhouse was already up, in her office, and looking at analytics. A projected map of the republic and the Great Lakes was very dark and comforting. The only confirmed red points were in Marquette, as the Command point for its area, and at Big Bay. A yellow point out in the woods showed where the intelligence had originated. "The agent just parked out on the road, I assume," she said.

"Actually, sir, that's a parking lot for a scenic area. Thomas Rock Lookout, it's called." Her intel chief of staff was obviously fresh out of bed, but he was functioning. Quite well, actually.

"Oh. What does SB say about the caller?"

"She's been implanted with this resistance group for some time. SB considers her highly reliable."

"And what about the Canadian side?"

"Nothing, sir. The antagonists here ..." he moved his pointer to Big Bay "... have been told that there'd be a group in multiple boats, coming across from Pic River, up here, on the north shore, to reinforce them, but there's nothing happening. Satellite confirms there's no boats, no camps, no people. The only shipping underway on Superior is known, commercial."

"And the Mounties?"

"Canadian authorities have no intel on anything like this, they assure us."

"All right. And nothing else is happening?"

"As you see, the map is dark."

"Okay, Tom. Now ... the big question. What the hell?"

"Excuse me, General." The only other person in the room was Jeri Klein. She looked somewhat disheveled, too. "This is very, very early on, but what our people and SB think is that we're being provoked."

"I am, for sure. By whom, though?"

"It's almost pure speculation, so far, but there are hints that this may have been a thing gone wrong. Something that was supposed to be canceled, and part of it didn't get the message."

"And if they had, who would have been messaging them?"

"We don't know yet. But if I had to guess ..."

"Guess."

"Naval Branch."

§

There were four assorted pickup trucks, two crew cabs and two standard two-seaters. "Not exactly a panzer division," said one of the men riding in the bed of the lead truck.

"Ah. We'll get there. We got what we need." His colleague craned his neck around the cab. "Still dark. We'll have just about time. To get set." Both of them had old US-made assault rifles. Neither of them wore any kind of formal uniform, but still, they looked alike: commercial hunting camouflage jackets, cargo trousers, lace-up boots. Only their headgear varied, and then only in the messages, brand names, or logos on the front.

"Hope we don't hit a deer. That'd be bad," the other man observed. His colleague didn't reply.

The driver was thinking, primarily, the same thing. He kept his eyes on the road at the farthest point the headlights would reach, scanning just a degree or two to either side. In the passenger's seat, his rider's job was to watch the wing mirror and keep count of the vehicles behind. Nobody wanted to become separated; they needed to arrive together, without delays or confusion.

Their tactical problem was that their approach route was limited to just this one road. Little dirt tracks went off left and right, but they led nowhere, at least nowhere that got them to Big Bay and the target. And the reinforcements they'd need, thirty minutes or less after the cat got out of the bag.

"Curve's comin' up, here. I seen two deer here the other night," said the passenger.

"Yeah. Watch that mirror." Silence. The road turned sharply north, and they passed a rusting yellow "watch out for snowmobiles" sign. Here and there driveways went off left or right, usually leading into darkness. Once in a while, a small house or mobile home would have a light burning. On the left side, what had been a gas station appeared and vanished.

"We're there," the driver said. "Knock on the back window." The two in the back already knew. The truck slowed, and the driver shut down the lights. Some kind of log building showed up, and he turned left. They drove, all four vehicles, less than a block. Before the upcoming cross street, they pulled over in line, and stopped. They got out, using the doors or jumping down. Somewhere, a dog barked.

"Game time! Do it just like we said!" the driver shouted. He turned and ran in a kind of crouch diagonally away from the street and toward a small stand of trees.

Two hundred meters straight north, the SB trooper assigned to the south wall triggered his issue phone. "I have lights on the County Road. Down south."

"Identify, dammit. Who's talking?"

"Sorry. This is Bradley. The lights are out now! Looked like three or four trucks. Just interior lights, not headlights."

"Got it. Everybody copy that? Looks like action on the south side." Samuels tapped the Private with her. "Get over on the south and keep Bradley company. I'm going over to the west side." As she was moving, she called Battalion. "This is Big Bay. We think we have people on County Road, south of us." At the same time, a woman in a house directly across from the line of trucks was also calling emergency numbers, reporting men with guns on her street. The residents who'd actually gotten the warnings were nervous and paying attention.

In Marquette, all of this was being fed to a command center, normally a conference room. SB's Brigade and Battalion had their respective officers there, and Field Branch had a liaison group as well. In his office, the Division leader was in touch with the capital. The command center pinged him: "Possible movement." He passed that right along to AoR. Then he asked his aide, "How are we coming with the helicopter?"

In Big Bay, the attackers knew the ground well – two of them had lived in the village – and they knew that a small area of pines lay off to their left, between them and the base. They cut diagonally into it and moved north. Ahead, where the trees ended, was a playing field and an unoccupied house. Their idea, worked out on a map and a few drive-by reality checks, was to come out of the woods and split into two. One group would make a dash for the base, over ninety meters of open ground, heading for the south door. The others would angle left, run up the roadside, and shelter behind the empty house. When the attack on the south door was underway, they'd cut around and go for the north side entrances.

There were holes in this scheme. For one thing, group one would have to cross paved, coverless tennis courts and a parking lot. There might be a parked vehicle or two, but the bulk of it was flat and open. On the other side, the second group would cross a smaller open space, farther from the base, but once there, their only cover would the abandoned house and a shed. Once they left it, they'd be exposed to the whole west wall of the school, and there was no door there. They had to get past and around to the north before there was any entrance. The saving grace was just darkness. They were gambling on surprise and their dark clothing.

Inside the base, Samuels still hadn't seen anything. She'd heard from Marquette that a civilian reported the same thing her south window man had, and she was acting on the assumption that it was all real. Outside, it was still dark. She looked down at her watch: 0520 hours. "The trucks showed up seven – no, nine minutes ago. If they're coming ... maybe it's time. Yeah, now." She triggered her phone. "Phil?"

"Yes, ma'am."

"Go ahead and hit the lights."

The attackers were ten or twelve meters out of the woods and moving ahead. Suddenly, the tennis courts lit up like daylight. Down in the basement, Phil had light switches for the whole place.

At the south windows, both the troopers there – watching from two separate classrooms – saw both groups. "Contact!" shouted Bradley. He had one waist-high, tilting window open, and by kneeling, he could cover the whole area with his rifle. The trooper in the next room was in the same situation.

"Shout 'HALT', and fire one shot high!" said Samuels. Both of the troopers did just that.

Out in the parking lot, the eastern group were momentarily panicked. One tried to run back, two of them bolted for a parked school bus. Two more ran forward, and another dropped to his knee and fired three rounds at the back of the school. Inside, Samuels heard the shots. She ran out into the corridor and toward the south rooms. "Fire for effect!"

Bradley and Carol, the trooper in the next room, had both seen the shooter. Both of them were better-trained, recruits or not, and both of them fired twice, aiming at the same point. The attacker, who had been getting up off the ground, spun around and then pitched forward onto the parking lot. He lay still.

On the west side of the open space, the group of attackers had a better choice. They were already in the middle of the tennis courts, but they had a shorter sprint to shelter, a shed belonging to the abandoned house. And instead of two defenders firing from the south windows, there was only one at the west side. When the lights went on, they were out of his angle of view. Then, as they dashed ahead, a single large tree gave them some cover. And finally, as they ran the last fifteen meters to the shed, the SB trooper was looking the wrong way. He had the idea that his threats would come straight in from the west, and by the time he saw the motion off to his left, four of the targets were under cover. He fired twice at the trailing men. One of them fired back, still running, and got lucky. The trooper, Lou, crumpled to the floor.

Samuels heard the shooting as she was moving. There were two rooms along the west wall. The first one was empty, but in the second, she found Lou. He was breathing but badly hurt. "Phil!" Samuels shouted into her phone. "Room seven! Wounded man! Come and get him out of here!" There was a crashing of glass. The west side attackers were in cover behind the shed, and they were ducking in and out, firing blindly at the base. "Jesus!" Samuels shouted involuntarily. She was already kneeling by Lou, and she stayed down. The three feet of brick wall below the windows was doing its job nicely. "Phil!" She said, "stay low when you come in."

In the basement, Phil was trying to acknowledge the calls, but he was forgetting to trigger his phone. Walkie-talkie mode wasn't something he used often. "I gotta go up!" he said to the civilian. "Somebody's hurt!" He started for the stairs.

"Hell, I'll help," the woman shouted. "I'm a big girl!" She was actually terrified, and the thought of being alone in the basement was worse than running into a gun fight. Phil was already going up, and if he heard her, it wouldn't have occurred to him to order her to stay. He'd never actually been in command of anything, his whole life.

Back in room seven, Samuels moved to the corner of the windows, stuck her rifle out the very edge of the tilting pane, and fired three rounds in what she hoped was the right direction. Then, she dropped down and changed positions. When she popped up the second time, she could see the shed and suddenly, muzzle flashes from the nearest end. They went high, bringing down glass from the higher windows, and she sent two more rounds, better aimed this time, at where the muzzle flashes had been. To her left, on the south side, she heard more firing from her people and also from out in the open spaces. An absurd thought came to her mind: "I've been in SB for seven years. Nobody ever shot at me before!"

§

From forty meters above the water, you could see that there was shore to the left, but no detail. Then there was a glow, then there were obvious lights. "Something's lit up over there," said the copilot. "That's the bearing to the objective."

"Tell Command," said the woman flying the helicopter. They were flying the shore line, and Big Bay Point was about to take them two K north, away from the lights. The mission was to round the point, then turn back southwest, make sure the harbor was threat-free, and then come in on the back of the SB base. In the jump seats behind the cockpit, six Field Branch troopers, a sergeant, and a medic were strapped in. Hung off one of the stub wings, there was a pair of belt-fed automatic rifles.

The copilot spoke briefly to the radio, listened, and said, "Understood." He turned to the pilot. "They acknowledge, and they say the road column is underway."

"Good," was all the pilot had to say about that.

§

In room seven, Samuels turned sharply, swinging her rifle around. "Don't shoot, don't shoot!" Phil yelled. "Just me!"

"Dammit, don't do that! I nearly shot you! Get Lou out of here. He's bad!"

"Okay. I'll ... Oh, the lady from downstairs is here, too!"

"What? All right, fine. Get her to help you! I'm ..." she meant say "busy", but another burst of fire hit the windows, high again. Somebody swore, but Samuels was focused on keeping the opposition heads-down and didn't pay any attention. When she turned back from the window, Phil and the civilian were gone, and Lou's feet were vanishing out the door, obviously being dragged. She turned her attention to status-gathering.

"Bradley, report!" Silence. "Bradley!"

"Yes, sir! I'm here! "

"What's going on?"

"We're ... um ... shooting. Firing, I mean."

"Right. I can hear it. How many are there? "

"Two at least. Behind a bus."

"Are you all right?"

"Me? Oh, um, yes. I'm okay. Sir."

"Just take it easy. Shoot low and slow, just like training. Stay cool. Carol?"

"Yes, Corporal. Same as Bradley. The windows in here are all shot up."

"Just stay down. Below the brick. Pop up to shoot and get back down. And move back and forth."

"Yes, sir. "

Another four rounds from the shed came in. This time, only one hit the windows. The rest tore up the gutters overhead. Samuels low-crouched to the back wall, outside the worst of the broken glass, and dropped to her knees. She crawled across the room, then back up to the outside wall and let off another two shots. She dropped below the brick. Somebody fired outside, but nothing hit room seven. Something about "the broad side of a barn" flickered across her awareness, but again she was busy with her phone.

"Janet, report." The north wall trooper was the newest, even greener than Bradley.

"Yes, Corporal. There's nothing ... I don't see anything, I mean here. Is everybody okay?"

"Just hang on over there. We're doing all right. I ... wait a minute, I have to talk to Command." There was an "urgent" call showing. "Samuels," she said.

"What's the status, Corporal?"

"We're holding the post, sir." She made the assumption that it was an officer calling. Everyone outranked her, anyway. "One casualty, serious. At least one of the ... the hostile force ... is down. We need, um, reinforcements." She stopped herself from saying "help".

"An FB team is ... five ... no, seven minutes out from your location. Confirm that your north side is the point for contact with you."

"Yes, sir. I just checked with the north wall, and my trooper reports no activity. It's all on the south and west, so far. West is a bigger threat at the moment."

"Understood. Expect FB personnel, commanded by a sergeant, coming in by helicopter, any time now. And a much larger force by land, in fifteen to twenty minutes. Wait one ..." There was a burst of firing from the shed, this time breaking glass again.

"Corporal, are you there?"

"Yes, sir. Taking fire in this position."

"Your air reinforcements are moving in on your north side, now. They will call you as soon as I sign off. Use 'muskox' as a recognition word. Repeat: 'muskox'."

"Understood, sir. 'Muskox'."

"Out."

Another set of shots hit the wall. Samuels stuck her rifle up to window height and fired twice. Then she went back to the phone. "Janet, I'm back."

"Yes, sir."

"We've got a helicopter coming in just north of you, somewhere. They're our people, understand?"

"Yes, sir."

"They'll drop troops off, and then they'll move toward us on foot. Don't shoot at anyone who isn't shooting at us."

"Yes, sir."

"And stay down, but if you hear someone yell "muskox", yell it back. Right?""

"Muskox?"

"Right. That's how we know the good guys from the bad guys. You good?"

"Yes, sir."

"They make me feel so old," Samuels thought. She selected the "whole team" contact. "Listen up! We've got reinforcements coming in any minute now! Make damn sure you know what you're firing at! Recognition word is "muskox"! Confirm that." One by one the remaining four troopers checked in. From the east side, Shanita, her oldest hand, said, "I got it, boss."

Samuels sneaked a look over the window sill. "Holy shit!" Twenty meters away, two men with rifles were running hard, straight at her. There were muzzle flashes from the shed, but nothing hitting. "You bastards!" she shouted, purely out of reflex, pulled the trigger, and swept the barrel right to left across the runners.

§

The Republic's aircraft purchasing policies were formally documented, using very formal language. But they could be summarized quite simply as "Anybody but LockBoeing or Antonov". The AoR's flight lines, therefore, were populated with a range of fixed and rotary-wing craft, from a range of outside manufacturers, and most of them were tweaked in design to meet local needs. There were only two helicopter types in use, one small search and rescue ship and a much larger two-rotor design. Its similarity to the old US workhorse, the CH-47 Chinook, was evident, but it was a new ship, from the ground up. All the Republic's military aircraft were given millennial-based designations, and this model was called the 21HH-2, Twenty-first-century Heavy Helicopter, version 2.

The one that was now coming southwest from the empty, unmolested waters of Big Bay, was fuselage number 7, and it technically belonged to Field Branch. This morning everyone on board did, too, including the pilot and copilot, the troops, and the medic. Everybody but the Sergeant, a man named Frank, was still strapped in; he was up, standing behind the seats in the cockpit, watching the ground.

"We are feet-dry," the pilot said, as they flew over the shore line. "Closest place to set down would be about here ..." She pointed at a spot on a zoomed-in image. It was an open area directly across the street from the SB base. "If the threat is off this way ..." She pointed at the back of the school building and then at the western edge of the block "... we might get some small arms fire, coming in."

"Where else?" the Sergeant asked.

"Here?" The pilot moved her finger right. She touched an open space, possibly a lawn, on the other side of another large building. "That's the next-closest place, half a block is all. With the base and this church or whatever blocking the fire."

"How about over here?" He pointed at a spot further northeast.

"Foliage. Trees. And I'm not sure that ground's very level. Let's go here. In front of this hotel or whatever it is."

"Done. And then what? So we stay out of your line of fire?"

"Can't say yet. I need a target designation first. I'll take off as soon as you're out, but I'll wait for you to call a target."

"Good. Let's go."

The pilot banked the ship left and dropped down. The helo followed a road briefly east, then back around south, and the edge of the village slid below. "I got the church ... and the base," said the copilot. "And there's the landing. Looks like just a lawn." In the back, everybody had a hand on his or her harness release.

"We're goin' in," the Sergeant said. "At my command ..."

The ship, slowed, flared, and started to settle on a sloping patch of grass. Suddenly it hovered, hesitated ... The copilot shouted, "There's a dog in the way! No ... there he goes! Set her down."

"Unhook!" said Frank. "Go, go, go!"

§

Behind the shed, west of the base, there were suddenly just two of the original seven shooters unhurt. Out in the open area, their unfortunate friends had just staged the twenty-first-century version of a bayonet charge against fortified musketry. Some time ago – specifically, the sixteenth century – this had been identified as a bad idea. The two were both down, and there was no way the remaining west group could do anything about it. Three more of them were out of the fight, too. Whoever that bloodthirsty Commie government goon was behind those menacing windows, he was a good shot. All three of the wounded had been hit by return fire when they stepped out of shelter. Their wounds were on arms and shoulders, and they weren't trivial. Now the two men left standing were confronted by a devastating idea. They were outnumbered and deeply, deeply in trouble.

Inside room seven, Samuels, the bloodthirsty Commie government goon, was down herself, unhurt but staying below the windows. The remaining insurgents were doing the only thing they could think of, firing sporadically at the west wall and wondering what in the name of God they should do.

In open space south of the school, sheltering behind a school bus, two more hostiles were trying to see what the action off to their left was about. They were still bathed in harsh light, and every time they moved, their shadows moved, too. This brought a shot or two from the troopers in the west side rooms. The two behind the bus knew they'd lost one of their number right at the beginning, but they had no idea where the rest of their group was. In fact, it was scattered behind them, three hiding behind small pieces of cover and one crouched behind the trucks, back where they'd parked.

"Where the hell are the other guys?" one of them shouted.

"Where are the damn reinforcements?" said the other. And then, they heard the helicopter.

Inside the north wall, Janet was as alert as she'd ever been. It seemed as though she could see through the darkness as well as if it were noon, and the moving shadow that blocked the stars to her right was crystal clear. Her first thought wasn't "Oh, it's the helicopter," because she was flooded with adrenaline, head to toe. She didn't really have a first thought; she just stared at it as it blocked what little amount of light there was beginning to be, then vanished again.

Suddenly, her phone woke up. "Janet! North wall, report!"

"Yes!" she said. "Yes, sir!"

"Yes, what? You see anything?"

"I ... yes, I did. Something. Out there."

"What?"

"I ... oh, I think ... I think it must have been the thing. The helicopter!"

"Christ almighty," Samuels thought. "Stand by, Janet. Shanita, you there?"

"I'm here, Corporal."

"You got any action on your wall?"

"No, sir."

"Get over to the north door, and give Janet a hand. I think the 'copter's here!"

"Moving now."

"Bradley, Carol ... sound off! What's happening?"

"We're still keeping tabs on the two we know about," Carol said. There were two shots, right on the heels of this last sentence.

Bradley chimed in. "That was me. One of 'em tried to move off right. Um, west, I mean!"

"All right. Bradley, move to the east wall. I just sent Shanita to the front door. I think our backup's here. Carol, hang on there. Report anything. Anything."

"Yes, sir! Oh, you bastard! Get back in there!" Two shots.

"What?"

"They're trying to go off west! Like Bradley said!" A burst of three shots. "Got him ... I mean ... Oh, hell. I hit him!"

"Calm down. Calm down. Keep your eyes open. We're doing all right. Just stay calm." Samuels saw an incoming call. "Samuels," she shouted.

"Corporal, this is Sergeant Frank. Muskox."

"Right, muskox. Muskox. Where are you?"

"We're on the ground and headed for your north door. There's seven of us. Let your people know."

"Yes, uh, sir. Yes, Sergeant."

"Janet! Shanita! We've got seven friendlies coming in from the north. Look ... look sharp. Use 'muskox' and bring 'em in. Oh, wait, they've got a sergeant. Do what he says. If they want to be in or out." The shed boys suddenly decided to shoot up the west wall again. Broken pieces of glass fell around Samuels. "I'm moving to the next room."

Outside, the Field Branch people moved fast, and as soon as they were out of the helicopter, they had a clear line of sight to the base. The Sergeant had a night scope, and the north door jumped out at him. "Follow me," he said. "Medic."

"Yes, sir?"

"Stay by me. You'll be goin' in. Command says they got at least one casualty." He moved off at a trot, sweeping his night eyes back and forth. The troopers spread out as they reached the street. The geography became clear to Frank: just a long building wall, no obvious opponents visible – "they're supposed to be on the south and west" – and one evident door. "Gotta be the north door, there." He was essentially talking to himself. "Get across the street, here. Then right and left, secure the corners."

Five long paces and they were there. He waved at the right three people in his line. "Go that way, secure the corner of the building." To the other three: "Go on over there, secure that corner." Ten more long steps and he was at the north door. "Muskox! Muskox!"

Inside the door, Shanita saw the outline of a large man, visible, sort of, in the very first of the morning glow. "Muskox!" she shouted back. Janet repeated it.

"Muskox!" Frank said again, "Field Branch. I need to see your commander." A strange mix of relief and disappointment hit Shanita.

"I didn't even fire a round. Damn," she thought. But, "Yes, sir," she said. She opened the door. "Come on in. I'll call Corporal Samuels."

§

On the helo, the pilot pulled up on the controls and got the machine back in the air. "Tell Marquette we've dropped the soldiers. Let's see if we can find something to shoot at."

In the FB base, the message got spread out quickly. Field and Security commands heard about it, and very shortly afterward, so did the little group in General Newhouse's office.

"Sir," said the intel aide, interrupting a conversation with Jeri Klein, "The air-deployed reinforcements are on the ground. And they report that the bay is clear. No evidence of any other antagonists."

"Is that what we're calling them?"

"Publicly, yes, sir. We used that term during separation. Internally, of course, we can use anything you want."

"Poor, deluded bastards? Suckers? I'll tell you, if anybody in this gets hurt, anybody at all, I want Petronas charged."

"Well, we've already crossed that line, sir. Several of the attackers are reported to be casualties, at least tentatively, and one of our people, too."

"Son of a ... Damn him."

Three hundred kilometers north, there was a suggestion of pink in the east. It was just 0530 hours. In the Alpena Field Branch post, a sergeant shook one of the bunks in the sleeping quarters. "Sir? Excuse me, sir?"

"Okay, okay. What?" said the sleeper.

"I'm supposed to alert you. Your Captain? Captain Matthew, I think ..."

"Matthews. "

"Yes. She says you need to go to the Naval Base as soon as possible. 'Right the hell now' were the words she used. Apparently there's a situation of some kind, up in Eighth Division."

"All right. All right. Do me a favor and get my troopers up ... right over there." E waved an arm at the next two bunks. "I'll call Matthews."

§

At the front door of the SB post, Sergeant Frank split his team, right and left. "Down to the west corner! Down to where you can see along the wall. Nobody comes down this way, bad guys or civilians or whatever. If you see incoming fire, return it."

"Sir!"

"You three, go around this corner and set in between the base and the other building ... church, whatever it is. Nothing comes down along that wall from the south. And nothing from the east unless it's our people."

"Have we got more people on the ground, sir?"

"We will. They're coming in from the south. Lots of 'em. Any time now. Move." He turned back to Shanita. "All right, let's go see your command. And you got casualties? Where's your aid point?"

"The wounded are in the basement, sir," she said. "It's on the way to Corporal Samuels."

"Right. Medic, come on with us, and we'll drop you off. Let's move."

They pointed the medic at the basement stairs, and then Shanita and the Sergeant went on toward the west rooms. "Let me call ahead, sir," she said. "Let her know we're coming."

"Do it."

"Corporal Samuels ... Corporal? Are you there?"

Samuels was watching the shed, raised up just enough to see over the bottom window pane. Nothing was visible. She keyed her phone. "Samuels. I'm in room six now. What's happening?"

"The FB Sergeant and I are coming to you. We're right around the corner. Oh, muskox."

"Muskox. It's the second door. Watch the door to room seven. It's open, and it wouldn't stop incoming, anyway. Go by fast."

They turned the corner into the west hall. There was glass on the floor, and blood, too. They ran past seven, paused at the door to six. "Muskox," Frank said, and they entered. "Are you Samuels?"

"Yes, sir. Keep low. They've got a line of sight right into these rooms."

"Okay. Here's the deal. I've got three troopers down at your northwest corner..." He pointed. "... and they'll fire on anyone shooting back this way. And three more are at the other side, same thing. You got any weak points? Or a better idea?"

"I have just one person on the south wall, and there are hostiles sheltering out in the open space there. And one other guy on the east, where it backs up to the church. If your people are at that corner, we better let my trooper know."

"Good." He turned to Shanita. "Can you do that?"

"Yes, sir." She'd had her phone in hand all along. "East wall. Bradley, wake up."

"I'm here. Shanita?"

"Right. Samuels and the new ... Sergeant say to watch out for FB people coming south along your wall. "

"Okay. So ... they're here?"

"Duh. Yes."

Samuels and Frank were both looking out the window. "You say they're in that shed?"

"Behind it, at least. I don't know if they're inside or not. All the shooting's been from the corners."

"And what is it, the shed? Anything explosive or toxic in

there?"

"No, it's not part of the base, but we checked on it. Just some hand tools and an old lawnmower."

"Any problem if it gets damaged?"

"Not for us. It belongs to that house, and that's been unoccupied as long as I've been here. Four ... no, five months."

"Good. As the old thing goes, hold my beer and watch this." Like the other people in the room, his phone was in his hand. His rifle was slung and his sidearm holstered. "Air one, muskox."

"This is air one. Go ahead."

"Got a target. From the west wall there's a house, and just south of it there's a shed. The shed is your target. Engage from the northeast."

"Understood."

"Keep low," Frank said. "The helo's gonna do some shooting."

Behind the shed, morale was disintegrating. At this point, it was just a question of which way to run. Straight west was one option, but there was just a gravel alley behind a few houses, then kilometer after kilometer of pine and birch woods. They could angle south and pick up an old back road, but it just led around to the highway, again. "We gotta get back to the trucks," one of them said.

"I guess ..." the other one started to say "...what the hell's that?!" The helicopter had circled around north, then come in at nearly ground level between some houses. It popped up over the last of them, moved the remaining fifty meters south, slipped across the road, past the west wall corner, and tagged the shed in its targeting system. The pilot thumbed the trigger.

"Jesus Christ!" Samuels had never seen belt-fed mini-guns operate. The shed vanished in a dust cloud, and something inside, probably the lawn mower's gas tank, exploded. The burst lasted a little more than three seconds, then the helo pivoted and moved back behind the base.

"Guess there was something in there," Frank said. He touched his phone again. "That looked all right, air one. You want to just hang on for a bit, here? We'll see if there's any more firing from over there. Or ... maybe this is better. How about you circle way around to the east and check out the road coming into town? See if you can spot the trucks coming in?"

"Understood. We'll go wide around."

"Now," said Frank, "let's go take a look at the south wall."

§

E's conversation with Captain Matthews was short, and the signal-to-noise ratio was high. A lot of information was transmitted in a short time, leaving E with nothing much to say except "Yes, sir."

According to the Captain, there were three immediate situations to be covered. First, there was the little unpleasantness going on in Big Bay. The summary: some very bad things were happening, and AoR command was blaming it on Naval. Second, and as a consequence of that loss of confidence at upper command levels, Naval was to be commanded for the duration of the emergency by Security Branch officers. And third, due to random situations, absences, assignments elsewhere ... E was the senior officer present in Alpena.

"I'm what?" she had asked.

"You are it. Right at this moment, the nearest SB

Captain is in Saginaw. Field doesn't have anybody above Sergeant at their Alpena post. So you, Acting Lieutenant Gorsky, are in command of the Alpena Naval Branch base until relieved."

"Yes, sir. What ... um ... are my orders?"

"Contact the person there who thinks he or she is in command, and tell them they aren't. If they don't like it, tell them to check their secure mail. If they still don't like it, you can place them under arrest."

"Okay." *Holy shit!*

"Order them to stand down any operations they may be running except search and rescue. If any. I don't see anything like that working, I mean, active. But that stuff goes on as usual. Nothing else. Not even admin. No, um, personnel actions, nothing. "

"Right."

"And secure their classified area. Everybody out, Field Branch personnel at the doors. Nobody gets in without your okay."

"Yes, sir."

"Sorry to stick you with this. But you're the highest ranking officer within two or three hours, even by air. Things are ... oh, hell, it's a cluster, frankly. A real cluster. Call me if you need to."

"Yes, sir." *How many times did I say that in the last two minutes? I sound like a recording.*

Her troopers, one of whom was Margie, the National Service Private from the island, were up and looking anxious. "All right, folks," E said, "We've got a situation, here. Let's roll."

"Excuse me, Lieutenant." The Field Branch Sergeant was back. "I have a squad of troopers for you. My command said you'd need support?"

Oh, hell, yes, I need support! "Thanks, Sergeant. Have they got transport?"

"Coming around from the back now, sir."

"And ... this is probably a stupid question, but ... are they, um, armed?"

"Yes, sir. Standard gear for supporting Security."

"All right. Good. All in a day's work."

§

Samuels and Sergeant Frank left Shanita to watch the west wall. "Sir," she said, "There's casualties out there."

"Yeah, there are. When the area's secured, we'll look after 'em. All right with you, Private?" There was only one answer for that, and she was alone before she could say it. "Damn," she thought. "Hardass."

Samuels and Frank went down the hall and, cautiously, around the corner. The two non-coms were at Carol's room door when they heard firing from outside. Both ducked. "South side," said Samuels. "Carol, talk to me!"

"One of them out there shot at something! Not this way!" Another three rounds. "He's shooting south, I think!"

"We're coming in. The Field Sergeant and me. Muskox."

"Okay. Muskox!"

Frank went left around the room's walls, Samuels to the right. Carol was down in the right corner, looking out at the lit-up grounds. The school bus, parked east-west, fifty meters away, was clearly visible, bright yellow in the overhead lights. "He's behind there," said Carol. "And there's the one I sh... the one I hit." There was a second dark shape on the gravel, this one a meter or so west of the bus.

Frank keyed his phone. "East wall, you got anything?"

"Negative, sir. We're in contact with the SB private on this side, nothing else."

"You're not taking any fire from the south?"

"No, sir."

"Air one, what are you seein' down south?"

"Air one. We're just getting in position to see. Wait one ... ah, all right. I've got trucks coming in on the south road. And ... some of them already in place along that lateral street, south of your position. Confirmed friendlies."

Frank looked at Samuels. "Help is here. We got people in behind the hostiles."

"Oh, good," she said. "Good." Carol was quietly crying.

§

In the basement, the Field Branch medic told Phil that, as he thought, Lou was gone. "You couldn't have done anything for him. I couldn't have. "

"Yeah, I tried, but ... I don't think he made it down here, even."

"All you can do is try. Good job with the dressing, anyway." It actually wasn't very good, but medic training included some basic psych techniques for survivors. You tried not to send anyone away from a crisis wondering if there was more they could have done. "She's okay," he added. "You got her wound cleaned up, got the bleeding stopped. She'll be good." He bent over the civilian. "You hear that, ma'am? You'll be fine. Just stay quiet, and we'll get you out of here and you'll be ... uh, what do you do, here, again?"

"Auditing educational programs."

"Okay. Yeah, you'll be back doing ... that in a couple of weeks."

"Thank you. Thanks for your help. Thanks, Phil."

"Oh, you're welcome, ma'am. Good of you to help out." He stopped. "Oh. I didn't get ... I didn't hear your name, even."

"Kristin. Kristin Horstel."

§

General Newhouse glanced at her wrist. "Dammit, I didn't put my watch on. What time is it, Doctor?"

"It's 0618 hours," said Jeri.

"We haven't heard anything from Big Bay in ... what? Half an hour, Jim?"

"Oh, uh, no, General. Our last update from Marquette Command was ... seven minutes ago." The aide was more nervous than usual. When Newhouse started losing track of time, everybody had reason to worry.

"Well, poke 'em, anyway."

"Yes, sir." He stepped to a terminal.

"How is Canada reacting, Doctor Klein? Anything from them?"

"Just an expression of concern for people affected by the violence, routine offer of assistance, etc. No specific complaints or queries. And I wouldn't expect any reaction to our Pilot Ruby position immediately. They want status quo on the lakes and on their borders, and we essentially said we do, too. So it shouldn't be inflammatory. Shouldn't upset them."

"Yeah. Oh, and Jim? Find out how the, what did we call it? stabilizing? ... of the Naval Bases is going."

"One minute, sir. Marquette is responding ... oh, good! The road convoy is there, they've got the antagonists ... um, jargon, jargon ... basically, surrounded. Some have surrendered already."

Newhouse closed her eyes. "All right. Casualties?"

"They don't say ... just that some have surrendered."

"I mean our people. Did we lose anyone?"

"Oh, let's see. We had one injured some time ago ... oh, dear. Now reporting one dead, killed in action."

"Damn it!"

"And a civilian hurt. Not badly."

Newhouse made a growling sound. "That's not what I wanted to hear. Let's make sure we take care of everybody involved, SB, FB, civilians. Deaths, injuries, property losses ... the works."

"Yes, sir. That's covered under section ..."

"Yeah, yeah. Just make sure it happens. Doctor Klein, do we need help from our friend from the committee? Where is he, anyway? Thought he'd be here."

"No, I didn't expect him. He's AIR – Attitudes, Ideas, and Responses. 'What does the Republic think about X?' Once something's actually happening, he's off working on the next challenge. We'll probably hear from him tomorrow, just as soon as Council starts asking 'What do we do now?' They'll call him, and he'll be talking to us."

"That sounds like a great job, but I'd be terrible at it. Jim, what do we know about the bases?"

"Marquette is taken care of. Security has a major from their base in nominal charge there. And Traverse City has a Field Branch captain standing in until Security can put someone in place. Alpena ...oh. This is interesting. The only ranking officer in reach was an SB lieutenant."

"A lieutenant?"

"They've got a captain headed there, but he's three

hours away by vehicle. And everything flying is doing surveillance. So this lieutenant is stepping in."

"I don't suppose we have anybody here ...?"

"Not any quicker than that, sir. "

"All right. I want to know how that's going, though. That's where this crap started."

§

"This is always fun." Una was visibly happy. She and Meg were getting to go grocery shopping at the giant farmer's market, right across the street from the capital complex. "It was a golf course before Separation," she said. "But nobody plays golf now. Nobody I know."

"You got my list?" Karen asked. "Make sure you get the greens I got on there. And don't get the chicken from that silly guy with the chicken hat. Get it from Dusty or the Amish people. Get the eggs from them, too."

"I know, Karen. I've done this a million times."

"Million times. Ha! I sent you for duck that time, and you came back with rabbit."

"That was one time! I know what's what, now."

"And be careful with the money." She turned to Meg. "Most of the people at the market don't do credit cards. So people bring cash. And that always makes me nervous, walkin' around down there with cash."

"We'll be careful," Meg said.

"Come on, let's go," said Una. "Let's catch this tram and not have to stand out there waiting for the next one."

§

E's SB truck led the way through the town. Behind her, three Field Branch trucks with canvas sides on the beds carried the muscle. FB liked a dark brown and green camouflage pattern on their vehicles. Inside, the clothes were the same forest green for everybody. Only the recon teams in Field got camo uniforms.

At the gate, two Naval recruits were in the guard booth. One of them was busy watching their communication screen for updates on their bewildering orders. The other one kept an eye out for whatever it was that they were supposed to allow in. At 0620 hours, Commander Pérez, the man one-down from the Captain in charge of the base, had sent a bizarre message to all hands, implying that Security Branch people would be arriving and issuing orders. Then he called the gate and said that no one was to get in or out except that someone – no name or rank specified – from Security or Field would be coming in, and they were to come in, no arguments. And let him know when they arrived.

When E's little convoy turned off the highway and into the short street toward the gate, the uncertainty increased. The lead truck stopped, and the driver held out her ID.

"I'm Lieutenant Gorsky," she said. "I'm in acting command here, now, and the FB people behind me will relieve you."

This wasn't quite what they'd heard, and so there was one phone call's worth of delay, but E and her cohort drove in, leaving two FB privates to hold the fort. The Naval Branch recruits walked back up to the entrance, looking somewhat uncertain. E parked her truck head on, five meters short of the steps up to the door. The Field Branch vehicles turned half around and backed in to flank her. Their passengers began dismounting.

As E was getting out, a Naval Branch Commander – one step down from Captain – came out the door. He seemed to be unarmed, and E took that as a good sign. "Good morning, Lieutenant," he said. "Who's in command of the group?"

"I am."

"Oh. I ... see. I ..."

"You were expecting a more senior officer?"

"Well ..."

"I'm the senior Security Branch officer available here. So, I'm it. There's a captain on his way, but his ETA is unknown, so it's me, for the next few hours at least. Let's go inside and get this thing underway."

"I ... all right. Yes. I was ordered to cooperate with ... whoever arrived. Captain Bird is the base Commander, but he was called to Headquarters, yesterday. So, please come in." He indicated the doors. "We can use the conference room here ..." he waved at a door on the left. "... or is this classified?"

"The management of this situation isn't. We'll be addressing classified programs, but not in detail. So this will work as a start, anyway." Margie was right behind E. "This trooper is acting as my aide, and she'll be keeping minutes of our conversation." E had promised Margie a promotion, in name, anyway, on the way there. "And Sergeant Keller ..." she waved at the woman in charge of her FB people "... will accompany me to detail her personnel as we identify tasks." Pérez was, by this time, ready for anything, and he just nodded. They arranged themselves around the meeting room's table.

"Point one," E began. "We need to close your secure area. Get everybody out, and confirm that they're out."

The Captain looked mildly shocked. "That's ... " He stopped. "How long will that be in place?"

"I have no idea. But we need to do it right now. "

Pérez closed his eyes tightly and opened them again. "Very well."

E looked at Keller. "Sergeant, go with whoever Commander Pérez assigns. Get a list of people who come out of the closed area, post a pair of your people to ensure no one goes back in, and keep it closed until I hear otherwise from above."

"Yes, sir." Keller got up and went out of the room. Pérez called someone on his phone and gave them appropriate tasks.

"Next," E said, "we'll need your Operations people. Command wants any operations being run out of Alpena canceled or put on hold, except ..." She held up a hand as the Commander was about the make the obvious objection." ...for Search and Rescue work. That goes on, of course. Are there any SAR ops running right now?"

"I can get a complete answer from Operations. I'm aware of one missing-swimmer search going on down the coast, ten or twelve klicks."

"A list of anything else will be more useful. Some of those efforts may be classified, but they still all stand down until we hear otherwise."

"I'll get the orders going out. We can confirm the list later on, I assume? When we can use the secure area again?"

"Right. Go ahead and get the stop orders working, then." There was another pause while errands were handed out.

"Now, finally, this third one is going to sound odd, given that we just handed out a lot of work to people, but except for the things we've put in motion, everything else here needs to stand down. Admin, personnel, logistics, training ... the works."

"Do I ... dismiss people?"

"No. But everybody just stops doing what they're doing. I've got the gate covered, and the FB troopers can patrol the fence and the docks. When your assets start coming in ... the ones we just cancelled ... you'll need people to work on the, what? dock work? Landing? So it's not everybody-go-home day. But just keep the lights on. Dimly, please."

"Okay. This is what I really have to call highly unusual."

"*You* have to call it that? I don't remember 'take over Naval base' being in my position description, either, Commander. Maybe I missed it."

§

From Karen's house, Una and Meg took a tram east to downtown, then another one south on the Main Street line. Una was chatty, talking about growing up in the city. "My dad was faculty. Mom, too. Dad didn't agree with the Separation, and he went back to the US. But Mom stayed."

"And you went to school here?"

"Yeah. For a while. But, you know, Mom was busy, and I don't think I picked the right department. I ... just kind of drifted."

"How did you get to Karen's?"

"One of the grad students told me about it. It's been nice. But I'm ready to go back."

The line went down a hill, past older-looking commercial buildings. At the bottom of the hill, there was an entire block of rubble, with a permanent-looking fence around it. "What's that?" Meg asked. "Like, a disaster or ...?"

"That's a park. There was a big, expensive apartment thing. Lots of 'em. But it was so bad, so badly made, that it just fell down. Like, boom. With people living there."

"Did it just happen? Are they going to clean it up?"

"No, that was years ago. After Separation, they made it a monument. Like a park. See?" She pointed to a sign: "Greed". "It's called Greed Park."

"This is all new to me," Meg said. "We never ... had any need, any reason to come over here."

"There's a local sight." Una pointed to the right. Half a dozen young men were trotting down the sidewalk, wearing shorts and nothing else. "It's supposed to be healthy, running barefoot. It ruins your feet, your arches. But they don't think so. Larry calls 'em the Joy Boys. It's supposed to be joyful, I guess."

The tram stopped. A woman got off by the back door, and three other people got on, two with baskets or bags for the market, one in Field Branch uniform. "Oh, that reminds me," Meg said. "If you go back to school, what about doing your service afterward? Would you want to be in the Army?"

"Well, it's a lottery, right? You might get the Army, or Public Services. Or teaching. If it's, like, something you can't do, like you're in a wheelchair, and you get the Army, well, it's just 'Okay, try again'. I don't really think about it much. I can do it, if I have to."

The tram tracks went up a hill, coming out of the small valley. On the right, there were homes and businesses, and on the left, the north side of the government buildings. They got off, stepping out into a group of people waiting to get on. Una had a backpack, besides the shopping bags. The tram started off, and as it unmasked the view across to the government complex, Una said "Oh, that's funny. Look at all the greenies."

"The what?"

"The soldiers. Something's going on. There's never that many here on market days." There was quite a large contingent of field branch troops, standing around the entrance, looking stern.

"I guess we have to go this way," Una said. The pedestrian crossing to the capital side of the street was closed off with barriers. A handmade sign said "CROSS OTHER SIDE". The small plaza in front of the main entrance had its flip-up steel barricades raised, and there were both green and blue uniforms standing around. "Too bad. You can see the poet's wall better from across the street."

"The what?"

"See? Over there." On the south side of Capital Avenue, the ground rose almost vertically for several meters, and the embankment was faced with a brick wall. There were paintings and texts on the length of it, from Main Street east to the market entrance, half a block away. The most striking image was a simplistic representation of Edgar Allan Poe.

"I guess some of this used to be downtown. But the building had a fire, and they moved the pictures ... the part of the wall with pictures ... out here. And then the rest of it's newer."

"What's the writing?"

"Quotes from poetry and things. I haven't read a lot of it, but some of it has names. And you know, titles."

As they crossed to the south side of the street, Meg could see some of the nearer texts, but the angle was too acute to read them. "I like the first one on this end," Una said. "I don't know who it is, who wrote it, but I like it." They got their walk signal, and as they got nearer, Meg could see the text in question. "The Heroic Struggle of the Little Guys to Finish the Mural." There were four names credited, and something about a theatre.

They walked east, Una pointing out quotes. A very large portrait of Anais Nin looked down at them. "I like this one, too." She pointed ahead to an off-white rectangle, hand-lettered with the last two lines of *Dover Beach*.

Meg stopped and read it aloud. "Swept with confused alarms of struggle and flight, Where ignorant armies clash by night."

"Let's go, we've got a lot of shopping to do. I'll introduce you to some of my farmers." The market was Una's favorite chore. Meg looked at one more inscription, just a block of text reading "*Rus in Urbe*". Below it, made to look like graffiti, red scrawled letters said "*Romani iti domum*".

On the other side of the street, more shoppers were walking down the railroad bridge, coming in from the neighborhoods on the east side. Among them, there was a young man wearing a backpack. He had sandals on, and jeans; his shirt was long and untucked, made of white linen, almost a tunic. He had long hair and a full beard, and the general impression was that of a badly westernized lithograph of Christ. He was staring straight ahead, clearly alone, and the way he looked was just enough out of the ordinary that people were leaving a small bubble of open space around him.

At the east end of the government complex, just past the round, fifties-starship auditorium that was now the Council assembly space, the official staff entrance was as secured as the public one. The SB people on duty were doing exactly what they should be, watching the passerby, looking hard for a second at each face as it came by, doing what the facial-recognition software boys had given up on a decade ago. A sergeant with some years of experience in this kind of work nudged the trooper beside him. "Look at that," he said. "Long hair, there. Watch him."

"Yes, sir. Is he, um, known?"

"Nope. But he's in a state of some kind. Staring. If he looks over here ... Whoa! Watch out!" The man turned directly toward the barricade, still staring but also unslinging his backpack. "Stop! Stop right there!" The man ran the last three steps, swung the backpack by the straps, and threw it at the entrance. "Down!" The pack flew a meter and a half, struck the top edge of the steel flip-up, and fell on the outer side. The man shouted something, turned, and ran south across the street, heading for the market entrance. Behind the barricades and shielding, men and women in uniform were on the ground, fumbling with weapons and radios, waiting for the explosion.

A westbound tram driver hit his brakes, and the bearded man ran in front of the vehicle, on into the market, still yelling. At the first booth, Una had just put half a kilo of tomatoes in a canvas bag. She took a step away from the farmer's booth, looking down at her wallet and not ahead. She walked into the man's path, and he tripped over her. Meg had just turned back from the display of vegetables. "Look out!" By then, the man was up, and Una was trying to reach her bag.

"Fiend of hell!" the man screamed. His hand came out from under the shirt, and in it was a knife. In three short motions, he stabbed Una in the side, recovered his balance, and ran south. Meg ran to Una. The shouts and the running man alerted two SB people down the market's main aisle. Una said something. Meg tried to see where she was hurt, but she was doubled up, with her hands pressing on the wound. The man saw the Security Troopers coming, spun around, and ran back toward the entrance. Meg saw him, grabbed the shopping bag, and threw it at his feet. He tripped on it and came down hard on the gravel. Meg jumped back, pointing at him and screaming.

"Judas!" the man shouted, getting up. The knife was still in his hand, and he took a step toward Meg. The faster of the SB people ran in on him, hit him with a tackle, and took him to the ground. The man got his knife hand free and tried to roll over. The other trooper came running up with a weapon drawn, shouted at him to drop the knife, and when he didn't, shot him in the left shoulder.

§

"Now, Commander," E said. "With those little things checked off my list, I'd like to bring up my original reason for being in town, here."

"Oh. I didn't realize ..."

"No, SB didn't just grab the first random lieutenant and send her down here. I was here to look into some things related to a specific investigation. I have some questions about a homicide up in Seventh Division, and I was trying to get some intelligence from this command yesterday, but I wasn't getting anywhere." Pérez reacted.

"That was you?"

"What do mean, me?"

"I heard from Captain Bird that there was an investigation there. He ... oh."

"Oh, what?"

"I think ... there may be a problem."

"Look, Commander," E said, "This whole situation is nothing but problems. Which one have you just discovered?"

"I was instructed not to ... not to discuss that operation. With anyone."

"By Captain Bird? "

"Yes."

"Well, Captain Bird isn't the base commander right now. I am. Discuss it with me." Pérez closed his eyes for a second.

"Yes. I see. I think we need to have another person here. The Chief Petty Officer who commanded the boat. At the point you're talking about. May I call her?"

"Oh, yes, please. I tried to talk to her yesterday. She wasn't available."

"All right. And ... Lieutenant, if you have the means to do it ... "

"What?"

"Can your people check to see if Captain Bird is actually at Naval Headquarters?"

"Probably. Do you think he isn't?"

"He left very suddenly, yesterday. And it was after you were making calls and inquiries."

§

General Newhouse had just had an update from Big Bay. She was as angry as she could remember being. Eight people dead. Civilians hurt. Four simple-minded rustics who'd certainly get life sentences. For what? For what? A very unwelcome thought: "Because I put the wrong guy in command of Naval." In this very office, sitting across that desk, she'd looked him in the eye and thought, "He'll do. He's the best of a bad lot, but he's trainable. He'll do."

The door opened. "General, the whole government complex is on lockdown!"

"What?!"

"Some kind of attack on the main door. The attacker is down, but the whole facility is on level zero for the moment."

A red haze appeared in her vision. "Tell General Hallstatt to get some of his people from outside HQ. Arrest Admiral Petronas. And get me a glass of water. Please."

§

While Commander Pérez summoned the Chief Petty Officer, E called Captain Matthews. There was a brief delay, then she answered. "Make it quick, Gorsky, I've got Major Vogel on my other line. He wants to hear what's up, anyway. So, what *is* up?"

"I'm about to have a talk with the Chief who was out in the lake, poking around the island. Finally. And the guy in charge here, when I showed up? He was second in command. He thinks we should see if the real base commander is actually at Naval HQ, down in the capital. Captain Bird. The guy here thinks he may be, um, AWOL. Or something like that. He took off yesterday, just about the time things started to get interesting. Especially me calling up his people and asking about kayaks." It wasn't her finest, most polished narrative report, but it would have to do.

"Are you saying the commander bolted?"

"His number two guy thinks it's possible."

"I'm shaking my head in dismay. You can't see it through the phone, but I am. But, fine, I can see if this guy's really down at their HQ. Have you heard about Big Bay? Or the thing at the Capital Offices?"

"Big Bay, up in Eighth Division? I just heard that something happened. No details. What about the capital?" The conversation was becoming informal, but formality was becoming an obstacle, anyway.

"I can't go into it all now. Have to get back to the Major. But there was shooting at our post in Big Bay. Bad stuff. And somebody tried to throw some kind of backpack bomb or something at the government offices."

"Holy ... all right, Captain, I'll get all that later. Tell the Major I've checked all the boxes in the orders you sent, and now I'm poking into the corners I couldn't get into on the phone, yesterday. "

"Okay. I'll call you again in, what? a couple of hours.

Out."

E closed her eyes. *Calmly, calmly. I'm a goddam Naval Base commander. For at least another couple of hours. Have to exhibit serene, professional leadership in the eyes of my terrified subordinates. Even if the barbarians are breaching the walls. Even if I have absolutely no idea what the hell is going on.*

This train of thought was interrupted by Pérez and the Chief. "Lieutenant, this is Chief Halber. She was in command of PC112 on the day you're asking about."

"Sit down, Chief." E had her neutral face on, again. "As Commander Pérez has, I'm sure, explained, I'm in temporary command of this base. I need to hear about that missing kayaker patrol, and I am ... removing ... any orders you might have had about it. About not discussing it. Clear?"

"Yes, sir. Very clear. As long as there's something in writing to the effect that you're countermanding Captain Bird's instructions, I'll answer any questions you have."

"Fair enough." E tore a sheet out of her notebook. She wrote two lines, signed them, and slid the page across the table. "Now, then. You were in command of the boat?"

"Yes, sir."

"What was the mission? Specifically?"

"We were to locate a member of Field Branch, take him and his gear on board, and return to base."

"Who issued those orders?"

"They came from Captain Bird's office. He signed them."

"What happened?"

"We reached the center point of our search area. We didn't sight any small craft, but we then carried out a box search, and within thirty minutes sighted the small craft that had been described to us."

"What kind of boat was it?"

"A plastic, rotomolded kayak. There was one occupant, using a paddle to propel it."

"Was there gear on board?"

"The occupant was wearing a pack. Nothing else was visible. There may have been additional gear inside it."

"What then?"

"The person in the kayak was identified as the Field Branch corporal we were instructed to assist. We maneuvered to bring him alongside. He was not expert in handling the kayak, and as we approached, he lost control of the boat and capsized."

"Capsized?"

"Rolled over."

"And ...?"

"We anticipated problems, based on the description of the boat. We were prepared to carry out a rescue, but the occupant ... well, panicked. We did get a line on him, finally, but he was unresponsive when we brought him aboard. Our attempts to revive him were not successful."

"He drowned."

"Yes, sir."

"That's too bad. What about the boat? The kayak, I mean?"

"In the attempts to rescue the corporal, my crew lost sight of it. We assumed it sank."

"And you reported all of this to ... what command?"

"Here, sir. Directly to Captain Bird."

"And then what?"

"We were ordered to return to base, bringing the casualty in, in a concealed manner. Wrapped in a tarp. Captain Bird's aide and a person in civilian dress, not known to me, assumed responsibility for the body."

"Two people just took the body from you?"

"Yes."

"What did they do with it?"

"I don't know, sir. They loaded it into a vehicle, and the civilian drove it away."

E couldn't conceal a slightly shocked expression. She glanced at Pérez, and he looked much the same. "Commander," she said to him, "Were you aware of any of this?"

"Not until yesterday. I heard from Chief Halber that things had gone wrong, but I didn't know the details. Especially about the body."

"Why did the boat go back to the island the next day? Was that the same boat?"

"Yes, sir. We were ordered to conduct another search for the kayak. It was not successful."

"Well. Well, well, well. That's ... a startling report, Chief. I appreciate your assistance." E was watching the woman closely. Was there anything more to this? *Just ask, Gorsky.* "Is there anything more I should know? You'll probably be called to repeat that at some point. If anyone is charged. "

"I'd just like to say, sir, that ... that the whole thing is disgusting. I'm disgusted."

§

In the National News studio, the Government Affairs desk was working at top speed. In seconds, it would be broadcasting a "special," and there was no guarantee that the Council's Press Officer, Doug Fitch, would be on-line. Their front person was ready with a what-we-know paragraph, in case Fitch didn't make it, but she was still hoping.

"Three, two, one ... and go!" The director pointed at her.

"Good afternoon. This is Marta Kelly, in National News studios, with an update on the ... " The Director pointed behind her. "... the situation developing. She glanced at a monitor, then went on. "With us now is Council Press Officer, Douglas Fitch. Mister Fitch, this is the second time we've spoken today."

"Yes, Marta. And I do have more to talk about than I did this morning. It's certainly what we'd call a good-news-bad-news day. "

"What can you tell us about the attack on the Capital Buildings a short time ago?"

"It was actually an attack, although one that was easily thwarted by Security. A young man who was known, it's just become clear, to the Health and Safety Department as being mentally ill threw a bag or a pack at the defensive positions outside the staff entrance. As it turned out, the bag did not contain explosives or biological materials."

"What was in it?"

"A strange collection of items." He looked at a paper. "There was a modern copy of a medieval bible. A crucifix. A small stuffed toy – a bear or a dog or something – a copy of a novel from the 1950s, *Naked Lunch*, by someone named Burroughs. A bottle of chlorine bleach. Oh, and the infamous *Atlas Shrugged*."

"The libertarian bible, I think, someone called it?"

"Yes. Obviously, none of that caused any damage or injuries. Physical, at least. But after throwing it, the man ran into the farmer's market across the street, and for reasons we don't know, stabbed a woman who was shopping."

"Is the man in custody now?"

"Yes. He was injured, too, and he's now in the Security Branch Medical Detention facility. The victim is in the National Hospital, here in the capital."

"Do we know her condition?"

"I don't have that, yet. I know she was taken to the hospital with some urgency. But we're still waiting to hear."

"What about the incidents in the Upper Peninsula? Is there any connection with what happened here?"

"Nothing that has emerged yet. Given the timing, most people here in the capital weren't aware that anything was going on, and Security has told me, just minutes ago, that they have no indication so far that the attack here was connected."

"What can you tell us about the attacks up north?"

"What has been released so far is that twelve or thirteen young men, known to be involved with a resistance group, staged a planned attack on the Security Branch post in a small town called Big Bay. The attack is over now, with seven of the attackers killed and five in custody. There may or may not have been one more of them, and the area is being searched now."

"What about government and civilian losses?"

"Unfortunately one Security Branch private was killed, and a civilian is known to have been injured. There was a lot of physical damage to the SB post and to some of the buildings surrounding it."

"What do we know about the motivation for the attack?"

"Very little information has been released so far. What SB and Field Branch – FB was involved in suppressing the assault – have said is that it seems to be isolated to the group who staged it, and although both Branches are on alert, they say there's no likelihood of more planned attacks. The person I talked to asked me to emphasize 'planned'. When something like this happens, there's always the possibility of copy-cat events, following on in the next days or weeks. So a state of alert is being maintained."

"And obviously I have to ask, is any of this related to the organizational changes we discussed this morning?"

"No one I've spoken to has suggested anything like that."

"Well, thank you, Mister Fitch. I'm sure we all hope that the rest of the day is good news, instead of more bad." She looked into the camera. "And that's what we know, at this moment. Marta Kelly for National News."

"And cut. 'Good news instead of more bad'?"

"I know, I know. It was all I could think of. You want to come over here and make this stuff up?"

"Better you than me."

§

A hospital waiting room is a depressing thing at night. As many people will testify, it's not that cheerful in the late afternoon, either. National Hospital – really an entire medical complex – was scattered around a hill on the north side of the capital. The trauma center was actually near the center of the whole thing, and its public area had an east-facing wall of windows. If you looked east, you could see trees in the distance, the rail station, the river, and some sports fields. Typically, people who gathered there weren't interested in the view.

Karen Mather was there, sitting where some chairs were clustered together. Larry and Meg were with her. There'd been a lot of talking and some crying, and now they were just waiting. Survivors of traumatic incidents sometimes remember small aspects of them, suddenly, things that surface later. Meg had been sitting with her eyes closed; now she opened them. "He called me Judas," she said.

"What's that, honey?" said Karen. "He what?"

"He looked at me. And he called me Judas."

"He's sick," said Larry. "Mentally ill. He was saying all kinds of things, after Security got him."

"I know ... wait, how do you know that?"

"Larry knows stuff," Karen said. "Sometimes he talks out of school." Meg was no longer listening. She could hear her uncle, and her mother, and her father, talking about the world, and the devil, and God. And ... lying. Lying, lying, lying. A single tear fell.

"Excuse me," said a woman. "Hello, Karen."

"Well, Jeri. Hi. Haven't seen you in a while."

"No. I've been a little busy. But I thought you'd be here."

"Yeah. She's one of my people. You met Larry, I think? And this is Meg. She was there. This is Doctor Klein. Old, old friend of mine."

"Hello, Larry. Are you looking for a job, yet?"

"Not yet, no. I'm kind of ... my hands are a little bit full, right now."

"Meg's new with us," Karen said. "She's Una's roommate."

"Karen's house is a good place to be." She fished a tissue out of her pocket. "Do you need one?" she said, holding it out to Meg.

"Oh, I guess I do."

"I've been in this place..." She waved her hand at the hospital, generally. " ... a couple of times, myself. I came out on my feet. I changed careers once, because of it, but that was all right. I needed to, anyway."

"I ... " Meg focused on Jeri's face. "I think I'll change some things. I think I need to."

"I didn't know that," said Karen. "You were laid up, here?"

"Yes. A broken wrist once, plus breast cancer. And later, I got shot. That was the one that got me to switch jobs." Meg had lost track, already. She was staring at the window, not really seeing any of the coming and going outside, just thinking hard, along some new roads.

"I have to go," Klein said. "I need to change clothes, at least – I've been up since four o'clock. Maybe eat, too. That would be good. Do me a favor, though?" She was looking at Karen. "Text me when you know anything about your person."

"I will. Thanks for coming. Did I say? Her mom's – Una's mom – is an OB-GYN here. On duty now, dealing with babies. But she knows what happened."

"Okay. Meg and Larry, good luck. Good luck to your friend, especially." Klein turned and walked back toward the outside doors. Karen frowned at Larry.

"You want to stay in her good graces, boy. She'd be good to work for."

"I know. But I've still got a year at this. Then I'll think about next things."

"Well, just ... Oh, oh. Here we go." Two people in scrubs were walking toward them, a man and a woman. "That's Una's mom, on the left, there."

"Hi, Ms. Mather," said the woman. "This is Doctor Singh. He's been working with Una." She took a long breath. "It's been hard, but ... she's going to be all right." Singh smiled.

"Yes, she's in very good heath, your friend. Except for

the wound, of course. But she should recover."

"Wonderful! " Karen said. "If I was younger, I'd say hallelujah."

Meg met the surgeon's eyes. "Thank you. Thank you for letting us know."

"She will be here for four or five days," Singh went on, "We have to watch for infection very carefully. And then, she will have to be very quiet and rest. And we will have to see her several times more. To be sure that all is well."

"And that's what I have to ask you about, Ms. Mather. I'd love to have her at home, but ... " As Klein had, Una's mother gestured at the hospital. "... things here are overwhelming, right now. I've got two women with bad presentations, and they're both likely to go into labor, right in the middle of the time Una'd be home, and ... could she... would you be able to have her at your house?"

"Doctor Gregory, I was going to insist on it. She needs to be with us. There's always somebody there, always somebody to jump in. She needs to be there."

Meg raised her hand. "I'll help," she said.

§

"Late in the day, Captain. We need to find him if we're goin' to find him." The helicopter was on the ground, again, back on the hotel lawn. Sergeant Frank was trying to impress on a Field Branch captain the difficulty in ferreting out the one remaining attacker by using troops. The last time the subject had been seen was right at the end of things, as his colleagues were being rounded up. He'd bolted out from the ruins of the shed, west of the SB base, and he'd run on to the west, back through a group of houses and into the beginning of patchy woods and clearings. That unwelcoming terrain ran for forty kilometers or more, straight west to the shore of Keweenaw Bay. "Let's let the 'copter look for him."

"Sure, why not? They can fail faster than we can."

The helo crew, back from ferrying the dead trooper and the wounded civilian to Marquette, was happy to help. The 21HH-2 spun up, lifted off, and turned west. "Can you have the FB units mark with smoke, Captain? So we know where the friendlies are?"

"Right." Small patches of blue smoke began to appear. The helo flew west along a street, then out over the scratchy woods below. The pilot was watching the horizon and the compass, the copilot had his eyes on a heat sensor.

"Houses on the right, still. Nothing much ... wait ... no, never mind, somebody's got a gas grill going. Panning left, two-sixty degrees relative, two-sixty-five ... Oh, yeah. Somebody's out there, all by himself."

They came around sharply. The contact showed as a red patch projected on the pilot's windscreen. "I see it. Targeting ... hold on." In the middle of a small, square clearing – a potato field, probably – a man was standing up, with his hands high over his head. "This is Air one. We have your guy. Three hundred fifty meters from the base, bearing 246 actual. Appears to be surrendering."

"Are you sure? What's he doing?"

The pilot had the video magnification zoomed in. He could see the rifle lying at the subject's feet. "He's outstanding in his field."

§

In Ottawa, in one of the more obscure Canadian national government buildings, one minor official walked in on another. He closed the door and sat down. "What are we going to do?"

"About what?"

"You know what I mean."

"No, I'm afraid I don't."

"About the problem we've just had."

"I don't know about any problems. Everything in my area is running very well."

"Do you mean to ..."

"Look, even if I knew what you were talking about, I wouldn't have anything to say about it. Whatever it was."

"People died."

"Oh, my! That's terrible! How did it happen?"

"You know perfectly well..."

"No, I don't. I try not to know about awful things. And you shouldn't, either."

"Are you serious?"

"Yes."

"I see. All right. I can do that. If you can, I can."

"No doubt about it. You know, supervising fisheries inspections in Newfoundland is not my idea of a career finale."

"Or customs and immigration in Sainte-Anne-des-Monts."

"No, hardly. Have you had lunch yet?"

"No, now that you mention it. Where should we go?"

§

At 1520 hours, one of the Field Branch troopers met E coming out of a restroom. "Sir," he said, "There's a captain in your branch at the gate. He says he's here to take command."

"Oh, thank God. Welcome him in. I'll be in the conference room over there." She walked back to the room herself and swept the sandwich wrappers off the table. Then, hearing the "Over this way, sir" chatter from outside, she got her phone out. As the door opened, she began speaking clearly into it. There was, of course, no one on the other end.

"I don't care how difficult it is! We've been dealing with this all day! Just get it done. I want to hand this base over in top notch condition ..." She turned around. "I have to go. My relief is here. Good afternoon, Captain. I'm Gorsky."

§

In the government complex, General Newhouse had managed to sleep, leaning back in her chair, for some small period. She woke by herself, probably from the slight sounds of the evening staff relieving the day teams. It took her a second to realize the implication: the base wasn't locked down anymore. She touched the desk button. "Jim," she said, "are you out there?"

"Yes, General."

"What's ... um, happening? I nodded off, there."

"Sir, the salient points are like this. They got the last of the attackers at Big Bay. He surrendered. The attacker here was a mentally ill person. The civilian he injured is reported as likely to survive. The attacker probably will, too. So those are the, um, positive points. On the negative, Admiral Petronas is, um, missing."

"What? How long?"

"The report says 'since midmorning'. Security went to his residence, and the only person there said that he and his assistant left around 1030 hours. In his vehicle."

"I don't get ... what 'assistant'? He took a government person with him?"

"No, sir. Apparently this was a personal, ah, employee. A 'companion', is the term the report used."

"Well, who answered the door?"

"The report says she was his 'secretary'. She denied knowing anything about itineraries or destinations."

"Son of a ... Get General Hallstatt on the phone."

"He's actually here, sir. I asked him to let you, um, rest a few minutes more."

The conversation was short. Hallstatt had already taken action, and when he'd explained it, Newhouse had to agree that it was all that could be done. Petronas and whoever was with him were using a personal vehicle, not a government car. Its description and identifying numbers were known and had been broadcast.

"General," he said, "We've closed off the formal exits, the obvious ones. The southern two, down into the US. The bridge and tunnel into Canada on the Detroit River. The bridge at Port Huron. And the Mackinac Bridge, up north. What that leaves is ... the whole rest of the Huron and Michigan shorelines. And of course, any place at all in the Lower Peninsula, if he's not trying to get out."

"What do you think he's doing?"

"Running. I don't think he'll try to stay here. In the Republic."

"That would be a very bad idea for him."

"I think, realistically, he'd have to be doing one of three things. Trying to get out on the south, into the US. Trying to do that across Lake Michigan. Or trying to get into Canada. We've got External Relations working on backstopping Canada."

"What if he was just going there to go on into the US?"

"He'd still have to go out through our exit formalities and in through theirs, and we have all that, um, handled. Notifications, etc."

"And none of that has triggered anything?"

"No, sir. So that leaves some kind of clandestine exit, almost certainly by water."

"But ... he left in a car. What if he just drives south and tries to get across the border, you know, illegally?"

"People try that, periodically. There are physical and surveillance means to prevent it."

"Can I assume, though, that a government branch commander might have some advantage, say in terms of knowing about those means?"

"Except that Security changes them around frequently. And we don't publicize them except on need-to-know."

"But that's not the case with the lakeshores? "

"On incoming traffic, it's much the same. But to be blunt, we've spent most of our development and analysis money on that incoming side. We have less technology aimed at preventing people from leaving."

"Sure. I know. If somebody wants out, let 'em go. I remember helping to make that policy."

"Yes. And in general, it's been a good thing. It's only occasionally we need to prevent someone ... Oh, excuse me, sir, it's my 'urgent' ring." He answered the call. "Very well. I'm with the General now. I'll brief her."

"What now?"

"The SB officer who took over Alpena? She reported that there was some question whether Captain Bird, the one originally in command there, had actually come down here. He wasn't ordered here or anywhere else. He's missing, too."

Newhouse looked down and massaged her forehead with one hand. "Can I assume that you've worked out the charges against these people? For when we catch them? Notice that I said 'when', not 'if'."

"I did notice that, yes. "

§

Having turned over the Alpena base to its new commander, E then asked him for a favor. He had quite enough on his mind as it was, and once he'd confirmed her clearances, he was happy to order poor Commander Pérez – now superseded twice in one day by people he technically outranked – to get E a space in their secure area. She made sure that her two SB troopers had a place to sit, and promised them she'd be back shortly, "After I clear up a few things."

The first task was to send Captain Matthews a summary of the missing sniper story. That done, she then looked into what nooks and crannies of the base's secure servers might be open to her access. The more she looked, the more it became clear that ... the door was wide open. To her amazement, they didn't seem to have structured the document storage by programs and their accompanying clearance levels. *If you're in, you're in!*

Figuratively, she backed away and shut the door. What was the governing rule? If you saw a classified document left on a table, what were you supposed to do? Report it. But what if you were investigating a crime, and it might be evidence? *When in doubt, ask your boss.*

There were secure phones in this closed area. *Kind of old-fashioned, but what the hell?* She tried Matthews' number, and, surprisingly, Matthews picked up, and E identified herself. "Yeah, Gorsky. Got your mail. What number is this?"

"I'm in the secure area here, sir. They have these old desk phones. Have you got a minute?"

"About a minute. Go ahead."

"I came in here to send that message, and then I discovered that I can see just about everything on their servers. There might be something about Silverman. Or Captain Wright. Am I okay with looking at this stuff if the system lets me?"

"You're cleared for all of their stuff."

"I am?"

"Yeah, didn't I go over that? You and a bunch of our people – me, even – are cleared for anything NB's got. Their security groups were told that this morning, and they must have jumped on it. Oh, hell, that all came down after you left. So I didn't get to tell you. But, yeah, have a ball. Did your relief guy show up, or are you still sipping grog on the quarterdeck, down there?"

"I've turned command over to those more qualified, sir. And no grog in sight. Their coffee isn't even as good as ours."

"Find all the dirt you can. I'm deep in some of my own, up here. I get to snoop on the Marquette people. So ... oh, hang on. This is a need-to-know for you. Both Admiral Petronas – you know, the head man – and the guy you were replacing down there, Bird? They're both officially wanted. AWOL. Gone like turkeys through the corn."

"That's ... remarkable."

"So if either of 'em shows up, there, cuff 'em and let me know. We'll split the reward."

"Very good, sir. Goodbye." *I wonder what Captain Matthews had for lunch? And how many of them?*

§

Sergeant Edmore set his grocery selections down on the counter. The IGA out north on Ontario Street had the widest selection of food in De Tour, and he knew one or two of the employees. He bought his staples there, mostly on his way back to the island, coming down from the Soo. This time, he was stocking up for a couple of weeks, at least. All the way back down, he'd been hearing about the Big Bay crisis and getting his marching orders from Company. He might not get back over to the mainland for a while.

The gist of it was "close the border off". Why a shoot-out over on the west side of the UP would threaten the border here, about as far east as you could get, wasn't clear to him, but as a man does who's counting the months to retirement, he said "Yes, sir," and got on with it. He checked his grocery list once more, put it all in the passenger's seat, and headed off to the ferry dock. He turned down the stub street, the one that ran right out onto the dock, shut the engine off, and waited for the boat. He was the first in line. A woman he knew pulled in behind him, and they waved at each other out their open windows. Behind her car, another truck drove in. Out on the lake, the superstructure of the ferry detached itself from the island and began visibly approaching. "Home again, home again," Ed hummed.

The driver of the third vehicle opened his door and got out. He walked up to the car ahead of him and spoke to the woman in the driver's seat. Ed overheard enough to know that he was asking about room on the ferry. The other driver assured him that there'd be plenty of room. He asked something else, and Ed heard the answer: "Oh, about twenty minutes. You can see it coming." That apparently satisfied him. The man went back to his truck.

Ed looked at his phone. It was 1650 hours, and, formally, he was supposed to be back on duty at 1800. "Might as well sign in," he thought. He called the SB base at Cedarville, spoke to the Corporal at the Company desk, and reported himself as on duty. "I'm at the ferry now. I'll be at the island base in forty-five or so." He heard a short description of the night's orders. They were the same as the day's, mostly. Get patrols out along the east shoreline, keep an eye out for any kind of cross-border shenanigans, a higher level of detail in any incident reports he might file: all recognizable symptoms of command-level paranoia. He'd been through it before. It usually boiled down to drugs or bad people or both, going one way or the other. He acknowledged and hung up.

As short-run ferries go, the PRS Dog Islander was reasonably large. She could handle five large vehicles on each side of her deck, more if any of them was smaller than the average pickup truck. As you drove on, a deck hand pointed you left or right, balancing the load. Ed went down the right side, the car behind went left, and the other truck came in behind Ed. He noticed that it had an aluminum row boat in the bed. People carried boats around with them, up here; nothing unusual in that. But his practiced eye made him think, "Might be over three and a half meters. It's hanging over the tailgate. Maybe I'll give him a look when we get across, see if he's got it registered." For the first time, he noticed that there was a passenger, too.

§

Roughly half way up the center of the Republic's Lower Peninsula, there are a pair of large lakes, Houghton and Higgins. For decades, they'd been recreational magnets; lucky people inherited "the cottage" from their parents, others bought or built. After Separation, the annual "going up north" vacation economy declined, but to some extent it was replaced by people moving in full-time. Government and technical workers could get on-line from the lakeside communities as easily there as elsewhere. Real estate values were normalized across the country and interest rates fixed, so if you didn't need to be down south, and you could cope with the weather, why not live here? The bait and tackle shops made room for year-round clothing; the burger bars hired people who could actually cook, and the management became acquainted with the concept of a wine list. One of the two small civil airports closed, but the other one turned into a combined Security and Field branch base. And like every other such establishment in the Lower Peninsula, this particular afternoon, its people were out on the roads, looking for a specific car.

Right around 1700 hours, one of these SB patrols was driving a primary road around Houghton Lake's south shore. On the right side: businesses and the lake. On the left, there was a web of small streets, lined with small cottages. The passenger was scanning the parking lots on his side, and the driver was alternating her attention between the road ahead and the lanes leading inland. They went by one of them, and she said, "Hey!"

Ten minutes after that, Security Branch Base Houghton Lake knew that Admiral Malcolm Petronas' personal car had been identified, and it knew that a neighbor had seen a man and a woman leave it in the driveway, go briefly into the associated cottage, and then drive away in the pickup truck that normally lived there. And, even more interestingly, this had taken place at around 0800 hours that morning.

§

"Bad news, General. Security says they found Petronas' car at Houghton Lake, and he was apparently there, getting a truck of some kind, way early this morning.

Plenty of time for him to be over the bridge and into the UP before our watch order went out."

"Son of a bitch," said General Newhouse.

§

With its usual *thunk*, the ferry came up against the dock at Landing. Ed, having been the first one on, got to be the first one off. He waved to the deckhand, drove off the ramp and down onto the paved driveway, then pulled to the side and got out. The car came off next and then the truck with the boat. Ed stepped partly out into its path and waved it down. He came up to the passenger's side, and she ran the window down.

"Good afternoon," he said, smiling in a half-official, half-friendly way. "That was a nice short trip over here, wasn't it? I just want to check and see if your boat registration is okay."

"Registration?" said the driver. He was in his later forties, dressed in a sort of down-south casual way. The passenger was not in her forties. Not at all. More like late twenties, possibly; stretching a point, early thirties. "We just bought the boat. They didn't say anything about registration."

"It could be fine, sir. Anything under three and a half meters doesn't need one. And if you don't have one, it's no big deal. You can get a sticker right over there at our luxurious headquarters." He pointed at the SB base. "Just let me put a tape on it, and if you're good, I'll just wave you ahead. Otherwise, we'll go over there and get you squared away." He held up a ten-meter tape measure and took two steps back toward the boat.

Because it was still on the paved apron of the landing, the truck's rear wheels screeched and even smoked slightly as the driver hammered down the accelerator. Ed jumped back, and it was a good thing. There was

221

gravel directly in the truck's path, and it slid sideways, losing traction momentarily. Then it went straight ahead, following the road, and ran between the two buildings that, along with the SB post, were all there was to Landing. Ed ran back to his truck, keeping his eyes on the fugitives, jumped in, and went after them. He was just in time to see them turn hard right, going behind the post and off toward the east shore.

Later on, Ed had to resort to radio logs and the memory of Steve, his National Service trooper, in order to sort out the exact sequence of events. He couldn't remember, for example, whether he called in a vehicle-fleeing report before or after he got a broadcast warning about a couple of fugitives in a pickup truck, possibly trying to reach the Canadian border. But one way or the other, his little pursuit became very, very interesting to a large part of the Security Branch.

For the moment, Ed was tightly focused on keeping the malefactors in sight. He was surprised to see, as he turned behind them going east, that they then turned hard right, off East Ferry Road and onto the smaller, unpaved South Branch Trail. Inside the fugitive vehicle there'd been a brief disagreement over which turn was correct, and the driver turned right on pure instinct. "It's an island! How many roads can there be?"

"We're supposed to go east!" the passenger objected. "This is south!" She jabbed a finger at the compass indicator in the rear view mirror.

"Too late now!" The driver ran the speed up as far as he dared. Behind him, he could see the flashers that Ed had just remembered to turn on. The other thing that Ed remembered was that, on Dog Island or anywhere near it this evening, the total manpower available to the AoR, let alone Security Branch, was two people. Fifty percent of that force was now in pursuit of fleeing persons, and they outnumbered him by, again, fifty percent. Standing orders were that the SB post was to be staffed at all times, but, as the senior non-commissioned officer present and in light of the current situation, he made a tactical decision to supersede that requirement and augment the operational force deployed.

"Steve! Get in your truck, and get on out to East Shore!" There was the sound of a microphone being keyed, then released. "Steve! Do you copy?"

"Yes! Yes, Sergeant! I'm, um, the only one here!"

"Get on the road, Steve! This is ... it might be important!"

"Yes, sir!"

The driver of the truck was trying to drive, watch Ed in the mirror, and fumble with the mapping capability on his phone. His colleague was becoming concerned about this multi-tasking approach. "Give me that!" she suggested. "I'll find it!" By "it" she may have meant their destination, their current location, or even a gas station. As she'd already pointed out several times, they were dangerously low on fuel.

The driver tossed the phone to her, she missed it, and it went into the darkness of the foot well. "Damn it!" she said, and began to hunt for it. The driver, distracted by this, looked at her. Then he looked up and out the windshield.

"Yahhh!" he said, or something close to that. A large dog was trotting down the middle of the road, straight ahead. The man turned right and hit the brakes. The truck slid sideways, and the lateral motion was too much for the bungee cords holding down the boat. It flipped up and over the left side of the truck bed, hung there for a moment, and then disappeared into the foliage on the roadside. The woman made a panic noise, similar to the man's but at a higher pitch. The dog turned and kept running, on out into the woods.

"Son of a bitch!" The driver managed to recover from the slide, and he got the truck moving forward again. "Check the boat!"

The woman looked out the back window. "It's gone!"

"Son of a bitch, son of a bitch, son of a bitch! ... Look out!" Ahead, South Branch Road met Little Lake Road and formed a Y. The man braked hard and took the course of least resistance. The left turn was easier, and that's the way he turned. He had to slow down almost to a stop to do it without crashing into the woods, and his associate took the opportunity to implement a program she'd been considering for the last hundred kilometers. That is, she opened her door and jumped out. She fell, rolled over once, and sat up. By then, the truck was too far away for her to hear the driver shout, "Biiiiitch!"

She stood up, collected herself and assessed the surroundings – thick pine woods on three sides, gathering dusk, and nothing else except a hand-made sign, pointing right toward "Little Lake". She heard Ed's truck coming up behind, and she turned and waved. Instead of stopping, the vehicle with its flashing lights and high beams went on by, slid around the turn, and tore off, still in pursuit. "Now what am I going to do?" was her only immediate thought.

Ed was generally a chivalrous individual. But in this case, his natural inclination to assist a fellow human being had to take second place to an increasingly specific set of orders from higher and higher up in the SB chain of authority. The gist of them, translated into colloquial speech, was "Get that bastard!" and so he was trying to. He did, though, call Steve and advise him that the miscreants had separated.

"I'm busy hanging on to this truck. But there's a woman on the road, right where South Branch splits from Little

Lake. She bailed out. Where are you?"

"I'm up on East Ferry. Like you said."

"Right. Okay, keep going. We'll have to pick her up later, then. This guy's only got one more choice. He could go on East, when he hits Ferry Road, you know, go up to East Shore. Or, he could go west around, by Peters. I don't know why he'd do that, but he might."

"You think he might stop somewhere, Sergeant? A house or something?"

"I'm right behind him. If he does, I'll see it. That's why I need you down here. In case we have to do a foot chase."

"Oh. Right."

Ed switched back to his main SB comm channel. There might be some help from Company just getting to the ferry, over at De Tour. And there was supposed to be all kinds of help coming from further off, a helicopter, even. But "further off" was the key term, there. Right now, it was all on Steve and himself. "I wish I knew who this guy is, even," he thought.

Ed didn't know who he was chasing; he wasn't able to formulate his tactical plans from full knowledge of the target. His assumptions about the arrival time of help were based on the Security Branch's usual level of concern over random criminals. Therefore, he assumed that no help would be arriving before his suspect either crashed, bailed out, or encountered Steve, coming down the road from the north. The problem with that thinking was that people much more highly placed in the military organization had a much more specific idea about the target and also a much greater ability to deploy resources. Fifty-five kilometers north, one of those resources was charging down a runway.

Forty or more years before, a Brazilian aircraft manufacturer had starting building small turboprop ground support aircraft. Cheaper to buy and fly and maintain than jets, they sold well to countries with internal wars and no native aviation industry of their own. These little fighters – that's what they were – grew up, got faster and more deadly, and shortly after Separation, a current version of them became the only fixed-wing combat aircraft the Field Branch used. Now, one of them – the only one in Seventh Division territory – was the only asset the AoR had that could be on station over Dog Island quickly. And it was on its way. "What the hell are we supposed to do?" the observer asked the pilot.

"No idea. Scare somebody, maybe? What's our time to target?"

"Eight or nine minutes."

The road was going generally southeast. The fugitive was exceeding the bounds of reasonability, in terms of his speed, but he had the excuse of having no choices. Except for driveways and hunting trails, there was nothing but woods on either side. Then, the road turned slightly to his left, and the entrance to a single-lane plank bridge appeared. To his exhausted brain, it looked impossibly small. At his speed, it was at least highly dangerous, if not quite impossible. He jumped on the brakes, and for a second time, the truck swerved. It went onto the bridge at an angle, clipping the railing with the right rear quarter panel. The driver cut back the other way and the front wheels found enough grip on the planks to straighten out and keep turning. The truck now veered the other way, dropped one rear wheel off the bridge, spun as the other wheel gripped, and somehow the whole thing came off the other side. It was sitting sideways across the road, but at least it was upright.

Ed, knowing that the bridge was coming up, had backed off, and he saw the predicament. He slowed more, thinking the chase was over, but the driver, performing better than any self-driving algorithm could have, cut the wheels the right way, hit the gas, and powered back onto the road. Sheet metal was banging around on the right side, but he was still mobile.

The plane was moving fast. "There's De Tour, off to the right," said the observer. "Aim for the east side of the island. They think there might be action over there. "

On land, the next relief from the trees-road-trees scenery would be a T intersection with East Ferry Road. Go left, and you'd be headed back north, up toward the cluster of houses at East Shore. Go right, and you'd be running west along the shoreline toward Peters. Ed's estimate of the driver's rationality wasn't high, and so he reported their location only. "Unit 32, approaching South Branch and East Ferry. Subject vehicle now damaged, still rolling."

"Air five, we're feet wet past De Tour. We're coming down the east shore. No, um ... nope, no boats observed, no water traffic."

"Company to Unit 32. You're going to have an air unit overhead in a few minutes!"

"32, understood. What kind of air support? Rotary?"

"Negative. An E335."

"Uh, understood." Ed wondered what use a ground-attack plane was going to be. "I need people," he thought. "If they want this clown alive, that is!" Ahead of him, the truck braked and ... turned left. "Unit 32, subject has gone north, up the shore. North on East Ferry Road. Following."

"Understood. Is subject showing lights?"

"Affirmative. Headlights on, tail lights on."

"Any other traffic? Besides you?"

"Negative."

"Air five, did you copy that? Subject and pursuit running with lights on."

"Understood."

The road here was inland almost a half a K from the shore, a tunnel through the woods with a strip of deteriorating pavement running through it. It bent left, pointing back north. For the first time since Landing, the man in the truck was headed where he wanted to go. He was a few minutes late.

"Air five, I have the vehicles in sight. Rolling in hot."

"Understood, Five. Unit 32, look away."

"What the hell?" Ed dropped his eyes to the dashboard, and his foot came off the gas. Ahead, the man was looking directly down the road. In front of him, the aircraft dropped down to nearly the treetop level and came tearing down at him. On the pilot's head-up display, projected on the windscreen, the truck's lights were obvious.

"On my mark. Three, two, one ... drop!" The rear seat man touched a control. In front, the pilot turned on the landing lights. Four extremely bright illumination flares popped out of the plane's launcher and ignited.

The world as the man in the truck could observe it became nothing but bright, blinding light. He repeated his earlier observation, "Arrrrrgh!" Some deep set of memories and logic functions interpreted the phenomenon as a huge vehicle bearing down on him. He twisted the steering wheel hard to the left. His truck left the pavement, struck a small tree, mowed down a clump of sumac, and buried its wheels in mud. It slid three feet and stopped.

"Thank you," said General Newhouse, speaking into her phone. "Let me know when they actually have him in custody."

§

Sitting alone in the classified area at the Alpena base, E had to stand to see a wall clock. She'd guessed at 1800 hours, but it was only 1620. Searching and reading, searching and reading: a slow way to spend time. *Profitable, though.* She shook her head rapidly back and forth like a dog getting water off its ears. *What a mess.* She was logging each document she read and noting whether or not it was relevant. The items of interest were, obviously, in the minority, but they were astonishingly toxic. Simple searching was turning up a three percent hit rate – likely sources of evidence – and so far, half had been actually valuable. The image that was forming was at once fascinating and odious.

The main threads had to do with Silverman, his background, and his life just before he fell, face down, behind that house in Peters. He was not a new recruit. He'd been undercover with other target groups before getting involved with the church and its pharmacy business. Specifically, he'd been one of an angry group of men – specifically men – living in the various small communities around Marquette. The initial contact reports described a man who wanted a more affluent life than the one he was leading. His commitment to the rather basic, extreme-libertarian views of the group was far less than he claimed. He'd made the logical assumption that the new government would be willing to recruit people who knew people. Specifically, they'd want people who could help keep tabs on who might be more than just an armchair rebel. The group he was involved with was, at that time, no more than that, but he believed that it could be made more interesting and therefore, more valuable. He found that his initial feelers along these lines met with a cautious interest. He was given a couple of simple tests – being asked to report things that the government already knew, for example –

and he passed.

Unfortunately for him, the obvious government around Marquette was the Naval Branch, and that was who he contacted. They brought him on board, and he reported and snooped and provided names. Security Branch wasn't aware of him. Then, when he was accidentally identified to SB, they put pressure on Naval to borrow him and use him in one of their down-country efforts. It involved careful insertion into a church group, one that was suspected of fostering a local resistance effort of its own.

This was nothing E had heard of, specifically, but she knew that this sort of intelligence gathering was going on. She also knew that it was rigorously restricted to being only that: intelligence gathering. All of SB had an across-the-board prohibition on provocation. You could spy on people, but you couldn't encourage them to break the law. The more she read, the more it became clear: Naval Branch was not operating under those rules.

The downstate program was called Log Happen, and it was, she read, brought to a quick close when it turned out that it wasn't really a resistance group but a pharmaceuticals export-smuggling scheme. *Nothing like a price differential across a border to give people ideas.* SB stepped in, shut it down, and arrested everybody that Silverman had identified. Publically, they took him, too, but then he entered their informant-protection programs. And there things sat for several months. The next document in the directory was a brief and panicky report from a Naval Branch officer who had been Silverman's contact.

Subject: Emergency Program Implementation

The information source known as Mike Silverman contacted this office and made demands relating to his current SB protective situation. He stated that unless he was moved out of the program (ref: Ice Way) to another location closer to the Upper Peninsula (Divisions 7 or 8, SB), he would inform his SB contacts of his work with NB program Mask Roger. Strongly recommend that NB comply with this request. Subject has demonstrated greater knowledge of Mask Roger than anticipated. Source of that knowledge not known as of this point.

E read that message twice. *He held up the bank, somehow.* She realized that, right there, there was a motive for Silverman's removal. How good a motive would depend on what "Mask Roger" turned out to be.

§

Ed drove cautiously up to the suspect's truck. The doors were still closed, and his experience suggested that people fleeing from an accident usually left them open. So there was probably someone inside. He steered his vehicle so that its headlights illuminated the scene, and he turned on a bright investigation light as well. Then he called his backup. "Steve, this is Ed! Where are you?"

"Just arriving at East Shore."

"Keep on south, then. He's wrecked out, about two klicks south. You'll see the lights when you get here."

"Yes, sir."

Next, he called Company. "This is unit 32. Subject wrecked his vehicle. I'm on scene. Subject is probably still in the truck. Advise."

"This is Matthews. Go get him, Sergeant. Don't let him get out on foot."

"Understood." "Why? Is he some kind of runner?" Ed wondered. He unsnapped his sidearm holster, glanced at the pistol to be sure it was actually loaded, and stepped out. With the door in front of him, he shouted at the truck in the mud. "Sir? Are you all right, sir?" No answer. He looked north, up the road. No sign of Steve, yet. "Oh, well. Here we go." He stepped around the door and, being very careful, moved toward the target.

As he closed in, he gave up the fight with his inner voices and drew his sidearm. The flares were dying down, and instead of just their reflections, he could see at least solid shapes through the truck cab's back window. The one on the driver's side moved slightly. "Sir ... in the vehicle! Stay where you are! This is Security Branch! We want to see if you're okay!" The shape moved again.

Staying closely tucked into the truck's left side, Ed moved in. He reached a point where he could tell the driver's head from the headrest, glanced down quickly at the door handle, then looked back at the head while he reached out. The handle moved for him – the man must have unlocked the door – and Ed gave it a push. The door swung open about half way, then hung up against a shrub. "Sir, are you hurt?" The man moved slightly and turned his head back toward Ed's voice.

"Do you know who I am?" The voice was a parody of a military "command voice". It was pitched too high, and there wasn't enough breath behind it.

"No, sir, I don't. But you're under arrest. For ... a range of things. Take off your seat belt." Nothing. "I said, take it off!" The man nodded slightly and unsnapped the harness. "Now swing your legs out. Keep your hands out." The man turned at least part way, shoving the harness aside. He scooted outward, and Ed used his left hand to help him stand up. "Are you hurt?"

"I ... my chest ... hurts. The seatbelt." He was shorter than Ed, and he had a day's worth of beard stubble. Standing there, he seemed to gather his wits somewhat. "I don't intend to answer any questions," he said.

"You don't have to, sir. Turn around so I can secure your hands. Then you can rest in my vehicle. There's medical help coming." This last was a partial lie, since Ed had no idea what kinds of help were actually coming. But there was no point in saying it. Sooner or later, some kind of physician would be on hand. He got the cuffs on, made sure the man had no obvious weapons, and walked him back toward the SB truck. As they got there, Steve arrived.

"Get this guy in my truck," Ed said. "I gotta image his. See if there's anything exciting in there." The vehicle had a typical dual seat cab. There were suitcases in a heap in the back seat, a purse on the floor of the passenger's side in front. A phone was lying on the floor, too. He took pictures of all that, plus the truck's controls. His own phone was making all kinds of noises and demands for attention, but he let it go for a minute more. Instead, he walked back to his truck and opened the back door.

"Sir, one thing I noticed with your vehicle: you've got the all-wheel-drive turned off. You want to keep it in four-wheel up here. You never know what kind of terrain you'll run into." Somewhere close by, a canid of some kind – dog, wolf, coyote – let out a long howl.

§

An increasingly chilly hour later, Steve crossed the bridge on South Branch Trail. Since the wreck scene was getting cluttered with Security and Field Branch people, Ed detailed him to go find the passenger. He drove slowly north, following Ed's directions. "What I'd do if I were in that situation – totally lost, out in the dark – I'd walk back the way I came. You see what I mean? So look for her up north along the trail."

"Yes, sir," Steve said. "Do we know her name?"

"Nope. What's-his-name over there won't even admit there was anyone else in the truck."

The road bent left, heading back toward the center of the island. It was full dark, and he took care not to overdrive the range of his lights. Another ten minutes, another slight turn, and ... in the headlights, a pedestrian. The woman must have heard him coming, because she was jogging back toward his truck, waving her hands. The evening was already chilly, and she seemed almost comically underdressed for it. Steve stopped, and she came up to his door. "Good evening, ma'am," he said.

"Are you the police?"

"Yes, ma'am. Security Branch. I'm Private ..." she cut him off.

"I'll tell you anything you want about that jackass! Anything!"

"Oh, well, fine. But first let's get you ... let's go back to the post. The SB office. You look cold."

§

On the southern tip of St. Joseph Island, the piece of Canadian shoreline closest to Dog Island, four men were getting tired of staring through binoculars. "I think he got popped," one of them said.

"With all that traffic on the ferry ..." said another one.

"And that plane buzzin' around ..." said the first speaker, "I don't think we need to wait. "

"Another wasted night. Just like up north, there."

"Good damn thing that one got canceled. From what I heard. They were ready and waitin'."

"Yeah. Let's go on home. Maybe stop for a beer, someplace."

§

It was getting dark out. In his room with green walls, the

man was finishing a document. Outside the door, his assistant was sending invitations to a discussion. There weren't many people on the list.

"... our view of the recent events, our public view should be that we have not adequately funded social development in our deeply rural areas. We need to ensure that social opportunity exists for everyone, regardless of where they are, and regardless of how stringently the wild areas of the Republic are conserved. We will suggest that ways of improving the integration of deep-rural populations will be forthcoming.

"This will, of course, cause concern among members of the public, many of whom will assume it means opening up wilderness areas to development. Our counter will be, obviously, that no such thing is intended. Instead, we will suggest, the idea is to provide opportunities for the most remotely rural populations to migrate to other areas, areas that offer more substantial economic and social support.

"Once that notion begins to achieve levels of acceptance, we can begin working on specific ways to define, very narrowly, the individuals most susceptible to resistance ideology, and begin defining means to relocate them to more settled areas – without, of course, making it clear that we are selecting for particular ideological points of view."

He leaned back and stretched his arms over his head. "Some of my colleagues will paraphrase that sentence," he thought, smiling. "'Get the bastards out in the open where we can watch them'," they'll say. 'Language is language,' I'll reply. 'But you catch more atavistic, egomaniacal simpletons with honey than you do with vinegar'."

§

In Alpena, the sun was long gone. E finished a sentence

in her summary and realized that she'd revised it three times. *Time to get some sleep. Or try to.* She saved the file to the SB classified cloud and sent it to Matthews' secure account, as well. She long-blinked three or four times, trying to get her dry eyes to water.

She shut down the machine she was using, policed-up the desk, and locked the drawer. *I'll sleep. Until 0400. Then, it'll be bad.*

In fact, she managed to stay asleep until 0500 hours, more or less; a dream woke her. She was chasing some nebulous thing through an office, jumping over desks, surfing on rolling chairs, skimming lunch plates at it like a discus thrower. She opened her eyes. *Alpena. Shit. I'm still in Alpena.*

Her first concern was, did she really keep Matthews up to date? *Has she read that report? How much hell is this going to raise? If Petronas makes it out of the country ... or Bird, for that matter ... that would be bad.*

Mask Roger was at the center. A Naval Branch highly-classified program. Run by the Admiral's office, with Bird handling the actual work. Using – the only word that fit – dissidents in the Republic and ex-pats in Canada to create an emergency. One that Naval Branch could suppress, by itself. And make SB and Field Branch look ... foolish. Incompetent. Poorly led. *Especially that one.*

Why? Because Petronas wanted it. There was nothing more about reasons in the documents she'd read. But if NB gained power in the Republic, so would the Admiral. Bad enough. But worse, from E's point of view, were the things not in the plan. It called for an attack by armed dissidents on an SB post. There'd be more of them coming across the lake in fishing boats. There were rough numbers, estimates of timing and cost. But nothing at all about risks and casualties. *They knew people would get hurt and killed. Not a word about it.*

And there was nothing about Canada. The program took their cooperation for granted. The attack from boats was starting at a river mouth, clear up on the north shore of Superior. In Canada, that is. They had to know. The phrase that came to mind was a piece of drama from a thriller she'd read. Here was Eden Bienvenue Gorsky, acting Lieutenant, ex-economics geek, assigned to a tiny piece of land on the edge of the country, and reporting *an international plot. I wonder if I'll get my own comic book?*

She got up. Margie heard her and sat up in her bunk. "What time is it, sir?"

"0500, more or less. I'm going to the head. Nudge your colleague over there ..." she pointed at the other trooper, occupying the next bed "... and let's get started. I think I'll be getting some orders of some kind. As soon as Company wakes up."

§

Morning in a hospital is never pleasant, especially when you've been there all night. Karen and Meg had some kind of breakfast at the dining area. Larry went back to his local apartment. "Look, girl," Karen started, "We need some plans, here. I got to go back over to the house. For one thing, somebody's got to go get groceries. For another, we're gonna have a lot of unhappy people over there. I need to be there when they need a kind word. You see?"

"I see. I was thinking about that, myself. I'll stay here."

"That's what I was gonna suggest. Have you done this before? Waiting around a hospital when somebody's sick?"

"No."

"Well remember, these people have all kinds of patients, all kinds of overhead work, they're all busy as hell. You got to be on a schedule, pushing for information. When can you see her? What's the next thing they want to do? What kind of help will she need when she gets out? You gotta ask for that. Nobody's gonna find you, just to give you an update. Especially when her mom's in the building. They're gonna go to her, first. So just make a schedule. Every hour, you go bother somebody. Okay?"

"Yes. I will. I can be a pest if I need to."

"Good girl. Make a job out of it." Karen stood up, then reached for her phone. "Hello, Larry. He is? Well tell him nobody can see her right now. But if he comes over here, he can talk to Meg. Meg's in charge. Yes." She turned to Meg. "You remember Alan? The tall guy?"

"Yes."

"Larry says he's all jacked out of shape over this. He wanted to come see Una. I told Larry you were the officer in charge here, right now. So if he comes, well ... " She sat back down. "I'm gonna give you the quickest introduction to crisis counseling that ever was. He might need some."

§

As she anticipated, E got a call from Matthews at a bit after 0600. It was necessarily vague, given the sensitivity of the subjects, but E had already gotten access to the local Field Branch closed area, and they were able to carry on with the details from there. Matthews sounded tired and perhaps a bit hung over, and she seemed to share E's sense of conflict over the new intelligence. It was essentially approach-avoidance: they were happy to have answers, and they hated what the answers implied.

"The way I read this, the head of NB was going to stage a small rebellion in order to discredit the other branches.

Right?"

"That's what I believe, sir. Yes."

"Incredible. How in the hell ..." She dropped that subject, since the answer was obvious. The head of the AoR had put a viper in the army's bosom, metaphorically. And metaphorically or not, that wasn't the most diplomatic thing to say. "But there's good news on that front, anyway. They got him. And you'll never believe how."

"I won't?"

"Well, maybe. He and his 'assistant' – who, I'm told, is extremely attractive and twenty-eight years of age – took off in his government car, but they swapped it for a truck, somewhere up-country. Then, they bought a rowboat, crossed the bridge, and headed for ... guess where?"

"Are you serious? Sir? Dog Island?"

"Yes indeed. We don't know why yet, but everybody assumes they were going to row over to St. Joseph or somewhere across the border. "

"That's ... well, actually it's not a bad idea. Not a lot of resources out there."

"Oh, yeah? Tell that to your friend, Edmore. He got 'em."

"Oh, fabulous! Hurray for Ed! That's the best thing I've heard in days! Is he okay?"

"He's fine. He got an assist from a FB Tucano – dropped flares ahead of the car, and the guy drove into the ditch – but Edmore definitely gets the credit. He stopped 'em to see if they had a permit for their boat, and they ran."

"That's great, sir. I can't wait to tell Margie ... one of the troopers I have here with me. I borrowed her from Ed."

"So ... that's the good news. On the other side of the books, we don't know where this Captain Bird crook is."

"No. As I reported, we know when he left, but we don't know where he was going."

"And what about Wright? I didn't see anything about him in your document."

"I have an answer, but I don't have the documents yet. My plan is to go back over to the base and dig that out yet today. "

"But you know something?"

"Yeah. NB must have had contact with him all along – at least the whole time Ice Rink was going. And when ... well, when it was time to get rid of Silverman, they pulled Wright out and gave him a Naval Commander's badge and a new name. Otherwise, he'd have taken the blame for ... for me, not protecting, um, Silverman. The guy named Derecha who got shot – you know, on board the Detroit? – he was Wright. And apparently it was just bad luck. At least that's what the informal stuff suggests. But I want to find an actual report or a plan or something, before I say so officially."

"Okay. But you don't actually have to stay down there to look at their stuff. The Examination Court that's going to deal with the Admiral just defined everything they've got as evidence. Everything. In a day or two, it'll all be available here or any other SB secure area."

"Oh, good. That's ... better. I find this place ... a little depressing. "

"Really?"

"These people are all so ... I guess I have to say, ashamed. And angry."

"Sure. And your replacement down there, Captain Garman? He'll make sure nothing happens to the data. Come on back."

"With pleasure, sir. It'll be nice to be back north of the bridge."

§

Just twenty kilometers north of the Republic's border with the US state of Indiana, a small city called Coldwater straddled Highway R69. The highway on-ramp for southbound traffic ran directly behind the local Security Branch post, and this post had responsibility for traffic and traffic incidents from the city south to the large, busy border crossing. The crossing was primarily a commerce gateway, and the traffic in both directions was mostly large transport vehicles.

This morning, there was a set of messages, dealing with people of interest in the ongoing national case. One of the threads cancelled a watch order for a man and woman travelling together, and the others concerned a man, travelling alone, and possibly seeking to leave the Republic. There were descriptions and a picture, details of the vehicle he might be driving, and a specific order to detain him if possible. He was not to be allowed to leave the Republic.

At around 0730 hours, the SB post received a report of an accident, south of town, at the last exit before the border post. Two SB vehicles were nearby, and they were ordered to respond. An ambulance was started on its way from Coldwater. When the troopers arrived, the details emerged rapidly. A civilian vehicle had merged onto the highway from the west, heading south. A pair of large trucks were side by side in the right and left lanes of traffic, and the car was caught between them. The drivers of the trucks provided similar stories; the car failed to increase its speed and was struck from behind by one of the haulers, unable to slow in time. The car was forced sideways against the other truck, turned perpendicular to the highway, and struck again, this time broadside, by the first truck. The car rolled over and was shoved off the edge of the road. It was at rest there, upside down, as the troopers and the medical personnel examined it.

Inside the car, the only occupant was dead, having received massive injuries to the head. He was taken by the ambulance back to Coldwater's National Medical Center. The SB report on the incident noted that he had a large amount of US cash, a lesser amount of Republic dollars, a US passport, a Canadian passport, and a tattoo on his left bicep identifying him as a member of the Republic's Naval Branch.

By 0800 hours, as General Newhouse was finishing her preparation for the day's meetings, she was informed that Captain Dennis Bird, ex-Commander of Naval Branch Base, Alpena, had been located, deceased. "That's too bad," she said. "I had a lot of questions for him."

§

The entrance of the Ross Commerce Regulatory Center was a remarkable example of late twentieth-century inhumane architecture. Built for quite another purpose, it funneled visitors into a right-angled mélange of glass, brick, blocks, and cement. The Republic, as it acquired space in which to govern, hadn't bothered with aesthetics. "Does the roof leak? Does the heating work? Okay, fine." It added a few new signs inside and out and a new motto over the doors: "*Pauca sed Bonum*". Now once again, a small group of officials gathered in the green-walled office. With his usual grace, the man rose to greet them, exchanging a social word or two with each one, leaving business aside until the group was complete.

"Now," he said, when they were all seated in his guest chairs, "I'm afraid it's once more unto the breach, dear friends, for many of us. With another day comes another restricted program, and with your permission, I'll read you all into my new little effort." He looked at them, managing to seem as though he really was asking their agreement. Nobody moved.

"Very well, then. On your own heads be it. This program is the first individual effort in what will be a group of similar efforts. That umbrella group will be called Salmon. This first little project will be called Mousse."

"Salmon Moose?" asked General Hallstatt. "Like the animal?"

"No, mousse with 'ou' and two s's. It's an old, almost folkloric cultural referent. "

"Oh," said Hallstatt.

"It has the advantage that any of us could refer to it outside a closed environment, simply by doing this." He put his thumbs up at his temples, with fingers spread out. Jeri Klein suppressed a chuckle.

"Salmon programs will include virtually all classified programs that are driven by the recent crises. Mousse will deal specifically with one question and its corollary. That is, do we believe that a foreign government was involved in the Big Bay event and the other acts centered around Naval Branch command, and ... " he looked at Klein.

"And if so, what do we do about it."

"Exactly.

"Mousse, at least, will be driven by External Relations, with Security Branch providing assets as needed, assets in the area of intelligence gathering, primarily."

"Right," said Klein. "I don't anticipate our having to invade anybody or carry out any assassinations. Although we'd like to keep all our options open." This got a smile, at least, from General Newhouse.

"Just let me know," she said.

"Question," said Hallstatt. "Just to set the bounds. Are

we talking just about Canada? Or the US, too?"

"There are no limits, General. Personally, I doubt whether Switzerland has stepped outside its traditional neutrality and interfered with our affairs, but beyond that, I trust no one."

"Because so far ... I mean, in a whole twenty-four hours or so ... we're not seeing anything that points south. The investigation isn't even young, hell, it's newborn, but all we see right now is that part of this had to be somehow supported, covered, winked at, just ignored ... by Ottawa."

"Yes," said Newhouse, "But the question is, what will we find, going forward? And what will we do if...?"

"I believe," said the man, "that as far as the US is concerned, the conclusion is likely to be inconclusive. Were they involved? Certainly possibly, possibly certainly. But what I believe we must do is to rearrange our approach to what I'll call proactive intelligence." Klein nodded.

Hallstatt was cautious. When someone like the green office man or one of the big guns from the diplomatic world talked about rearranging something, any senior manager could get nervous. Fortunately, he was not prepared to play a passive-aggressive game. "What do we mean, 'rearrange'?" he asked.

"This is mostly my idea," said Klein. She looked at the man. "Do you want me to talk about it?"

"Of course. Please do."

"What we need in order to deal with these minor aggressions, from anywhere, inside or out, is more granular intelligence. What we have"... the implication was "what we're getting now" ... "is large-scale, strategic analyses, and we believe we'd be better off if we kept the structure Security has in place for that, but also put a large number of small, internal groups into play. In addition. People who don't do field work, don't do anything outside an office, really. They just listen and read, watch, develop leads and theories, test the theories – or turn them over to your more hands-on people for testing."

"Where do you see these groups living? Organizationally?"

"Oh, in SB. No doubt of that. You have the chain of command, the logistics, the facilities – we see these teams as sort of faux-companies. With a lieutenant in charge, but with only ten or twelve people. And reporting to a Battalion commander – a major, usually."

"Why would ... you know, I like the idea, but why would you call it a company? Companies have two hundred people, at least in SB."

"Um, actually, I think we just grabbed the title of a group that reports to Battalions." Klein said. "What we call it is the least of our worries. What would you suggest?"

"You're right. We don't have a formation exactly like that. FB calls their recon groups a team. How about team?"

"Fine with me, General," she said. "Team it is. And if you like that, wait, there's more. External Relations will pay for the staff."

Before Hallstatt could react, the man said, "Yes, that's the part that needs clear definition. ER will provide the funding, and some of the, I suppose you could say, user stories. Some of the things that need answers. But Security will be in charge. There's no question there."

Newhouse leaned back in her chair. "What you're proposing is a customer-supplier ... structure? Right? External pays for small teams to do intel work, some of which External defines. And SB sets the teams up. And manages them, personnel-wise, like their other people."

"Yes, that's the idea. I wouldn't say that External defines the work, strictly speaking. It requests specific output with a priority or a schedule. Security directs the work. And this is very important: it doesn't change the way Security does its other intelligence work now. It adds another approach."

"I like it," said Newhouse. "I have no idea whether it'll be more effective, but let's give it a try. Phil, are you okay with it?"

"Yeah. I am. I'm mildly annoyed that I didn't think of it, but I'll get over that. Let's go ahead."

"Very well, then," said the man. "Doctor Klein and General Hallstatt and I will begin to put it into play. We will meet again shortly to see the outcome of all that. Now ..." he picked up his tea cup "... I must see a man about a dog."

§

E and her gang of recruits left Alpena after breakfast. She let them exchange theories about the whole adventure while she just drove. She felt bad about having to keep them in the dark; neither of them was cleared for anything, let alone this kind of info. *When it opens up, I'll have to tell them about it. Shame to be on the front lines and not know what the war's about.*

They were getting to the point where the old highway began curving west around the tip of the Lower Peninsula. E's personal phone went off. "See who that is, will you?" She handed it to Margie.

"This is Lieutenant Gorsky's phone. Can I take a message for her?" Pause. "I don't know... I can ask her. Hold on, please. Lieutenant, a medical assistant in Marquette needs ... she says she has you listed as an Informed Consent Contact ..." She spoke back to the phone. "Is that right? Informed Consent Contact?" Back to E. "Yes, a contact for someone named Horstel. Does that sound familiar?"

"Kristin Horstel? Yes. I'm supposed to be what for her?"

"What does Informed Consent mean?" Pause. "Oh. All right. Hold on. She says you're supposed to be contacted if this person is unable to give consent. To a medical procedure."

"What on earth ...? Look, I'm going to pull over. Ask her to hold on just a minute."

It took another ten or twelve minutes to grasp, but the summary was that a person scheduled to undergo surgery was supposed to have another party to stand in and agree – or not agree – if something came up while the first person was under sedation. It appeared that the patient named Horstel had listed E as such a person and provided her phone number. There was an awkward tangle of conflicting regulations about confidential patient information – could the hospital tell E what the patient's medical condition was, before any surgery had taken place? And the patient was still conscious? And E had no idea that the patient was a patient? The Republic had made extensive and effective changes in healthcare finance, but healthcare bureaucracy had yet to undergo the same process improvement.

"Hold on a minute, if you will," E said. "Margie, you or Phil take over the driving. I have to get this squared away. No point in our sitting by the road here while I do."

They drove off. As the lake slid by on the right, E spoke with a range of medical people, and she finally found herself talking to an orthopedic surgeon.

"Okay, who are you, again?" he asked. E tried to keep her answer factual, leaving metaphysics out of it. "So, you're in Security. You're on the road someplace? And you're my patient's consent contact? And you didn't know it? Well … here, just talk to her."

"Hello, E." Kristin's voice was fainter than usual. "I'm sorry I didn't get to call you. You know, first."

"Never mind that, lady. What the hell's going on? Why are you in the hospital?"

"They didn't … I told them to let you know … "

"I don't know a damn thing! What's happening?"

"I got shot. In the fighting."

"Are you serious … you mean in Big Bay?"

"Yes."

"All right. All right. I'm going to have to process this. Why you were in harm's way … that can wait. But right now, just tell me how bad it is. And what they're doing." She had control over her voice, again. It was a pose, but it sounded better.

"I was helping … helping move a man. Who was shot. And then I got hit. In the leg. I think… in the bone, some bone … Doctor? Where did I get hit?" There was a voice in the background. "He says in the femur. On the left side. They're going to … fix it, I guess. Right?" Again, the doctor said something. "He says they're going to fix it."

"Fine. But I have to hear this from you. You want them to do that, right?"

"Yes."

"And if they need to do something else, while you're knocked out, I can tell them to go ahead? If it's necessary?"

"Yes. I put your name down. For that."

"You've had some painkillers already, I gather?"

"Something …" She was trailing off.

"Good. Let me talk to the doc, again."

Meg came back to what was becoming her couch in the waiting room. A trip to the restroom, water splashed on her face, a long look into that face – somehow she felt better. A tall young man was standing at the desk; she heard the admin say, "There she is, sir."

"Meg," he said. "Oh ..."

"Let's go over here," she said. "We can talk."

Alan was a very unhappy boy. His story was halting and sometimes hard to piece together, but the gist of it was: he'd known the attacker. They were living in the same house. He knew there were things wrong with him, but not ... mayhem. And he, Alan, hadn't done anything. Hadn't told anybody. Hadn't tried to help.

"Alan," she said, when he'd come to a pause, "You're not Karen. Or Larry."

"What?"

"It's not your ... job. To intervene. I'm sorry to say it, but ... you don't know how. It takes experience. And training."

"But I could have called ... somebody. The police."

"You could have. You just told me that you didn't think he was ... dangerous. What would you have said to the Security people? There's a boy here. He's acting ... what? What would you have said?"

"I don't know. I ..."

"Right. You don't know. And if you had called? What would have happened?"

"Maybe they could have stopped him."

"It's not against the law to be weird. They could have come to see him. And if he blew up, then, yes they'd take him into custody. And you'd feel bad about that. And if they didn't come, and he ... did what he did ... you could say 'I told them.' And nobody but you would care."

"But ..."

"Imagine it that way. You called Security, and they didn't do anything. And he hurt somebody. And we're talking about it. Would being able to say 'I told them' make you feel better? Or me? Or Una?"

"No. I ... guess not."

"I ... was from a place ... my family was religious. My uncle was a pastor. And it all blew up. They were doing awful things. My uncle, the church, my parents. All of them. If I'd known about it, honestly, I don't think I would have said anything. If it was somebody else's family, some other church, I probably would have. What does that say?"

"Why do you think that? That you wouldn't ..."

"Because I was ... trained ... to trust my family. I had no idea what was going on. At home or anywhere. And I'm just now coming to see that. Do you think you might have been trained to trust ... something?"

Alan sighed. It was the purging kind of sigh, the kind that empties the lungs and at least part of the mind.

"I want to come back to Karen's."

"I know. You should. She says she's got room. She's definitely ... got room."

§

E and the troopers got back to B Company by noon. She gave the kids a verbal pat on the back, and went off to see Captain Matthews.

"So, you're back," said Matthews. "Tired of the big city?"

"The temptations were hard to avoid, sir. But we resisted."

"I asked Personnel to check for me, and you're officially the only SB Lieutenant, acting or not, ever to command a Naval base."

"I can believe that. It was … interesting."

"And things here are going to get interesting, too. There's a buzz on, all the way up at Branch headquarters. A new organization – several of them, actually, one per Battalion. This isn't official, yet, but because we were out on the front edge of this nonsense, we get to do the first one. And when I say 'we', I mean you and me."

"New organization?"

"New formation, I should have said. They're calling it a 'Team'. With a lieutenant in command, and nine or ten signed-up NCOs – no National Service kids. Doing short-term, on-line, mostly quick-hit intel. Like Recon in Field Branch, but smaller, and virtually all the work done at a Battalion HQ, not out in the field. We – SB – own the Teams, but the diplomatic people, External Relations, ask the questions."

"Can the Teams cooperate? Share their findings?"

"Oh, yes. There's an IT operation getting off the ground, too. To make that possible. It has to be hyper-secure, of course, but yeah, the cooperation is essential."

"I like the idea, sir."

"Good. Because you're going to run the first one."

"Oh."

"Right. Couple of other little things I haven't covered, yet. One is that Major Vogel is going up to a planning job at Division. I'm going to run the Battalion and, eventually, if I'm a good girl, I'll get the promotion to match. And you're getting your bump up to real Lieutenant. And I said 'Hey, I know a Lieutenant who'd be good at running that first Team'."

"That's ... Thank you, sir. Do you perceive that the Army is acting a little ... faster than it usually does?"

"Yes. Oh, and I forgot to mention: Sergeant Edmore? He's getting a Lieutenant's slot, too. Army was really, really happy that the ex-head of Naval didn't make it out of the country."

"Great. Ed works hard."

"I know. And I know he's ready to retire. So they're giving him a ... what? A kind of phantom year of service. He can retire a year sooner."

§

Architecturally, the capital's Legal Center was a copy of a copy. There were buildings from the late twentieth century, trying to match a smaller group of structures from the early twentieth, themselves copied from even earlier styles. To paraphrase the Book of Matthew, the Victorian you will always have with you. In one of the small, highly secure examination rooms, the case of Malcolm Petronas was being examined.

If your experience with the law was limited to the American legal system, you would not have recognized it as a court. There were no flags, no robes, no swearing in any of the senses of the word. There was just the person being examined, his appointed Advocate, the Security Branch Case Presenter, and the Legal Department Examiner. And two Security Branch Corporals, in charge of the accused. There was a large screen for display of evidence and for any actual testimony, recorded or live.

"I have to remind everyone that this is a public proceeding," said the Examiner. "If we get into classified material, I need to know that before it happens. So I can mark that portion as closed." The Presenter nodded. The Advocate said, "Understood."

"There are a lot of individual charges against the accused. Let's take them in decreasing order, from the class threes to the zeroes. Go ahead with the threes."

"All right," said the Presenter. "Class threes. Four charges. He's charged with fleeing from Security Branch personnel. There's deliberately dangerous behavior – the way he was driving while being pursued. We have endangering a vehicle passenger – that would be Ms. Christianson – and damage to public property. He hit a bridge railing."

"Does the accused's Advocate want to dispute any of those?"

"No. Security has imagery and or testimony to confirm all of them."

"Remind me who Ms. Christianson is?"

"She was the passenger in the accused's vehicle. She's testified in support of several charges."

"Oh, yes. His assistant. I will validate all four of the class three charges, then. No class twos, is that right?"

"Yes," said the Presenter. "No self-directed crimes appear in this case."

"Go on with the class one, then."

"Class one, one charge. He's charged with lying to Security Branch personnel, during arrest and during questioning afterwards. Specifically, he denied that there was a passenger in his vehicle. There is SB personnel testimony to his making that statement at the arrest, and imagery of it while he was being questioned, later. It's demonstrated to be false by SB testimony – the passenger was seen in the truck – by imagery showing the passenger exiting the vehicle, and by the passenger's own testimony."

"Advocate?"

"The evidence is unquestionable. The accused says he was trying to protect Ms. Christianson from being involved."

"I will validate that charge, then. Now, the class zeroes, please."

"Class zero, the societal impact charges. There are four of them, as follows. One, a public official causing an unjustifiable danger to individuals. Two, a public official causing the unjustifiable injury or death of individuals. Three, a public official reporting inaccurately or falsely or failing to report to superiors and or officials. Four, a public official contacting a foreign government without authority."

The Examiner looked over the text version of the charges. "To make sure what's recorded here... " She gestured at cameras, "... matches what's in the documents, I'll ask you to clarify some of them. The danger to individuals and the causing death or injury? What are the actions that drive those charges?"

"There is documentary evidence that the accused directed Naval Branch personnel to plan and carry out an armed attack on the Security Branch post in the town of Big Bay. That's the 'causing danger' part. And when that actually happened, eight people died and one was injured. That's the second charge. It was no longer just danger, it was realized."

"All right."

"The third one, reporting; that's the synthesis of a long period of time when efforts were going on at the accused's direction that were not known to his superior officer and were in fact deliberately concealed. The fourth charge refers to his having had discussions with the Government of Canada concerning the Republic's intentions in a particular matter. I can't detail the discussions in this ... venue. Without closing the proceedings. But the nature of them – the discussions – is not the basis of the charge. The accused was not authorized to be in contact with Canada at all, without the knowledge of his superior and the External Relations Department."

"And the support for the charges?"

"As I noted, there are documents supporting the first two, endangering and causing. The third is supported by testimony from General Newhouse, the accused's superior officer. She's testified that none of the operations regarding resistance groups was reported to her, nor was the contact with Canada that's cited in the fourth charge. And no such reporting documents have been found. As for that fourth charge, again, there are copies of communications between the accused and unnamed Canadian officials, related to the classified issues I mentioned."

"No documents or testimony from the Canadians, though?"

"No."

"Advocate, what's your view?"

"We have two concerns. First, with reference to all four class zero charges, we question the assertion that the accused was responsible for them. A subordinate of his, Naval Branch Captain Dennis Bird, is also believed to have been involved. Security Branch listed charges against him as well as against the accused, but unfortunately he's deceased. His death occurred before he could be detained, and there's no testimony from him. Obviously."

"And you're questioning ... what?"

"That the causes of danger and injury and the failure to report, at least, may have been the fault of Captain Bird, not the accused."

"Has the accused stated that?"

"No. On my advice, he's elected not to comment on the charges until we go to appeal."

"Well, without his testimony, I'm not going to reject those charges. You can take it to appeal. Now what about your other issue?"

"As the Presenter said, there's nothing on the record from Canada. The evidence is only from references in documents found at the Naval Base Captain Bird commanded. That seems short of conclusive, as a charge against the accused."

"Excuse me," said the Presenter. "If you look at the source evidence for that charge, you'll see that the accused's personal communications indicate knowledge of contact with Canada. And there's nothing to indicate that Captain Bird was involved with that. There was plenty of other culpability for him, but if he'd survived, we would not have charged him with the contact issue."

"So ... I will validate all of the class zero charges. Advocate?"

"We will ask that the case go to Appeal."

"Of course. And did you say that the accused is not willing to testify here?'

"That's right. We'll look at that in Appeal."

"Then, based on these charges and on the evidence supporting them, I am sentencing the accused, charge by charge, like this. On the class threes, four charges times one month imprisonment each is four months. On the class one, one year. And on the class zeroes, life imprisonment times four charges. All of that is cumulative. And we're done."

§

The conversation between E and Kristin, this time, was unimpeded by pain meds. At least, not to the level of previous talks. But again they were on the phone. E was explaining, to the extent she was allowed to, what she'd been doing, how it might be connected with Kristin's experience, and why she couldn't just jump in a car and come to Marquette.

"So, I'm really tied to a desk, down here. Or out here. I guess I'm more east than south of you, right now."

"What ... made it all happen? The stuff we're hearing in the hospital is just crazy. The head of the Navy is out. The thing we had, here. And the thing at the capital? What's going on?"

"I have to think carefully about how I answer that. You know what I mean. "

"I know. Classified stuff."

"Yeah. But ... the simplest way to put it is ... bad things happened, but we think it's over with. And some smart people are trying to figure out why it happened. And how to keep it from happening again."

"Are you one of the smart people?"

"Well, in this context. That sounds egotistical, but in this context, yes. I'm helping, anyway."

"But is it safe to say you don't think there'll be more? More bad things?"

"Wow. Ah ... yes. From what I know, yes. And most of the people I work with think that, too."

"Okay. Then I'm not going to worry about it."

"You really know how to put a girl on the spot."

"To each his own. My mother used to say that. You know more about all ... this, than I do. So I'm just going to leave it. For now, anyway."

"I hope you don't regret it. I hope I don't regret it."

The talk shifted to the prognosis for Kristin's leg, how long she'd have to do what, when she could go back to work. There was a pause, and then Kristin cleared her throat. "I have to ask you something. Something kind of personal."

"The toilet paper definitely goes over the top of the roll."

"Right. But ... are you ... alone? Socially, I mean. Commitment-wise?"

E took a breath. "Yes."

"Because, you know I was with somebody, out in California? Right?"

"I heard that."

"And I'm not. That came ... to an end."

"I'm sorry." E was conscious of not being sorry, not at all.

"It was getting too, oh, middle-class. I guess. Curtains and china and silverware. And ... she wanted to adopt children."

"Oh, dear."

"We just decided to go ... our own ways. Before we made each other any unhappier."

"And you're okay? Okay with that?"

"Well, here's the confession part. I've been stalking you. Sort of."

"So you deliberately flung yourself into a firefight, just to get me on the phone?"

"No, it wasn't that well organized. But I got myself into this job ... up here, you know ... because you were up here."

"Well, for a stalker, you've been nice about it. You

bought me dinner, after all. But ..."

"Yes?"

"I admit to having some ideas, myself. Kind of like this. I'm going to get to 'go up to Battalion' with my boss. That's what we call more work for the same pay. And I'll be part of a team up there. Meaning closer to Saint Ignace. Oh, and I got promoted. But it occurs to me that when you're not running around ruining the careers of educators, you're more or less based there, too."

"Right."

"So what if we were to look for a house or something, somewhere around there? And we could be there when our glittering careers weren't taking us off somewhere else. And, you know, when we were both there at the same time, we could make dinner. And have our books and things. And sleep together, when we were there." She paused. "Or not. I mean ..."

"Oh, no. I'm okay with that. With all of that."

"Good. Good. I think we'd both enjoy some slight ... domesticity. But no china. And no children."

"Hell, no. Although we could have cheap china. And we'd need glasses. Like, one or two."

"So how about you carry on with getting the hell out of that hospital? And maybe look at some places on the housing sites? I'll do that, too – the housing part – and we can compare notes. Say, tomorrow."

"Tomorrow."

They hung up. E set her phone down. She kicked her feet out in front, stretched her arms up and back and held it. *Wow.*

§

"Karen?" said Meg. "Do you have a minute?"

"Sure, girl. Come on in."

"My mother called me. From where she's living now."

"Uh huh."

"I don't want to talk to her. And I don't want her trying to get me back ... there or back with my father. "

"She's in the US, right?"

"Yes. With her sister."

"And you're how old, now?"

"Nineteen."

"She's got nothing. Your father, either. Block their numbers. And if they try anything else, we can deal with that, too. We know people."

"Okay. Thanks. I've got work to do here. Helping Una. And Alan needs a lot of talking to. And I have go back to school, soon. I don't need my family anymore. Just ... " She made an inclusive gesture with her arms. "... this. This family. Anyway, thanks again. I have to get back over to the hospital. They're going to try getting Una out of bed today." She left.

"Son of a gun," Karen thought. "One of these days, that girl's gonna have a look at Engels and be surprised. She just did for herself what he wanted the party to do for the kids. I hope it works out better for her." The dog, Ginger, was lying under a table. She stretched and yawned.

§

Sheila Edmore got home a few minutes earlier than usual. She liked being home. Past the end of the street, she could see just the stern of somebody's fishing boat, headed upstream toward Lake George. When she turned into their driveway, she stopped short. Ed's Republic-official truck was there. The side door of the house opened, and Ed waved. "Surprise!" he shouted. A quick hug and kiss, two of them, in fact, and she asked, "What's up?"

"Well," he said, standing back from her, "Notice anything different about me?"

"Um, let's see." He pointed to his upper left chest. "You have a different ... badge, thing."

"That's right, dear. You are addressing LOO-tenant Wilber Edmore!"

"Oh, my God! How did ... what happened?"

"Come on inside. There's a bottle of wine open. I'll tell you the story of my heroic exploits. Oh, and they didn't just give me the badge. No more 'three more years', baby. It's 'two more years,' now!" The neighbors' Labrador trotted out from behind the garden shed and stood there wagging.

§

The Marquette National Medical Center was well out of the downtown, west along Baraga Avenue. Carol, wearing civilian clothes, was early for her appointment, and a nurse put her in an interview room to wait. It felt non-clinical for a hospital, but she'd never been to a psychiatric provider before.

Outside, a doctor walked rapidly through the office. He dropped one file of paperwork onto the specialist's desk – not, as he'd been asked over and over again, into the IN tray, just onto the desk. He picked up his next patient's folder, looked at the first document, and said to no one in particular, "What's next?"

"The patient's name is Douglas, Doctor. Possible PTSD related to the Big Bay incident."

"Well, where's the security? Is he restrained? Are they just bringing these people in here for us to deal with?"

"I don't understand ..." the specialist started to say. The nurse jumped in.

"The patient is a Security Branch Private, Doctor. Not one of the insurgents."

"Why isn't that made clear?! I don't have time to read the demographics! Why didn't someone tell me that?! Oh, never mind. Where is he?"

"She, Doctor. In room four." He made a small dismissing sound and went down the hall.

In a bit less than ten minutes, Carol came out. She stopped at the desk. "Do you need anything, any information from me?" Her expression and tone were as neutral as she could make them.

"Oh, are you done already?"

"Yes. I think that ... person needs more help than I do." Her voice trembled just slightly, and then she got it back under control. "Good afternoon." The staff exchanged looks.

As she walked back to the bus stop, she passed an older woman, walking with a cane. Out in the air, the woman caught up, and they exchanged a nod. A bus arrived; "DOWNTOWN" was on its destination scroll. It went east into the city, running through neighborhoods of old frame houses. Each cross street sloped downward, right to left. Carol was deep inside herself, the word "failure" coming up again and again. "The government is failing me. It failed that poor idiot I shot. I shot him. Politics put him out there in that schoolyard. We shot them. They shot at us. Lou got killed. I never even knew him. I never knew the guy ... the guy I shot." She looked up and saw the abandoned church that meant her stop was next. She reached for the bell cord, but the woman from the hospital pulled it first.

They got off the bus. Carol started up Front Street, then abruptly decided to walk through Marquette Park. It was at street level along Front, but dropped downhill toward the harbor. She reached a bench near the top and sat down. The view to the east was of the lake, a brick structure that had been a hotel, a small island called Ripley Rock, and the end of an ore dock. To the right, a mixed-breed dog was lying in the sun, staring out at the lake. Carol made an effort to keep her consciousness in neutral, just looking at the physical, undebatable things spread out in front.

"I like that view," someone said. Carol looked up quickly. It was the woman from the bus. "Mind if I sit down?" she said. "That's kind of a hike, up and over the park." She did seem to be breathing hard.

"Oh, please. Sit down." Carol moved over.

"Thanks. I live over there," the woman said, pointing at the ex-hotel.

"There? Is it apartments or something?"

"Yup." The woman looked around. "Funny thing, I've slept on this bench once or twice. More than that, some years."

"Oh." It was all Carol could think of.

"But now, we get the Support. Me and two of my friends, the crazy old birds, we call ourselves. We got one of those places over there. We do all right."

"So you live with some friends?"

"We're sort of a band. Fiddle music. Reels n' Ballads. We play kinda year round, now. Sometimes here in the park, sometimes in the government halls. Couple of the bars. We'll be at Vierling's tomorrow night." She paused. "We do all right," she said again.

"What do you ... do you have a name? For your band?"

"Like I said, The Crazy Old Birds. Well, guess I'll go on the rest of the way home. You take it easy." She got up, not without a certain amount of care, and walked off.

Carol looked down at the bench. It was the older kind, with wooden slats for the seat and back, bracketed into iron legs and supports. It didn't look like a place to sleep. She shook her head, got up, and started the walk back to the SB base, three blocks away. Somehow, she felt better.

§

The street was faced on both sides with elderly, red brick buildings. E's line of sight was limited, as though there were steep hillsides at each end. Somehow, there was no traffic, and she was walking down the center of an asphalt surface. A man paced out into the street, moving deliberately. In the middle, right at the central lane marker, he turned and faced her. He was dressed in black, with a black ball cap. His face would obviously have been visible, but for some reason, it made no impression. He stood there, legs slightly apart, waiting.

She felt at her side for a weapon, but there was nothing. The man had somehow become an adversary. She began walking toward him. He stood his ground, and neither of them spoke. A greater and greater sense of urgency flooded her consciousness, and she began to run at him. He adopted a fighting stance, knees bent, left arm forward, the right back. She tried to remember the kicks, the blows, the sidestepping move to counter a defense, but ... the light seemed to brighten. She slowed, still compelled to attack and correct some dreadful wrong. But ... the sidewalks were suddenly populated. Up and down the street, on both sides, there were dogs. Except for a pair of puppies wrestling with each other in the shade of an awning, all the canids were unmoving, sitting, standing, lying, watching her and her dark opponent. Who had vanished.

She stopped. The dogs looked at her, she looked back,

turning all around in a circle. Except for one, scratching himself with a back leg, none of them moved.

E sat up in bed, eyes wide, staring around. The room was momentarily unfamiliar, then it resolved itself into her temporary quarters at the Saint Ignace Battalion headquarters. Her uniform lay folded on a chair. The first hints of sunrise were lightening the window. She shook her head. *What in the hell was that about?*

§

About the Author

McConnell has been writing in one form or another for decades. Besides *Dog Island*, he's written a five-volume series of crime novels featuring a retired police detective and some unusual recurring characters – including a pair of dogs and, in one of the books, a pack of wolves. Most of his fiction involves the State of Michigan and the city of Ann Arbor, less-than-brilliant criminals, and extremely human men and women.

The Mac MacArthur series of novels includes:

- *Many Believable Lies*
- *Clash by Night*
- *The Least Weasel*
- *A Lair for the Wolves*
- *Driven by the Trades*

There is also a collection of poetry and short fiction, *The Run of Myself*.

For McConnell's books and for occasional bits of humor, see the ProcArch Press blog at
https://procarch.blogspot.com/